SWEETWATER
AND THE
WITCH

Titles by Jayne Ann Krentz writing as Jayne Castle

Sweetwater and the Witch	*Canyons of Night*	*Harmony*
Guild Boss	*Midnight Crystal*	*After Da*
Illusion Town	*Obsidian Prey*	*Orch*
Siren's Call	*Dark Light*	*Zin*
The Hot Zone	*Silver Master*	*Am*
Deception Cove	*Ghost Hunter*	
The Lost Night	*After Glow*	

THE GUINEVERE JONES SERIES

Desperate and Deceptive
The Guinevere Jones Collection, Volume 1

The Desperate Game
The Chilling Deception

Sinister and Fatal
The Guinevere Jones Collection, Volume 2

The Sinister Touch
The Fatal Fortune

Specials

The Scargill Cove Case Files
(writing as Jayne Ann Krentz)

Bridal Jitters
(writing as Jayne Castle)

Anthologies

Charmed
(with Julie Beard, Lori Foster, and Eileen Wilks)

Titles written by Jayne Ann Krentz and Jayn

No Going Back

Titles by Jayne Ann Krentz writing as Amanda Quick

When She Dreams	*The Perfect Poison*	*Affair*
The Lady Has a Past	*The Third Circle*	*Mischief*
Close Up	*The River Knows*	*Mystique*
Tightrope	*Second Sight*	*Mistress*
The Other Lady Vanishes	*Lie by Moonlight*	*Deception*
The Girl Who Knew Too Much	*The Paid Companion*	*Desire*
'Til Death Do Us Part	*Wait Until Midnight*	*Dangerous*
Garden of Lies	*Late for the Wedding*	*Reckless*
Otherwise Engaged	*Don't Look Back*	*Ravished*
The Mystery Woman	*Slightly Shady*	*Rendezvous*
Crystal Gardens	*Wicked Widow*	*Scandal*
Quicksilver	*I Thee Wed*	*Surrender*
Burning Lamp	*With This Ring*	*Seduction*

Titles by Jayne Ann Krentz

THE FOGG LAKE TRILOGY

Lightning in a Mirror
All the Colors of Night
The Vanishing

Untouchable	*All Night Long*	*Sharp Edges*
Promise Not to Tell	*Falling Awake*	*Deep Waters*
When All the Girls Have Gone	*Truth or Dare*	*Absolutely, Positively*
Secret Sisters	*Light in Shadow*	*Trust Me*
Trust No One	*Summer in Eclipse Bay*	*Grand Passion*
River Road	*Together in Eclipse Bay*	*Hidden Talents*
Dream Eyes	*Smoke in Mirrors*	*Wildest Hearts*
Copper Beach	*Lost & Found*	*Family Man*
In Too Deep	*Dawn in Eclipse Bay*	*Perfect Partners*
Fired Up	*Soft Focus*	*Sweet Fortune*
Running Hot	*Eclipse Bay*	*Silver Linings*
Sizzle and Burn	*Eye of the Beholder*	*The Golden Chance*
White Lies	*Flash*	

SWEETWATER AND THE WITCH

Jayne Castle

BERKLEY
NEW YORK

BERKLEY
An imprint of Penguin Random House LLC
penguinrandomhouse.com

Copyright © 2022 by Jayne Ann Krentz
Penguin Random House supports copyright. Copyright fuels creativity, encourages
diverse voices, promotes free speech, and creates a vibrant culture. Thank you for buying
an authorized edition of this book and for complying with copyright laws by not
reproducing, scanning, or distributing any part of it in any form without permission.
You are supporting writers and allowing Penguin Random House to continue to
publish books for every reader.

BERKLEY and the BERKLEY & B colophon are registered trademarks of
Penguin Random House LLC.

Library of Congress Cataloging-in-Publication Data

Names: Castle, Jayne, author.
Title: Sweetwater and the witch / Jayne Castle.
Description: New York : Berkley, [2022] | Series: A Harmony novel
Identifiers: LCCN 2022002034 (print) | LCCN 2022002035 (ebook) |
ISBN 9780593440254 (hardcover) | ISBN 9780593440261 (ebook)
Subjects: LCGFT: Novels.
Classification: LCC PS3561.R44 S96 2022 (print) |
LCC PS3561.R44 (ebook) | DDC 813/.54—dc23/eng/20220120
LC record available at https://lccn.loc.gov/2022002034
LC ebook record available at https://lccn.loc.gov/2022002035

Printed in the United States of America
1   3   5   7   9   10   8   6   4   2

Book design by Kristin del Rosario

This is a work of fiction. Names, characters, places, and incidents either are the product
of the author's imagination or are used fictitiously, and any resemblance to actual persons,
living or dead, business establishments, events, or locales is entirely coincidental.

For Harriet. Here's to popcorn and fireworks,
the keys to a happy life.

A NOTE FROM JAYNE

Welcome to my Jayne Castle world—Harmony. You're invited to join me on another adventure in Illusion Town. This is Las Vegas on Harmony but way more weird. The sign on the highway says it all: *The thrills are real.*

For those of you who are new to Harmony, here's a quick summary of the history of this new world:

Late in the twenty-first century, a vast energy Curtain opened in the vicinity of Earth, making interstellar travel practical for the first time. In typical human fashion, thousands of eager colonists packed up their stuff and lost no time heading out to create new homes and new societies on the unexplored planets that were suddenly within reach. Harmony was one of those worlds.

The colonists who settled Harmony brought with them all the comforts of home: sophisticated technology, centuries of art and literature, and the latest fashions. Trade through the Curtain flourished and made it possible to stay in touch with families back on Earth. It also allowed the colonists to keep their computers and high-tech gadgets working. Things went swell for a while.

And then one day, without warning, the Curtain closed, disappearing as mysteriously as it had opened. Cut off from Earth, no longer able to obtain the equipment and supplies needed to keep their high-tech life-style going, the colonists were abruptly thrown back to a far more rustic existence. Forget the latest Earth fashions; just staying alive suddenly became a major problem.

But on Harmony, folks did one of the things humans do well—they adapted and survived. It wasn't easy, but two hundred years after the closing of the Curtain, the descendants of the First Generation colonists have managed to fight their way back from the brink to a level of civilization roughly equivalent to that of the first half of the twenty-first century on Earth.

The four original colonies have evolved into four large city-states loosely united under the umbrella of a federal government. With no enemy nations to worry about, there is no standing army. But every civilization requires some form of policing. On Harmony those tasks are handled by three different agencies. Aboveground, the various police departments and the Federal Bureau of Psi Investigation (FBPI) take the lead. But in the ancient ruins belowground, law enforcement and general security are handled by the powerful Ghost Hunters Guilds.

Vast stretches of Harmony have yet to be explored, both aboveground and down in the mysterious and dangerous maze of green quartz tunnels in the Underworld.

Interestingly, an increasingly wide variety of psychic powers are showing up in the descendants of the colonists. It seems that something in the environment is bringing out the latent paranormal abilities in humans.

Of course, there are some people who don't need any help from the environment to unleash their psychic talents. Turns out a whole bunch of the members of the Arcane Society were among the First Generation settlers. So were a few of the Society's old enemies. (I know. Who could have seen that coming, right?)

Harmony holds mysteries and secrets and dangers, but, as usual, the real trouble is caused by humans.

SWEETWATER
AND THE
WITCH

CHAPTER ONE

"The witch will burn."

Ravenna Chastain could hear the chanting in the adjacent chamber. It was growing louder and more intense. The members of the witch hunter cult were working themselves up into a frenzy.

"The witch will burn. The witch will burn. The witch will burn."

Until a few minutes ago she had kept panic at bay by telling herself that help was on the way. All she had to do was stall for time. She had done her best, but the trial that had condemned her had lasted less than twenty minutes and had consisted primarily of a lengthy reading of the charges against her. *"You have been accused of practicing witchcraft. You have presented no evidence to the contrary. You must be cleansed."* At the end the Master had pronounced the verdict, which had never been in doubt: guilty.

She and the dust bunny were on their own.

The cult's head enforcer appeared in the arched doorway. He gripped a flamer in one hand. Such weapons were among the few that functioned in the heavy paranormal energy that circulated in the ancient ruins of the Underworld.

"Time to meet the cold fire, Witch." He selected a key from the metal chatelaine at his waist. "The Master and the Acolyte are waiting. The Guardians have gathered to witness the destruction of your powers."

Ravenna watched him through the bars of the cage. He wore a black, hooded robe and a black mask. His eyes glittered with a sick excitement. He called himself the First Guardian, but she knew his real name was Charles Granger.

"Tell me, Chucky, are you having fun with this crazy witch-hunting cult?" she asked.

Granger flinched. Panic flashed in his eyes. "How do you know my name?"

"Magic. I'm a witch, remember? That's why you kidnapped me. Don't tell me you've forgotten already. What's the problem? Short attention span?"

"You're going to be a flatlined witch soon." Granger shoved the key into the lock and opened the cage door. "Come on out."

"Doesn't it bother you to know that you're being used by a manipulative, deranged psychopath who gets his thrills using his talent to put innocent people into a waking coma?"

"Shut your fucking mouth. Your powers will be destroyed tonight. Tomorrow morning they'll find you wandering the streets. You won't remember who you are, let alone that you used to practice magic. You will be cleansed. If you're lucky you'll end up in an asylum."

"Between you and me, I don't think the jury is going to buy your rationale for helping Fitch psi-burn innocent people."

"The Order of the Guardians must fulfill its mission," Granger snarled. "We will rid Harmony of all those who practice witchcraft."

"Yeah, right. Do you realize just how ridiculous you sound? You believe in magic? Really? Can you even spell the word *science*?"

Granger grabbed her arm and hauled her toward the arched doorway of the glowing green chamber. Ravenna caught a flicker of movement out of the corner of her eye. The dust bunny was back.

"No, please," she said, willing her to remain in hiding.

She had no idea how much the creature understood, but dust bunnies were hunters by nature. That meant they probably shared a few basic takedown strategies with humans. For some reason, this one had apparently adopted her after she had been thrown into the cage. The dust bunny had been careful to remain out of sight when the cult members were around. She seemed to understand that they were outnumbered and outgunned.

If she revealed herself too soon in a valiant but futile attack on one of the enforcers, she would be killed. Dust bunnies were quick and fast, but they were as vulnerable to a flamer as any other living creature.

Ravenna was scared but she was also pissed. She was not supposed to be in this mess. Things had gone very wrong.

"Too late," Granger said, assuming she was pleading with him. He hauled viciously on her arm. "Nothing can save your magic."

"I wasn't talking to you," she said.

"Is that right? Who, then? I don't see any other members of your coven around."

"I don't have a coven," she said. She was a member of an FBPI task force team, but she didn't think that qualified as a coven. "I'm not really a witch, you know."

"The Master identified you as a witch. That's good enough for me."

"Seriously? I'd like to blame your failure to think for yourself on the defects of the modern education system, but I've got a feeling it's a symptom of a personality disorder instead. You're pretty much doomed to be a pawn for others to manipulate, aren't you? When Fitch gets arrested, which he will eventually, he'll go back to that high-security para-psych hospital for the criminally insane. But you'll probably go to prison. Once you're inside, you'll drift into the spiderweb of some other narcissistic psychopath. I'm sure there are a lot of them in there."

Granger used his grip on her arm to give her a violent shake. "I told you to shut up."

He pulled her through the doorway and into another chamber. The room was larger than the one in which she had been held prisoner for the past day and a half. Like all the ruins left behind by the long-vanished Aliens who had tried to colonize Harmony eons earlier, the proportions looked vaguely off to the human eye. But if you dropped your preconceived notions of what constituted good architecture, it was possible to perceive a refined elegance and grace in the impressive structures.

Issues of architectural design were not top of mind for her today, however. The real problem was that Granger was not the only cult enforcer. She had counted three, and they were all clearly ex-Guild men. They carried flamers but that was not their only weapon. They had been in the Guild at some point in their lives because they possessed a talent for working some of the strong energy that flowed through the vast maze of tunnels in the Underworld. They could create and manipulate small storms of acid-green "ghost" fire. A brush with a hot ball of that kind of energy could knock you unconscious. A seriously close encounter could stop the heart.

"The witch will burn."

The annoying chanting stopped abruptly when the small group of robed and hooded twits saw Ravenna and Granger in the doorway. An expectant silence shivered in the room. The evening's entertainment was about to begin. This was why they had invented the word *bloodthirsty*, Ravenna thought—or, in this case, talent thirsty. This bunch wanted to strip her of her psychic senses.

Like Granger, the other cult members were dressed in masks and hooded robes. There were fewer than a dozen in all. They were gathered around the man and woman seated on the glowing green quartz thrones on a dais in the center of the chamber.

They called themselves the Master and the Acolyte, but Ravenna knew their names—Clarence Fitch and Louise Lace. Fitch wore an impressive black-and-gold robe. His mask was gold. Madness glinted in his eyes. Lace was dressed in white from head to toe, including her mask.

"Bring the witch forward," Fitch intoned.

Granger shoved Ravenna toward the thrones.

"Oh, hey, don't stop whatever you're doing on account of me," Ravenna said. "Sorry to interrupt. Don't worry, I won't be staying long."

"She won't stop talking," Granger muttered. "Want me to gag her?"

"No." Clarence gave Ravenna a considering look. "We want to question her first."

"If you answer the Master's questions, he will let you keep some of your powers," Louise Lace said. She spoke in a reassuring, encouraging tone.

A murmur of astonishment and acute disappointment rippled around the room.

"But she's a witch," one of the Guardians said.

Clarence glared at Louise, who visibly withered.

"I am sorry, Master," she whispered. "I was trying to help."

"Silence," Clarence snapped.

"Yes, Master," Louise said.

Clarence gripped the wide arms of the quartz chair and pushed himself to his feet. He fixed Ravenna with his mad eyes. "You will answer my questions or you will die."

"Choices, choices," Ravenna said. She glanced at the door in one last burst of hope, but there was no sign of a rescue party. "What's your question?"

"How much does the FBPI know?"

"The Federal Bureau of Psi Investigation knows everything I know, of course," Ravenna said. "I work for them. The task force should be here any minute now. Guess they got held up in traffic."

There was a collective gasp. Stricken looks were exchanged. Louise stiffened in the big chair, clearly alarmed. But Clarence was enraged.

"You're lying," he roared.

Ravenna gave him a dazzling smile. She did not speak.

"She's bluffing, Master," Louise said. "You're not going to get anything useful out of her. It is time to strip her of her powers."

Clarence did not need much in the way of persuasion. "Prepare to be cleansed and purified in the fires of ice. When I have finished, you will no longer possess your dark powers of magic."

He advanced on Ravenna. A chilling energy shuddered in the chamber. Fitch was raising his psychic talent. He was, just as she had expected, a true flatliner, one of the monsters. And he was strong—very strong.

Ravenna retreated a few steps. She had studied the para-psych profile that had been assembled on Fitch during the years he had spent in an asylum. The medication that had dampened his dangerous ability had worn off quickly after his escape a few months ago, and now she was dealing with the full force of his frightening talent.

Fitch took another step toward her. Waves of ice pressed at her, seeking to overwhelm her aura. She retreated again but found herself up against a wall. She spotted the dust bunny crouched, unnoticed, on the far side of the chamber.

She had seen videos of dust bunnies in full attack mode, but this was the first time she had watched one prepare for battle. The little creature was sleeked out, all four eyes open. There was a saying about dust bunnies: by the time you see the teeth, it's too late. Her new pal definitely had a lot of teeth on display.

Once again Ravenna tried to send a silent message that the time was not yet ripe to stage a desperate attempt at escape. There were too many flamers in the room. The odds were not good. A distraction was called for.

Fitch stopped a short distance away. His eyes burned with excitement as he pushed the cold waves of his talent toward her. She felt her heart rate begin to slow. A great chill settled on her, icing her blood. She glanced at the door one last time and abandoned the last vestige of hope.

"It looks I've been stood up," she said to the room at large. Then she focused hard on the dust bunny. *"Now."*

Somehow the creature got the message. She zipped across the floor, her six paws a blur. She was heading straight for the Acolyte, who was looking the other way and did not see her coming.

Ravenna rezzed her talent to the max. A wall of paranormal flames roared to life and enveloped Fitch. She saw his mouth twist and his eyes widen in mortal fear as the fire swirled around him. She was vaguely aware of screams and shrieks from the onlookers. One particularly piercing cry reverberated through the chamber.

"Get it off me," Louise yelled. "Get it off."

The dust bunny had found her target.

Fitch stiffened, convulsed, and dropped to the floor, unconscious. Ravenna lowered her talent. The flames vanished. The room was in chaos.

"Fire witch," someone screamed.

"Time to go," Ravenna called.

Louise flailed wildly and managed to dislodge the dust bunny. The creature made an adroit landing and promptly dashed across the chamber to join Ravenna.

Ravenna was already running for the door. The dust bunny caught up with her just as she raced out into the hall.

They both nearly got trampled by the phalanx of Guild men and FBPI agents heading toward the chamber. Ravenna scooped up the dust bunny before she was accidentally struck by a large boot and flattened her back to the wall to avoid the task force team.

"You're late," she yelled as they thundered past. "Where in hell have you guys been?"

CHAPTER TWO

The thundering herd of agents and hunters ignored her and charged into the chamber. Ravenna heard a lot of shouted commands along the lines of *"Everybody down on the floor. Hands behind your heads."*

She went to the doorway, the dust bunny tucked under one arm. Together they watched the team put the cult members in handcuffs. On the floor, Clarence Fitch stirred and opened his eyes. Max Collins, the team leader, yanked him to his feet.

"What happened to you?" Collins demanded.

"The witch burned me," Fitch said. The words were slurred. "Tried to murder me."

"Right," Collins said, unimpressed. He shoved Fitch toward the nearest agent. "Cuff him."

"He's telling the truth," Granger said. "I saw it with my own eyes. Flames from across the spectrum. The woman is a real witch. You gotta believe us."

Collins shook his head. "Bunch of deluded idiots. Get 'em out of here."

He turned and headed toward the doorway, moving with the not-so-subtle swagger of a heroic agent of law enforcement who has just completed a successful takedown and knows there will be a commendation for same in his file.

Ravenna stepped back and to one side. The dust bunny chortled. She was once again fluffed. With only her innocent blue eyes showing, she looked like a large wad of dryer lint. Ravenna waited for her to leap free and disappear as mysteriously as she had appeared. But she made no move to leave.

Collins stopped in front of Ravenna. "What's with the dust bunny?"

"I have no idea," Ravenna said. "She just showed up after I was *kidnapped and locked in a cage.*"

Collins paid no attention to her accusatory tone. "Cute little critter."

"You should have seen her a moment ago when she was coming to my rescue—unlike, say, your FBPI team."

Collins frowned in concern. "Are you okay? You sound a little wired."

"Wired? Gee, I guess I am a little tense. Clarence Fitch just tried to ice out my talent. He was going to do to me what he did to those other three women—flatline my senses and leave me in a waking coma."

"Take it easy," Collins said. "Calm down."

She couldn't believe it when he reached out a hand and patted her on the head. This was the problem with being on the short side, she fumed. She stepped back out of reach. The dust bunny growled at Collins.

Collins blinked and hastily retrieved his hand. "Everything's okay now. The team is here. All the bad guys are on their way to prison or, in the case of Fitch, a para-psych hospital for the criminally insane."

Ravenna narrowed her eyes. "You cut it a little close, didn't you?"

"Sorry about that. One of the locators jammed. We got conflicting readings. Had to wait until the tech guy figured out what was going on."

"Better late than never, I guess."

"We got here in the nick of time, and that's what counts, right?" Collins said cheerfully. "By the way, Fitch and the others keep saying there was a for-real paranormal fire in that chamber. Any idea what they're talking about?"

She rezzed up a bright little smile. "Nope. Fitch is delusional. Thinks he really is a witch hunter. His followers are deluded, too."

A young FBPI agent appeared in the doorway. She had thought she knew all the members of the task force, but she didn't recognize him. His name tag was partially obscured by the locator attached to his bulky flamer-proof vest. He was in full takedown gear—boots, black trousers and shirt, and a utility belt studded with serious law enforcement hardware, including a flamer—but somehow he made the clunky outfit look good.

"We've got things under control, sir," he said. "But some of the suspects are insisting Ms. Chastain tried to roast them all alive."

"You know how it is with suspects," Ravenna said. "They tend to exaggerate."

The agent looked amused. "They say they thought Fitch was going to go up in flames and that they would all be next."

Collins frowned, and then his brow cleared. He patted Ravenna on the shoulder this time and winked. "You got hold of a flamer, huh? Aren't you glad I made you go through that basic weapons training course when you got assigned to my team? Nice work holding off that bunch until we got here."

"Just doing my job, sir," Ravenna said.

Well, no. Defending herself against a crowd of murderous cult followers was not in her job description, and they both knew it. She was the team's criminal profiler. She was not supposed to get close to the scene of the action, let alone end up in harm's way. But the sarcasm blew straight past Collins without disturbing his crisp FBPI haircut.

"Right," he said. "See you back on the surface. How about we get together to celebrate with a drink tonight?"

"Love to," she said. "But I've got to wash a load of clothes."

"Some other time, then," he said, unfazed. "Catch you later."

Collins vanished back into the chamber to take charge. The FBPI agent studied Ravenna.

"Got hold of a flamer, huh?" he said. He gave her a knowing smile. "Smart move."

"I got lucky."

"Pretty amazing luck. Not everyone could grab a flamer from a trained Guild man."

"Yay, me." She studied him. "I don't think we've met. I'm Ravenna Chastain, the team profiler."

"Oh, sorry." He glanced down at his vest and adjusted the locator so that his name tag was visible. "My name's Sweetwater. Jeff Sweetwater."

"Sweetwater?" Startled, she took a closer look at him. "As in one of the Amber, Inc., Sweetwaters?"

He winced. "Afraid so."

"I have to tell you, I'm a little surprised."

"That a Sweetwater joined the FBPI?"

"I suppose so. Never really thought about it. I assumed the Sweetwaters all worked in the family business."

The Sweetwaters controlled a vast chunk of the resonating amber market. Given that resonating amber was the primary source of power on Harmony, it followed as night follows day that the Sweetwaters were a wealthy, powerful clan. In addition to large mining operations, they ran a variety of research-and-development labs. They also funded high-tech medical facilities, academic chairs, and museums.

Jeff grinned. "A few of us have managed to escape Amber, Inc."

She smiled. "Good for you. How did you wind up on the task force?"

"I was pulled in at the last minute because one of the other members of the team couldn't get to the assembly station in time. By the way, I come from a long line of people who understand your kind of luck."

She wasn't sure where he was going with that remark and decided the safest thing to do was deflect it. "Like Special Agent Collins said, it's a good thing I took the weapons training class."

"Right." Jeff smiled again. "I'd better get back in there and at least try to look like I'm doing my job. You're not the only one who got lucky tonight. Being on this team is going to look good in my file." He turned and started toward the doorway. He paused and looked at her. "Nice profiling work, by the way. You've got the eye."

"Thanks."

Jeff disappeared through the doorway.

Ravenna found herself alone in the glowing hall. She cuddled the dust bunny, who showed no signs of rushing off.

"I need a drink," she said.

The dust bunny chortled.

"I've got a bag of pretzels at home if you're interested."

The dust bunny chortled again. It sounded as if she was in agreement with the plan.

"We can discuss my new career path," Ravenna continued. "I've had it with this profiling work. My boss takes me for granted and treats me as if I'm the team mascot. There are too many unhappy endings. Tonight I almost got flatlined. On top of everything else, I had to use my other talent. Fortunately no one is going to believe those cultists in there, but it was a close call. Mom is right. I need to find a new line of work."

The dust bunny blinked her blue eyes.

Ravenna was about to continue the one-sided discussion of her future when the team marched the perps through the doorway and led them down the hall. She watched them file past, trying to assess their demeanors. Most looked dazed and bewildered. Several cast fearful glances at her and then quickly averted their eyes.

Louise Lace appeared. Her mask had been removed. When she saw Ravenna, panic flashed across her face.

"Witch," she whispered.

She was led away.

Clarence Fitch emerged from the chamber, escorted by two agents. At the sight of Ravenna he flew into a wild rage and twisted violently in a vain attempt to get free.

"She's a witch, I tell you," he rasped. "She destroyed my talent. I tried to cleanse her but she's too powerful. She must die."

The agents ignored him and steered him after the others. When the last of the agents had gone past, Ravenna fell into step behind them, the dust bunny cradled in her arms. She was bringing up the rear, and not for the first time, she reflected.

"I'm serious," she said in a low voice. "I'm going to go home, open a bottle of wine and a bag of pretzels, and come up with a new career goal."

The dust bunny chortled. Ravenna glanced down and saw that the creature was gripping a long narrow object in one paw.

"That's a very nice pen," Ravenna said. "Where did you get it?"

The dust bunny graciously offered it to her to examine. She took a close look. Fashioned of some dark blue metal and trimmed in gold, it gleamed in the light. It was engraved with the familiar logo of the FBPI, but it wasn't an ordinary Bureau pen, the kind that came from the office supplies closet. It was the expensive version that was handed out to high-performing agents, those who made the Bureau proud. Agents who were being fast-tracked into upper management. Agents who were put in charge of high-profile task forces.

She was pretty sure the pen had once belonged to Special Agent Max Collins.

"We'd better get out of here before you get arrested for the theft of government property or something," she said.

The dust bunny seemed fine with that idea.

There were forms to file, but they could wait until tomorrow. The team would be celebrating at a nearby bar this evening, but she wanted to go back to her apartment, take a long shower, put on a robe and slippers, pour a large glass of wine, and ponder her future. Something had to change.

She expected the dust bunny to disappear before she and the others emerged from the Underworld, but her new best friend was still in the crook of her arm when she walked through the front door of her apartment. She opened the jar of pretzels. The dust bunny chortled enthusiastically and selected several. Munching pretzels, she set out to explore the small space.

Ravenna watched her for a few minutes.

"If you're planning to stick around, we're going to need a name," she said.

CHAPTER THREE

"You can't dump me," Ethan Sweetwater said. "I've got a contract with this matchmaking agency. You owe me one more date."

"To be clear," Ravenna said, "I am not dumping you. I am trying to explain that I cannot help you."

"I don't believe it. When my nephew Jeff recommended you, he said you have the eye."

"Your nephew met me one time, and that was several months ago, when I was doing criminal profiling, not matchmaking. This work is quite different."

Actually, it was not all that different, she reflected. It turned out that criminal profiling had a lot in common with matchmaking. The emotional drivers were key.

"Maybe you're not trying hard enough," Ethan suggested.

That was nothing less than an insult.

"I am a professional, Mr. Sweetwater," she said coldly. "I assure you I have given your case my closest attention. In fact, all four of us here at Ottoway, including Ms. Ottoway herself, have gone through the files several times trying to find good matches for you."

She did not add that there were only two reasons Ethan Sweetwater—aka the client from green hell—was still on the books. The primary one was the contract. It stipulated that he was to receive a minimum of ten matches.

The second reason, of course, was that Bernice Ottoway, the proprietor of Ottoway Matchmakers, was desperate not to lose such a high-profile client. The Sweetwater name carried a lot of weight, not just in Illusion Town but throughout the four city-states. A successful match for a member of the notoriously private clan that controlled a huge chunk of the amber market would give Ottoway a major promotional hit. It also would do a lot for her career, Ravenna thought. Sadly, a successful outcome did not appear to be in the cards.

"We will be happy to refund your money and refer you to another agency," Ravenna said. Mentally she crossed her fingers. Bernice Ottoway never returned a client's money if she could help it, but surely she would understand that Ethan Sweetwater was a hopeless case.

"I don't want to waste my time starting from scratch at another agency," Ethan said. "I was assured that here at Ottoway the process would be efficient and professional."

"It would have helped if you had been more forthcoming on the Ottoway questionnaire," Ravenna said.

"Don't try to blame this on me, Ms. Chastain. I'm the client, remember? The customer is always right."

He was standing in front of her desk. He reached down somewhat absently to scratch Harriet behind her ears. The dust bunny was in the process of rearranging the pens in the tray. She paused to chortle appreciatively.

Ravenna stifled a groan. She and the entire staff at Ottoway might have a problem with Ethan, but Harriet's relationship with him was just fine. *Uncomplicated*, she thought. *Unlike mine.*

"I must tell you that, according to the after-action reports I received from the nine dates I arranged for you, your dating technique leaves something to be desired," she said.

"There you go, blaming the client again. If I've got a technique problem, you should help me fix it."

Ethan adjusted his black-framed glasses, turned away from the desk, and crossed the office. He took a stance at the window overlooking the quiet residential street.

She liked watching him move, Ravenna thought. He reminded her of a specter-cat, all prowling grace and elegant strength. He had the eyes to match. They were a dark amber gold and infused with the cold heat of controlled power—the eyes of an apex predator. The amber stone in his gold signet ring was the same color.

Eyes like Ethan's probably made some people nervous, she thought. Maybe that was the reason he chose to wear glasses. Or maybe he thought they went with the rest of his persona. He was an engineer by training and profession, and he had the pocket protector and chunky multifunction watch to prove it. Just to complete the fashion statement, he wore cargo trousers, a button-down shirt, a narrow, nondescript tie, and a slouchy jacket that looked as if it had been chosen for comfort and convenient pockets, not style.

But just as his nephew had somehow made the bulky FBPI vest and utility belt look good, Ethan managed to pull off the same sartorial miracle. Maybe it was because of the unmistakable aura of power and control that charged the atmosphere around him.

If you did not know what he did for a living and if you substituted dark glasses for the black frames, it would be easy to imagine him as a professional assassin. *One who only targeted the bad guys,* she assured herself. Well, maybe. Regardless, you would not want to be one of Ethan Sweetwater's targets.

"I sincerely regret that Ottoway Matchmakers was unable to find the right person for you, but occasionally we fail to bring about an ideal match," she said. "I assure you we deeply regret our inability to be of assistance."

That was nothing less than the truth. Bernice Ottoway was going to be very unhappy about the failure.

"I'm a busy man," Ethan said. "I'm trying to build my amber and quartz analysis business here in Illusion Town. I've made time for nine dates—*nine*—arranged by you. Every single one has been a disaster. So much for your agency's slogan."

He had a point, Ravenna thought. The words on the front door and on the firm's business cards made a proud boast: *When you're ready for Covenant Marriage, the best way is the Ottoway.*

"I assure you I devoted a great deal of time to your case," she said.

She had worked hard and succeeded in turning up nine potential matches. True, they had been less than ideal, but given the limited amount of personal information Ethan had provided and the not-so-hushed-up scandal in his past, she thought she had done remarkably well.

Harriet chose that moment to abandon her pen collection and vault down from the desk. She bustled across the floor and bounded up onto the windowsill to see what had attracted Ethan's attention.

Ethan reached inside his jacket, took out a pen, and offered it to the dust bunny. Harriet bounced up and down a few times and accepted the gift eagerly. She fluttered down from the windowsill, raced back across the office, and jumped up onto the desk. She added the pen to her collection and hovered over it, gloating.

"I'm afraid you're going to have a hard time getting that pen back," Ravenna said. "Harriet is a very possessive collector."

"It's all right," Ethan said. "I've got another one." He glanced at the tray of pens. "Out of curiosity, are they all stolen?"

"Of course not," Ravenna said, indignant. "Some were gifts. The rest are found objects."

"Forget the pen," Ethan said. "I don't want it back. Let's talk about my next date."

Ravenna reminded herself that her goal that afternoon was to remove Ethan Sweetwater from the roster of clients in a way that would not reflect badly on the Ottoway agency. She had delayed too long as it was. She was not sure why she had not given up trying to match him after the abject failure of the first three dates.

The odd thing was that back at the start she had been certain she could find Ms. Perfect for him, in spite of the scandal. But she was still new at the matchmaking business and it was obvious now that she had a lot to learn.

She had joined Ottoway less than six months ago, shortly after moving to Illusion Town, and until Ethan, she had racked up an unbroken string of successes. Her intuition for matchmaking was proving every bit as accurate and reliable as her talent for criminal profiling. It was glaringly obvious, however, that she had run straight into a solid quartz wall with Ethan Sweetwater.

He turned away from the window, his amber eyes glinting behind the lenses of his glasses. "I don't want my money back. I'm trying to find a soul mate for a Covenant Marriage. I want my forever match."

"Don't we all?" Ravenna said through her teeth.

She was horrified to realize she was in danger of losing her temper. That would be extremely unprofessional. But Ethan had hit a nerve. He wasn't the only one who wanted a good match, or at least one that appeared to be a distinct *possibility*. She needed a match, too—badly—and she was in a hurry. Time was not on her side. Her grandparents' wedding anniversary was coming up in a few days.

She had abandoned hope of finding a real match in time for the big event. She was now trying to find someone who could get her through the harrowing ordeal of the big Chastain family celebration. She was so desperate she had been toying with the notion of hiring an actor to play the part of prospective fiancé. Talk about humiliating and, in the long run, futile. But the future would have to take care of itself. She was no longer searching for Mr. Right. She needed to find Mr. Right Now.

The pressure was getting intense, and it wasn't as if the upcoming family gathering was the only problem she was dealing with. Her day had gotten off to a bad start when she found the barbecue grill fire starter on the front step of the quaint little Colonial-era cottage she had purchased two months earlier. The fire starter was the third ominous package that had been left at her door. It was clear now that she had a stalker.

To her surprise, Ethan Sweetwater did not appear annoyed by her sharp tone. Instead, he watched her with a speculative expression. The eyes of an engineer trying to decide how to deal with a system malfunction? Or those of a hunter stalking prey?

After a moment he removed his glasses and proceeded to polish the lenses with a small square of cloth. His direct, unshielded gaze sent a shivery thrill through her, lifting the fine hairs on the back of her neck.

"I've been wondering why an employee at one of the most exclusive matchmaking agencies in Illusion Town isn't married," he said. "It's interesting that with the full resources of Ottoway at your fingertips you haven't been able to find Mr. Forever for yourself."

She managed a steely smile. "My marital status is none of your business, Mr. Sweetwater, but for your information, matchmakers never date their own clients. Well, almost never."

"But it happens?"

"Rarely. It's not illegal or anything, but it's considered bad policy."

"Why?"

"It's an axiom in this business that matchmakers are terrible when it comes to finding a good match for themselves."

He looked startled. "Seriously?"

"Seriously." She cleared her throat. "As it happens, I'm registered at another agency."

She did not add that she was having less luck at the Banks agency than he was at Ottoway. Thirty-six dates now and counting.

Ethan's brows rose. "Any luck?"

"No."

Ethan looked much too intrigued by that information. "How many dates have they arranged for you?"

"That, too, is none of your business."

"That many, huh?"

"I suggest we change the subject," Ravenna said.

"Right." He tucked the polishing cloth into a pocket and used both hands to put on the glasses. "Speaking of marital status, the bottom line here is that you owe me one more date."

"I've gone through our files again. I'm afraid I was unable to find one more suitable candidate."

"How about an unsuitable candidate? Maybe I'll have better luck if we just roll the dice."

"I never roll the dice when it comes to matchmaking. I thought I made it clear, I am a professional. If you want to take risks I suggest you try one of the casinos. Here at Ottoway we do not play games with our clients' matrimonial futures."

"Too bad. It might be interesting."

"This has gone far enough." She clasped her hands on her desk. "I take full responsibility for this agency's failure to find the right match for you."

"As well you should. You were pretty damn positive that you could find a wife for me back at the start."

"I'm afraid I was overly optimistic," she admitted. "It's true that while you are a strong talent, your para-psych profile is not exotic."

His smile was suddenly ice-cold. "Meaning I'm not one of the monsters?"

Unlike me, she thought. *Lucky you, Sweetwater.*

"Precisely," she said. "You're a paranormal engineer. That is usually a very stable talent, even when it is high-rez, as it is in your case."

"Good to know I'm stable. Is that a polite word for *boring?*"

She flushed, aware that she was walking the very narrow line between explanation and insult. The vast majority of the descendants of the First Generation colonists from Earth had developed varying degrees of psychic talent. Even a five-year-old kid could generate enough energy through tuned resonating amber to turn on a rez screen or unlock the front door of the family home. Some people exhibited above-average talent, and Ethan was obviously one of them. Powerful talents with unusual para-psych profiles made a lot of people nervous.

But Ethan's profile was not dangerous or unstable. He was just a very good engineer. Her father and brothers were very good engineers who specialized in para-psych medical technology. Stable.

"Unfortunately, there are other factors at play here, Mr. Sweetwater," she said.

His jaw flexed and he got a grim, knowing look. "Is it the Kavanagh affair?"

"That was, of course, a complication, but for the most part I was able to overcome it long enough to book those nine dates."

It was true the nine matches she had produced so far had been hesitant about Ethan because of his vague responses on the extensive personality questionnaire. He had listed gardening as his only hobby and checked *N/A* (for *Not Applicable*) and *Decline to Specify* for many of the questions.

But it was the fact that he had been the *other man* in a notorious love triangle that had created the biggest stumbling block. Eighteen months earlier the media had gone wild with the story of what became known as the Kavanagh affair.

Covington Kavanagh had been a fast-rising star in politics. He was on a trajectory that would have taken him all the way to the presidency of the Federation of City-States. But his ambitions had been crushed when his wife, Bethany, had engaged in an affair with Ethan Sweetwater. The scandal had been huge. The media had splashed the headlines across the front pages of the newspapers and featured the story on the evening news broadcasts. There had been talk of a divorce, a rare and career-damaging move because the Kavanagh marriage was a Covenant Marriage.

Marriages of Convenience were dissolved all the time. They were designed to be short-lived. But the dissolution of a Covenant Marriage was not only an extremely expensive and lengthy process, it carried the weight of a heavy social stigma. Kavanagh's political career would have been derailed by a divorce.

The whole sordid business had come to a miserable end when Kavanagh had suffered a heart attack and died. The family had blamed the death on the stress of the scandal. Specifically, they had blamed Ethan Sweetwater.

When the headlines eventually faded away, Bethany Kavanagh had disappeared from the elevated social circles in which she had once traveled. Ethan had left Amber, Inc., the Sweetwater family business, and moved to Illusion Town.

So, yes, the scandal had been a problem when it came to finding a match for Ethan. But not surprisingly, the powerful Sweetwater name had overcome the initial concerns of all nine matches. There had, however, been no second dates.

Under normal circumstances Ottoway Matchmakers would not have accepted a client who had been involved in a high-profile scandal—or one who had failed to complete the questionnaire, for that matter. But Bernice Ottoway had made an exception for Ethan. After all, he was a Sweetwater.

"It's up to you, Ravenna," she had said. "If you think you can handle this client, he's all yours."

In spite of the negatives, Ravenna had been certain she could match Ethan. Everything about him fascinated her. She was sure the matches she selected would be equally intrigued by him. But there was no denying that something had gone terribly awry on all nine of the dates that she had arranged.

Each of the nine after-action interviews had revealed the same list of complaints. Ethan had been described in various shades of dull, boring, uncommunicative, and obsessed with his small engineering analysis business. Candidate number nine had declared Ethan "a complete waste of time" and insisted that an additional match be added to her contract to make up for the "poor quality" of the Sweetwater date.

For his part, Ethan had been less than helpful. Each of the nine candidates reported that he had ended the date early, saying he had to get back to the lab to finish an analysis of a specimen.

"Obviously you are no longer optimistic about finding a good match for me," Ethan said. "I get that. But I'm not ready to give up on your services."

"That's very gracious of you, Mr. Sweetwater," Ravenna said. "But you don't understand. This agency is giving up on you."

He considered that briefly, frowning a little as if trying to translate her words. Then he crossed the office in a few long strides, leaned forward, and planted both hands flat on the surface of her desk. His eyes heated.

"If you dump me before I get all ten dates specified in the contract, I'll sue," he said.

That did it. Now she was getting mad. She smiled her iciest smile.

"No, you will not sue, because when the *Curtain* and the other local media outlets discover that a member of the Sweetwater clan is suing one of the most elite matchmaking agencies in town because he was *unmatchable*, there will be headlines. Again. There will be pictures. Again. There will be interviews. Again. The story of your role in the Kavanagh affair will be dredged up and splashed across the front pages. *Again.* There will be questions—lots and lots of awkward questions. Your family will not be happy about that. It's well-known that the Sweetwaters have always gone out of their way to maintain a low profile in the media."

Okay, she was bluffing—a little—but they both knew that it was all true. The Sweetwaters had a long-standing tradition of trying to keep the family name out of the glare of the media. In addition, it would look ridiculous for a member of the clan to sue over something as humiliating as a failed attempt at matchmaking.

Ethan got a calculating look. "You play a tough game, lady."

"I am not playing games."

"Neither am I. You owe me one more date."

She took a sharp breath and started to rise from her chair, preparing to tell him one last time that she was firing him. That was when the outrageous idea struck with such dazzling force that for a moment all she could do was stare at him.

No, it would be incredibly reckless. Ethan would probably refuse, anyway. But if for some reason he accepted the deal, it just might work.

She sank back down into the chair and did a single staccato drumroll on the desk with her polished nails.

"You're not going to give up and go away quietly, are you?" she said.

"No," he said, "but I have an idea."

"So do I. You want one more date? Fine. You'll get it. With me."

He went very still and watched her with his specter-cat eyes. "You?"

"I happen to need a date. A family event. My grandparents' anniversary. It's a big overnight affair at the Silver Lake resort in the Silver Mountains. You know what those celebrations are like."

He grimaced. "Big family gathering and you're not married. There will be pressure. Lots of it."

"Yep."

"I understand, believe me."

"You, too?"

"Yep."

On this topic, at least, they were in complete accord, she thought. Family was everything on Harmony. For two hundred years the institution had been woven into the basic structure of society by a rigid network of laws and customs. Sooner or later almost everyone got married, and the only kind of marriage that mattered was a full Covenant Marriage. The pressure to marry became intense after a certain age. The tacky Marriage of Convenience, intended to put a veneer of respectability on what was nothing more than an affair, did not count. MCs were for young people who wanted to spread their wings and experiment before settling down into the real thing.

So, yes, when it came to family pressure, she and Ethan each had a solid understanding of what the other was facing.

He studied her as if she was an unfamiliar specimen of amber or quartz. Maybe he was trying to decide if she had any useful resonating properties.

"Let me get this straight," he said. "You want to satisfy the terms of the contract by asking me to escort you to a major family gathering."

"That's the deal," she said.

"Just to clarify, it would be a fake date."

"A date is a date, right? This is my best offer, Sweetwater. Take it or leave it."

"I'll take it."

She was stunned. "What?"

"I said, I'll take the deal. With one slight modification."

"Modification?" She was still coping with the shock of his ready acceptance of her offer. She could not formulate a logical response.

"I'll agree to act as your date for your grandparents' anniversary event if you'll act as mine tomorrow night."

"I don't understand."

"You aren't the only one who needs a last-minute date," Ethan said. "I need someone to accompany me to a business reception at the Amber Palace. Think of it as a failure mode analysis date."

"Failure mode analysis?"

"My dating techniques have evidently failed nine times in a row. I'm an engineer. I believe in conducting a failure mode analysis when things go wrong. Tomorrow night will provide the perfect opportunity for you to observe and assess my technique."

"Hmm."

"In addition, it will act as a stress test."

"Pardon?"

"A catastrophic failure at the anniversary party would be a major disaster for you, much worse than showing up with no date at all," Ethan continued. "It's a long drive to the Silver Mountains. We need to know if we can survive a road trip together plus the pressure of trying to act like a happy couple in front of your family."

"Hmm."

She suspected she was being manipulated, but maybe a failure mode analysis and stress test date was not such a bad idea. Ethan had a point. It was an all-day drive from Illusion Town to the mountains, a long, tedious road trip across the vast Mirage Desert. They would be locked together in a car for several hours each way. And then there would be the stress of trying to pretend they were a couple in front of her family, the people who knew her all too well.

She gripped the arms of her chair, mentally bracing herself. "You said the event tomorrow evening is a business reception?"

"The Amber Research and Technology Association is holding its bi-annual convention in town," Ethan said. "My family is in the amber business, in case you didn't know."

She made a valiant effort and succeeded in resisting the urge to throttle him. "Yes, Mr. Sweetwater, I am aware of your family's little amber business."

He surprised her with a quick laugh. "I happen to live here in Illusion Town, so Cruz asked me to represent Amber, Inc., at the reception. Between you and me, I have not been looking forward to it."

"Cruz?"

"Cruz Sweetwater is my brother. He's the CEO of Amber, Inc."

"I believe I have heard the name," she said very sweetly.

"I said I'd do him a favor and put in an appearance at the reception."

"I see."

Ethan gave her a dangerous smile. "Naturally, having signed up with one of the most elite matchmaking agencies in Illusion Town, I had assumed that by now I'd have a real date for tomorrow night."

"All right," Ravenna said, her voice very tight. She stood and faced him across the expanse of her desk. "I will do the failure mode analysis stress test date. I agree it would be a very good idea to see if we can be civil with each other long enough to get through a road trip."

"That's the spirit. There's nothing like a positive attitude to brighten one's day, I always say."

"Have you ever personally experienced a day brightened by a positive attitude?"

"No, I'm an engineer." He glanced at his chunky watch. "I've got to be on my way. The reception starts at seven. Cocktail formal. We won't have to stay long. I'll pick you up at six thirty tomorrow evening. What's your address?"

"It's 118 Midnight Court. But it's in the Dark Zone near the border of the Fire Zone. You'll never find it. The navigation systems don't work well there. Why don't I meet you at the Amber Palace?"

"I know my way around the DZ. I'll find you."

"Outsiders always get lost in the DZ," she warned.

"I'm not an outsider. I live there, too. Ruin Gate Lane."

She glared. "According to our files, your address is in the Emerald Zone."

"That's my business address. It's where the lab is located. I don't live there. I like my privacy. See you at six thirty."

He let himself out into the hall and closed the door very deliberately.

CHAPTER FOUR

Ravenna looked at Harriet. "Tell me I haven't just made the biggest mistake of my career."

Harriet chortled, selected Ethan's pen from the tray, and offered it to her. It was a very attractive pen made of silver mirror amber so beautifully polished she could see her own reflection in it. The cap was finished with a lovely little jewel of red-gold amber.

Intrigued, she took the pen—and got a little flutter of energy. Caught off guard, she smiled.

"It's tuned," she said to Harriet. "Mr. Sweetwater must be a very, very good engineer. I didn't think you could tune mirror amber."

What startled her was that the amber had not been generically tuned so that anyone could pick up the vibe and generate a little psychic energy through it. No, the elegant pen was sealed with a rez-Valentine lock.

"Who would have guessed that Ethan Sweetwater was the romantic type?" she said to Harriet.

Rez-Valentine locks could be installed in any object made of resonating amber, but they were used primarily in objects given as gifts—small figurines, paperweights, jewelry, music boxes. Trust an engineer to choose something practical like a pen, Ravenna thought.

Objects tuned with Valentine locks were sold as a set that included both the gift and a separate item also made of amber that was designed to resonate with the frequency of the gift. The person who gave the Valentine kept the resonating object. The locked gift could be unlocked only once by the recipient. When that was done, it sent out a signal on a unique frequency that could only be detected by the object tuned to resonate with the gift.

A rez-Valentine was infused with romantic symbolism. The giver was sending a message—*My heart resonates with yours. I love you.* If the recipient unlocked the gift and sent the signal, it meant that the love was reciprocated.

A wistful sensation whispered through Ravenna. She looked at Harriet. "Ethan must have had this made for the woman he assumed I would eventually find for him. He gave it to you today because he realized he probably isn't going to find Ms. Perfect through this agency. I'll bet he had already given up on Ottoway before he walked into this office today. I failed him, Harriet."

Harriet chortled and went back to arranging her collection of pens.

Ravenna tossed the rez-Valentine pen into the air and caught it. "So why didn't he take the refund? Why insist that Ottoway fulfill the contract? He must be one of those annoying people who are sticklers when it comes to the legal stuff."

The door popped open. Bernice Ottoway appeared. She was in her mid-seventies and endowed with a kind, warmhearted, grandmotherly air. But looks were deceiving with Bernice. She had not built one of the most successful matchmaking agencies in Illusion Town by being kind, warmhearted, and grandmotherly. She had a will of iron, and her razor-sharp business instincts were the equal of those of any of the powerful CEOs who ran the big hotel-casinos. She had, in fact, matched several of those CEOs.

"Well?" Bernice said. "Did you lose Sweetwater?"

"Not yet." Ravenna rezzed up an attitude of reassuring professional optimism. "Mr. Sweetwater has one more date on his contract. However, he has come to the conclusion that there is something off-putting about his dating skills. Judging by the feedback I've had from the nine dates I arranged for him, he's right."

"That bad, is it?" Bernice groaned. "Damn. I was hoping the Sweetwater name would be enough to make prospective dates overlook the scandal and a few minor imperfections."

"Apparently the imperfections are not so minor. Mr. Sweetwater and I discussed the matter at length. I agreed to accompany him to a business function tomorrow night to see if I can analyze his dating techniques and provide helpful counseling."

Bernice looked skeptical. "That is an interesting approach, but it's a bit fraught, don't you think? We would not want to give Mr. Sweetwater or any of his acquaintances the wrong idea."

"What wrong idea would that be, Ms. Ottoway?"

"The notion that Ottoway Matchmakers is a high-end escort agency."

Ravenna stared at her, horrified. "Absolutely not. I assure you my arrangement with Mr. Sweetwater will be handled in an entirely professional manner."

"See to it," Bernice snapped. "And make sure you produce a successful match for Mr. Sweetwater."

"I'll do my best, Ms. Ottoway."

"Let me be clear, Ravenna. You are in charge of the Sweetwater account only because he insisted on having you as his matchmaker. He said you came highly recommended by a relative. Under normal circumstances I would never have assigned such an important client to you.

You're the newest, most inexperienced agent in this firm. Granted, you've had some initial success, but if you fail to come up with a successful match for Sweetwater, you will be placed on probation. Is that clear?"

"Yes, Ms. Ottoway."

Bernice pivoted and left.

Ravenna looked at Harriet. "My life is getting complicated."

CHAPTER FIVE

"Okay, this is not good," Sybil Banks said. She brought the tunnel sled to a halt and climbed out from behind the wheel. "You're telling me that if you don't find a match for Mr. Impossible, you might lose your job?"

"Not exactly," Ravenna said. "Ottoway informed me I would be put on probation."

She got out on the other side of the sled. The vehicle was about the size of a golf cart and, at top speed, moved about as fast. Equipped with simple, low-powered amber engines—one of the few forms of technology that worked in the Underworld—tunnel sleds were the vehicles of choice when you wanted to move faster than a walk, cover long distances, or haul a load through the tunnels. The more sophisticated engines used to power cars, trucks, trains, and ships on the surface did not function in the heavy psi environment.

Sybil took hold of the rim on one side of the large kettle that sat in the back of the sled. "Think Ottoway is serious?"

"Yes." Ravenna gripped the other side of the kettle. "Ms. Ottoway didn't want to trust me with the Sweetwater match in the first place, but she had no choice. Now she's desperate not to lose such an important client. Ready?"

"Yep," Sybil said.

Together they hoisted the pot out of the sled and carried it down to the glowing quartz platform in the center of the chamber. Harriet, supervising from the dashboard of the small vehicle, chortled encouragement.

When they reached the round platform, they set the pot in the center. Ravenna removed the glass lid.

She and Sybil had discovered the strange Underworld chamber a couple of months earlier in the course of an exploratory hike through some of the tunnels directly under the Dark Zone neighborhood.

There was no way to know how the Aliens had utilized the spacious room, but with its high ceiling, stadium-like seating, and circular stage in the center, it looked so much like a human-engineered theater-in-the-round that it was difficult to think of it as having been used in any other fashion. It seemed logical that any intelligent, creative species needed some form of storytelling, and there was no doubt but that the long-vanished Aliens had been extremely intelligent and very creative.

Technically, she and Sybil should not be down here on their own. Private ventures into the catacombs that were undertaken without security provided by the Ghost Hunters Guild were strongly discouraged, but everyone knew they took place all the time. There were a number of reasons why people went down into the Underworld minus a security team, not the least of which was that hiring Guild escorts was expensive.

A lot of off-the-books forays were made by indie prospectors hoping to discover a cache of priceless Alien artifacts or a vein of some rare amber or quartz. If they got lucky they had every reason to keep the coordinates of the find a secret until they had registered the claim and figured out how to make it pay off. The last thing the indies wanted to do was alert the Guild. Rumors spread fast in the mining business. There was a long history of incredible discoveries in the Underworld, and an equally long history of claim jumping.

There were other reasons why individuals headed into the maze of tunnels. Some went below for the thrill of the experience. The paranormal currents were strong and unpredictable. Most people got a pleasant little psychic buzz from the atmosphere, but some individuals experienced profound terror, and others became dangerously intoxicated.

And then there were those who found the lure of the ancient ruins irresistible because it allowed them to exercise their talents to the max. *People like us,* Ravenna thought. She and Sybil had begun their private expeditions into the tunnels shortly after they had become friends. That had happened when Ravenna registered at Sybil's boutique—translation: one-person—matchmaking agency. *When it comes to Covenant Marriage, you can bank on Banks.*

"Everyone knows some clients are extremely difficult to match," Sybil said. "That goes double if the client is a high-end talent, which, according to you, is the case with Ethan Sweetwater."

"No doubt about it," Ravenna said.

Sybil's brows rose. "Are you still certain he's just an engineering talent?"

"That's what he put down on the questionnaire. It was one of the few questions he answered. There's no reason not to believe him. The Sweetwaters have been mining and conducting research and development on amber for several decades. It makes sense the members of the family would have a talent for tech."

"And you're still sure he's stable?"

"Yes. That's not just my opinion. Ms. Ottoway and I both agree Sweetwater appears stable."

"Powerful auras are usually very hard to assess when it comes to a para-psych profile. I've met one or two talents who are so strong they can shield the unstable frequencies."

"Sweetwater is stable, trust me. He's also as stubborn as a rock. I practically begged him to cancel the contract and accept a refund."

"Speaking as a professional, I have to tell you something isn't adding up here," Sybil said. "An engineering talent, even a very strong one, combined with the Sweetwater name should have made for a doable match, even factoring in the Kavanagh affair."

"I know."

"Maybe not the most romantic match in the history of Covenant Marriage," Sybil allowed. "Maybe not a match filled with grand passion. But so what? When it comes to a Covenant Marriage, smart people look for more important and long-lasting elements, such as trust and friendship and mutual respect. Sure, there must be a degree of physical attraction, but it doesn't have to be the whole swept-away-on-wings-of-rapturous-moonlight thing."

Ravenna frowned. "'Wings of rapturous moonlight'?"

"You know what I mean."

Ravenna grimaced. "I do, and I agree with you. The Kavanagh affair certainly didn't help, but I was sure I could find a good match for him. He suggested the problem is his dating technique, and after listening to the after-action reports from the nine matches, I'm pretty sure he's right."

"Even if that's the case, what makes you think he'd listen to advice? In my experience, people don't change; they want everyone else to change instead. Hang on, I'll be right back."

Sybil returned to the sled, picked up a large package, and carried it to the stage. Harriet chortled and bounced up onto the last tier of seats.

"Everybody makes mistakes," Sybil said. She opened the package. "I still can't believe I was so wrong when I matched you with Garrett Willis. He looked like a good match. Not perfect, but let's face it, we in the matchmaking business know there is no such thing as perfect. Still, the two of you should have been a reasonably comfortable fit. You're both strong talents. You have a lot in common. You each come from solid families."

"He's in the casino business, Sybil."

"So?"

"I don't think I'm cut out to be the wife of a casino mogul."

"In that case, you shouldn't have moved to Illusion Town," Sybil said. "Casino moguls are pillars of the community here."

"You've got me there," Ravenna said. "I will admit he seemed like a very nice person. It was a pleasant evening. I learned a lot about how to calculate odds and I got several tips on poker that may come in handy someday. Oh, and there was an interesting discussion about how to deal with psychic card counters."

"There, you see?" Sybil emptied the contents of the package into the kettle. "It wasn't a bad match."

"Willis wasn't any more excited than me," Ravenna said. "Afterward we both agreed to keep dating others."

"What went wrong with Clark Hatch? I was sure that one would work out."

"Again, a nice guy, but he spent the entire evening telling me about the plot of his next psychic vampire thriller." Ravenna brightened. "I did learn a few things about the publishing industry."

"So not a wasted evening."

"I'm starting to think I'm even harder to match than Sweetwater," Ravenna said.

"Nonsense."

"I'm serious. We knew it would be a difficult process, but it's turning out worse than I imagined, and we both know why."

"Your talent is . . . complicated," Sybil admitted. She crumpled the empty package. "But I'm not giving up on you."

"Thanks," Ravenna said. "Most professionals would have after so many failed dates. I'm at thirty-six and counting."

"I never give up on a client," Sybil said. "Well, almost never. Mostly I try to avoid the ones I know I won't be able to match."

"That's what we do at Ottoway," Ravenna said. She put the lid on the pot. "But apparently you can't just dump a Sweetwater."

Muffled chortles sounded in the distance. Harriet bounced up and down a few times, buzzed on dust bunny adrenaline.

"I think the guests are arriving," Ravenna said. "Brace yourself."

The pack of excited dust bunnies raced around a corner and dashed into the theater. There was much enthusiastic chortling as fifteen or twenty oversized wads of dryer lint took up positions on the benches. Once in place, they fixed their attention on the stage. Silence fell.

"Time to fire up the cauldron, oh great witch," Sybil said.

Ravenna shot her a stern look and then pulled a little energy out of the intense atmosphere. Flames leaped under the kettle and licked up the sides. It didn't take long before the first kernels of popcorn pinged inside. At the sound, the dust bunnies went wild.

Sybil chuckled. "See? Your talent for fire is good for something, after all."

"Right. Making large quantities of popcorn. Maybe I should get a job in a movie theater."

The initial pings changed to a rapid-fire series of small explosions. It wasn't long before the popped kernels pushed aside the lid and overflowed the kettle. Ravenna cut the power. The dust bunnies rushed toward the popcorn.

"That will keep them busy for a while," Sybil said. "Our turn."

Ravenna followed her back to the sled. They climbed into the front seat and sat down. Sybil opened the large bag of chips. Ravenna took out the bottle of Old World Zin. According to the label, the grapes were grown from vines that had been brought through the Curtain by some wine-making First Gen colonist. She filled two glasses and handed one to Sybil, who offered her some chips.

They lounged against the back of the seat, stacked their sneaker-clad feet on the dashboard, drank the wine, and munched while they watched the dust bunnies consume the popcorn.

The kettle was emptied just as Ravenna poured the second glasses of wine.

"Looks like everyone is ready for act two," Sybil said.

"Here we go." Ravenna rezzed her talent again.

A dazzling display of paranormal fireworks burst above the stage. The dust bunnies were euphoric. Ravenna smiled and whipped up another brilliant display.

"Great audience," she said.

Sybil gave her a knowing look. "You like doing this, don't you?"

"Using your talent always gives you a rush, you know that."

"Especially down here in the hot atmosphere." Sybil drank some wine and watched the fireworks flash and flare. "Harriet and her pals do know how to party, don't they?"

"Life is uncomplicated for a dust bunny," Ravenna said. "We humans could probably learn a few things from them."

"Has it occurred to you that the fact that we are down here in the Underworld entertaining a bunch of little critters with popcorn and fireworks suggests our aboveground social lives may be somewhat lacking?"

"Yes," Ravenna said. "That has occurred to me."

CHAPTER SIX

The witch walked through the botanical garden, savoring the energy of the exotic plants. Each specimen had been selected for its therapeutic properties. Medieval apothecaries had used such plant collections—called physic gardens—to supply the ingredients needed to brew medicines and remedies.

According to the legends, apothecaries were not the only ones who took a special interest in plants and herbs. Poisoners relied on them, too.

The witch stopped at a plot of herbs and collected some before moving on to the flowers that would be needed for the finished product.

Back in the lab the witch opened the herbal and studied the formula one last time. Getting access to the fully equipped facility with its state-of-the-art instruments and equipment had been a simple matter. Illusion Town College had been delighted to host a visiting chemist from the distinguished University of Resonance.

An expertise in chemistry made an excellent cover. No one questioned the credentials, which, technically speaking, were real. The witch had the degrees to prove it. But unlike most people in the field, the witch did not possess any paranormal talent for the work. The witch worked magic instead. On a world that used resonating amber and quartz to power everything from light bulbs to computers, it was easy to pass for normal. Most people could not tell the difference between witchcraft and paranormal talent.

Satisfied that all the required ingredients had been assembled, the witch began preparations. Modern technology combined with the paranormal-enhanced plants of Harmony guaranteed significantly more powerful results than the original version of the poison.

The interesting thing about medicinal herbs and plants was that, like so many other things in life, they had a dark side as well as a light side. That was nature for you. Anything strong enough to create a healing remedy was strong enough to create a poison.

Better magic through chemistry.

Chapter Seven

"I appreciate this." Gabriel Jones swallowed some of his Hot Amber beer and lowered the bottle. "So does Arcane and the Guild Council."

"The Sweetwaters are always happy to do a favor for Arcane and the Guild Council," Ethan said, gravely polite.

Gabriel raised his brows. "The Guilds don't have a long history of doing business with the Sweetwaters, but Arcane does. We know how the favors work."

Ethan smiled a bland smile. "You know that because Arcane and Guild favors work exactly the same way."

He and Jones, the new Guild boss in Illusion Town, were sitting in a bar at the edge of the gaming floor of a small casino located off the Amber Zone Strip. Way off. They wanted privacy.

It was late afternoon and the establishment was only lightly crowded. No one was paying attention to them. The steady ping, buzz, clang, and cha-ching of the slots created enough background noise to mask their conversation, in any event.

"The Jones family has a saying about the Sweetwaters," Gabriel said. "'Sooner or later the bill will come due.'"

"I'm deeply offended that you are under the impression we would charge for our services. According to Granddad, we only sent bills back in the old days when we were in a different line of work. We're in the amber business now, in case you haven't heard."

"Trust me, I remember that every time I rez the lights or turn on the rez screen."

"The good news for the Sweetwaters is that there is a lot more money in good rez-amber than there ever was in our old line."

"So these days you just do favors."

"Occasionally, and only for a very few, very trusted clients," Ethan said.

"Moving right along. Did you get the file?"

"Got it and read it. There's not much in it that isn't already on the public record. It's not exactly a secret that Taggert Spooner is the CEO of Spooner Technologies. He has every reason to attend the convention of the Amber Research and Technology Association. His company does a lot of R and D, and his customers include the federal government and some of the biggest companies on the planet. Why are you worried about him?"

"Before we get to that, I need to ask one question." Gabriel leaned back in the chair and got a considering look. "Has Spooner ever taken a contract with Sweetwater?"

"No. When it comes to amber tech we have our own in-house experts. We don't use outsiders if we can avoid it."

Gabriel's eyes narrowed a little. "I'm talking about the other kind of contract—the sort the Sweetwaters occasionally signed with Arcane back on Earth and in the Colonial days here on Harmony."

"No," Ethan said quietly.

Gabriel nodded. "Didn't think so. Just wanted to be sure."

"For the record, the Sweetwaters were never dumb enough to actually sign anything, not when it came to those kinds of contracts. We did business on a handshake."

Gabriel nodded. "Smart."

"The Sweetwaters didn't make it through the Curtain and survive on Harmony by doing dumb shit. Tell me why you're interested in Taggert Spooner and what you want me to watch for at the convention."

"Ever heard of Vortex?" Gabriel asked.

"Are you talking about that outfit that gave Jones and Jones so much trouble back on the Old World?"

"Yes. And for the record, Vortex wasn't just a problem for Jones and Jones and Arcane. According to the archives, an organization known as the Foundation was actively involved in hunting them."

"Never heard of the Foundation," Ethan said.

"Some kind of off-the-books government contractor, I think."

Ethan paused his beer in midair. "I was under the impression that Vortex had been taken care of before the Curtain even opened."

"You know how it is with legends. There's always some truth at the core. Apparently there were a few loose ends that were never dealt with. Now Arcane has reason to believe someone is trying to create a new version of Vortex here on Harmony. If so, we've got a problem."

"You mean Arcane has a problem."

"It's not just Arcane. The Guild Council is also concerned. Given my job and my family name, I find myself representing both organizations at the moment. What I'm telling you is strictly confidential, Ethan. The bottom line is that we don't know who we can trust."

"Except for the Sweetwaters."

"Our families go back a long way."

"I know," Ethan said. "Go on, tell me about Spooner."

"All we've got at the moment is a rumor that he may be using the convention as a cover to meet with an unknown individual who may have a lead on a very hot find in the Underworld. Arcane and the Council want to know the name of that person."

"Define *hot find*."

"At this point we have no idea what it is," Gabriel said. "What I can tell you with confidence is that if Spooner is interested, Arcane and the Guilds are interested."

"Maybe the hot find is just another routine amber or quartz strike. Indie prospectors file claims for new discoveries all the time and then try to sell them to a big company."

"Yes, but most of those discoveries don't amount to much," Gabriel said. "The fact that Spooner may be planning to set up a secret meeting indicates that whatever he's after is big."

"And may be completely legitimate. There's no law against staking a claim to a new amber or quartz mine."

"No, but there are laws that forbid possession of Alien artifacts of any kind that may have unknown or potentially dangerous properties."

"You mean weapons-grade Alien tech," Ethan said.

"Discoveries that fall into that category must be turned over to the government authorities immediately."

Ethan reflected briefly and shook his head. "No one has ever discovered much in the way of working Alien technology, let alone Alien weaponry. What makes you think this hot find may be different?"

"Let's just say that if this is in any way connected to a new version of Vortex, we need to know about it."

"All you want is a name?" Ethan asked.

"Yes." Gabriel paused for emphasis. "No further action is required, at least not at this time."

Ethan drank some of his beer and set the bottle on the table. "Meaning?"

"Meaning no further action is required."

"Good. Because I'm a tech guy. I don't do the *further action* stuff."

"Just get us a name," Gabriel said.

"I'll see what I can do."

"Thanks," Gabriel said. He started to say something else but his phone pinged. He glanced down, grimaced, and reluctantly got to his feet. "I've got to be on my way. Aiden, my administrative assistant, just reminded me my fiancée and I have an appointment with the wedding planner this afternoon. Something about finalizing the catering menu."

Ethan gave him a sympathetic smile. "Your upcoming wedding is going to be a major event here in town. I hear the studio is planning to coordinate the release of that movie they're making about you, *Guild Boss*, with the festivities."

"Don't remind me. Lucy and I would be happy to keep the whole thing low profile, but Aiden insists we have to pull out all the stops. Says it has to be an old-fashioned formal Guild-style Covenant Marriage wedding. He's renting the ballroom at the Amber Palace. The good news is that I get to wear the formal Guild boss uniform instead of a tux, but that's about the only good news."

"Your administrative assistant is in charge of your wedding?"

Gabriel looked grim. "Aiden is on a mission to rebrand the Guild here in Illusion Town. Says the wedding of the new Guild boss—that would be me—should be a headline-making event. Claims it will be good for the image of the organization."

"He's probably right," Ethan said. "Illusion Town loves big, flashy events. Consider yourself lucky. At least you've got an actual fiancée."

"This is true," Gabriel said. He looked remarkably cheered by the observation. "That reminds me, how are things going with the matchmaking agency? Or should I not ask?"

"Got another date tonight," Ethan said. He smiled a little. Unlike the previous nine matches, he was looking forward to this one.

"Yeah?" Gabriel's brows rose. "How many dates does this make?"

"Ten, but technically it's a failure mode analysis and stress test date."

"What the hell?"

"My matchmaker is going to assess my dating techniques and advise me on how to improve them. If I get through the evening, I will accompany her to a resort in the Silver Mountains to attend her grandparents' anniversary celebration."

Gabriel whistled. "Sounds complicated. Think date number ten is going to be any different than numbers one through nine?"

"Oh, yeah," Ethan said. A frisson of anticipation aroused all of his senses. "This one is definitely going to be different."

"What's she like, this matchmaker?"

Ethan pictured Ravenna in his mind. He saw her sunset-red hair bound up in a strict knot; her petite, gently curved figure clad in a crisp, snug-fitting blue business suit; her lagoon-green eyes burning with intelligence, determination, and control. And then he thought about the indefinable aura of power that whispered in the atmosphere around her.

"Small but fierce," he said.

CHAPTER EIGHT

The sweet scent of a flowery perfume slipped through the atmosphere, riding invisible currents of energy.

Garrett Willis was in his paneled office on the top floor of the gleaming tower that housed the Lucky Quartz casino and hotel. He was watching the array of computer screens on the wall. The displays covered the gaming floor, the bars, and the restaurants. There was another set of screens on the adjacent wall that captured the real-time images from the garage.

He had a crack security team on constant patrol twenty-four hours a day throughout the casino and the hotel, but he had been raised in the business. The importance of the owner keeping an eye on all aspects of the operations had been drilled into him while he was still in the cradle. The Lucky Quartz was a family business that had been handed down through three generations. He was in charge of protecting it for his as-yet-unborn heirs.

He tried to ignore the perfume, assuming it had somehow wafted in through the air-conditioning ducts. It was no longer alluring. Instead it was becoming cloying. It was also getting stronger. That should not be happening. The ventilation throughout the tower was state-of-the-art. He started to rez the button that would connect him with the head of maintenance.

Inexplicably, he fumbled, missing the button entirely. Irritated, he tried again. This time his arm was too heavy to lift. His vision was blurry. Bizarre visions formed in the atmosphere. Hallucinations. He wondered, vaguely, if he was having a stroke.

He was trying to rez the emergency number when the door opened. A woman in a tailored business suit and heels entered the room. There was something terribly wrong with her face.

"Who are you?" he managed, aware that his words were so slurred as to be almost unintelligible. "How the hell did you get past security?"

"I'm your new consultant," the witch said.

He finally realized what was wrong with her face. She was wearing a gas mask. He remembered the mag-rez stored in his desk, but he fell into a dream before he could figure out how to open the drawer.

In his dreamscape the witch took off her mask.

He came out of the darkness aware that he had dreamed but unable to remember the dream. Not that it mattered. He was surprised to realize he had dozed off at his desk, though. He never napped. He raised his head and sat back in the chair, moving cautiously because he was a little dizzy.

He blinked a few times to clear his vision and then got up to get a bottle of water out of the concealed refrigerator. A few sips helped.

The faint, lingering scent of perfume made him pause. There was something he had to do. Something important. It had to be done tonight. The woman was a threat to the family business. She would destroy it. He was the only one who could stop her. He had to protect the Lucky Quartz. It was the inheritance he was supposed to hand off to the next generation.

He went back to the desk, opened a drawer, and took out the mag-rez.

CHAPTER NINE

"What do you think, Harriet?" Ravenna surveyed the handful of potential cocktail-formal dresses suitable for a business reception that hung in the back of the walk-in closet. "Black is always a safe bet. You can never go wrong with a little black dress."

She had five little black dresses, all styled in varying degrees of sexy. One was discreetly sprinkled with black crystals. She had cycled through all five numbers several times over the course of the thirty-six failed dates.

In addition to the LBDs there were two other dresses that qualified as sophisticated evening wear. One was the long, elegant blue gown she had bought for her grandparents' anniversary ball. It was too formal for a cocktail reception.

The second option was the newest addition to her wardrobe, a knee-length green number. She loved it but it made her nervous. It was the sort of dress that demanded some attitude. She wasn't sure she could carry it off. Thirty-six failed dates had a negative impact on a woman's self-confidence.

But tonight was not intended to be a real date. She would be work-ing on this date, conducting a failure mode analysis. Oh, right, and a stress test.

"Maybe I'll wear the green one," she said to Harriet.

Harriet chortled in what she took to be an encouraging way. The dust bunny was on the dressing table, gripping one of her favorite acquisitions, a bright-red pen bearing the logo of the Dark Zone Delivery Service: *We Know the Zone.* She liked watching her own reflection as she waved it around in front of the mirror.

Ravenna did not have to wonder if Harriet had thieved the pen. The DZ Delivery person who had delivered last night's pizza had given it to her.

"All right, the green one it is," Ravenna said. She felt very daring.

She carried the dress, a slinky, long-sleeved sheath, across the bed-room and arranged it carefully on the bed. The dress was cut demurely high in front and just low enough in back to qualify as both elegant and discreetly sexy, according to Sybil, who had helped her select it. The shopping expedition had taken place after failed date number thirty-six. Sybil had suggested that perhaps Ravenna was not sending the right mes-sages with her little black numbers.

"Wearing it will be my own private stress test," Ravenna said to Harriet. "If I feel uncomfortable in it, I'll know I shouldn't wear it on a real date."

She wondered if talking to a dust bunny was a bad sign.

"You know, Harriet, it's going to be ironic if this date goes well to-night and I actually do take Ethan Sweetwater to Silver Lake. It would be the first time I've had a second date since I got serious about trying to find a husband. Dawson doesn't count. That fiasco happened back in Cadence, not here in Illusion Town."

Harriet chortled and waved the pen.

"I wish you could go with me tonight but I have a feeling you'll have a lot more fun on your own," Ravenna said.

She stepped into the knee-length green sheath and struggled with the zipper in back. Yet another reason to get married, she thought. It would be handy to have someone around the house who could assist with zippers.

She checked the time—a quarter after six—and decided it would be okay to put on the stiletto heels. Intuition told her that Ethan would arrive at her door at exactly six thirty. She went back to the closet and picked up the high-heeled, pointy-toed pumps.

To her surprise the doorbell rezzed just as she sat down on the edge of the bed to slip on the heels. Her pulse, already beating a little too quickly, abruptly kicked up.

"Wouldn't you know it?" she said to Harriet. "He's not the always-right-on-time type, he's the always-early type."

The doorbell sounded again. This time she thought it had a distinctly annoyed, impatient vibe.

"Not a good way to start a date," she told Harriet. "I must remember to note this in my failure mode analysis." She stepped into the pumps and got to her feet. "No wonder he made a bad impression on those nine dates."

In spite of having made up her mind that the evening was already a disaster, she checked her reflection in the mirror one last time. Her hair was anchored in a twist at the back of her head. A pair of amber-and-gold earrings dangled from her ears. For the most part she had kept the makeup to a minimum—it was a business reception, after all—but she had gone for a little drama with her eyes. More than one cosmetic counter consultant had told her they were her best feature.

Concluding she was as ready as she would ever be, she left the bedroom and stalked down the hall to the front door. Harriet bounded off the dresser and scampered after her. She scooped her up and tucked her under an arm.

When she reached the small foyer she yanked open the door, intending to tell Ethan Sweetwater that his dating technique was a disaster.

But it wasn't Ethan who stood on the front steps. It was failed date number thirty-six, Garrett Willis. Harriet started to chortle a greeting—she liked Willis, who had gifted her with a Lucky Quartz casino and hotel pen. But the chortle turned to a menacing growl.

Willis was dressed in classic casino mogul evening casual—a well-cut cream-colored jacket, dark trousers, and a maroon dress shirt with a wide, flared collar, open at the throat. His accessories included an impressive steel-and-obsidian watch and a massive ring set with a huge chunk of rare blue quartz. He wore his tuned amber in his belt buckle.

He also had a mag-rez pistol in one hand.

"Witch," he rasped.

For some reason she noticed the pupils of his eyes. They were pinpoints. Instinctively she tightened her grip on Harriet, who was trying to wriggle free.

"Garrett?" she said. "What's going on?"

"I have to destroy you," Garrett said, "before you destroy my family."

He sounded calm—unnaturally so. Ravenna stepped out of the heels and moved back into the hall. If she got a chance to run, she did not want to be hampered by the shoes.

Garrett followed her, the mag-rez never wavering. She tried to come up with a plan. She could pull energy here on the surface, but Garrett could rez the pistol more than once in the time it took her to generate some serious flames.

She glanced past him. Through the open doors she could see the front steps and the driveway framed by the overgrown hedges. There was no point hoping that a passing neighbor might distract Garrett. The little house on Midnight Court had been affordably priced because, as the real estate agent had pointed out, it was located in a very quiet neighborhood that was just waiting to go upscale. What that meant was that there were several empty residences on Midnight Court. No one was likely to notice the open front door and come down the driveway to investigate. She and Harriet were on their own.

"Garrett, this is me, Ravenna," she said, fighting to keep her tone quiet and reassuring. "And this is Harriet. You remember Harriet, don't you? You thought she was cute."

Not that Harriet looked cute at the moment. Ravenna retreated a few more steps. If she made it to the basement door and managed to get through it, she could lock it. She would be safe in the basement.

"I must stop you before you destroy my business," Garrett continued.

"I am not going to hurt the Lucky Quartz," she said.

"I regret that our relationship must end this way. I thought you were the woman of my dreams, the one I've been waiting for."

"What relationship? We had one date and we both agreed to call it quits."

"I didn't understand that you are a witch."

"Who told you that?"

"There is only one way to deal with a witch. You must die."

"Garrett, who told you I was a witch?"

"It doesn't matter. I know the truth."

A thought occurred to her. "Garrett, did you leave the burner and the torch and the fire starter on my doorstep?"

"Yes."

Great. She was dealing with a real psycho. Who knew that one of the most successful casinos in Illusion Town was owned and operated by a madman?

She took another step back. The basement door was closer now. She needed to buy time.

"You don't want to hurt me," she said. "You'll be arrested and put in prison. Your casino will be ruined if you're not around to run it. There is no one to take over, because you are still trying to find a wife for a Covenant Marriage. You don't have children yet."

"No one will ever connect me to what is going to happen to you. I'm a powerful man here in Illusion Town. I own one of the biggest casinos in the Emerald Zone. A man in my position has women standing in line trying to fuck him. The cops won't believe for a minute that I went out of my way to kill a bitch like you."

"You've really thought this through, haven't you?" she said.

He was right. In Illusion Town the casino owners were among the most powerful people in the community. Garrett Willis could get away with murder.

They were passing her office now. The door stood open. She pulled some energy. Fireworks burst inside her office, sparking and flashing in colors that came from the far end of the spectrum. Brilliant. Distracting.

Startled, Garrett yelped in alarm, spun around to face the doorway, and fired. The shot boomed in the confines of the hallway.

Harriet succeeded in escaping Ravenna's arm. She bounded down to the floor and raced toward Garrett, snapping at an ankle.

Distracted again, Garrett looked down, horrified. "No."

He started to aim the mag-rez at Harriet and evidently realized he was more likely to put a round through his own foot. Frantic now, he scrambled backward, kicking wildly in an effort to get rid of Harriet.

A fierce energy shuddered in the hallway. Flames from the paranormal end of the spectrum flashed to life and leaped around Garrett. He dropped the pistol and flailed wildly.

His eyes widened in horror. "Fire witch. You're a fucking fire witch."

"I left that off the Banks agency questionnaire," Ravenna said.

The fire blazed higher. Harriet released her grip on Garrett's ankle and darted out of range.

"Stop," Willis yelped. "Stop."

He tried to lunge toward Ravenna but the flames engulfed him in a whirlpool of energy.

Willis's mouth opened on a silent shriek. He convulsed and went down with a thud that shuddered through the old Colonial-era floor.

She was staring at Willis's crumpled form, trying to process what had just happened, when she caught the first wisp of smoke. The firestorm she had created was starting to move into the normal end of the spectrum. If she didn't get control, it would set the cottage ablaze.

She shut down her senses. It wasn't easy because she was rezzed on adrenaline and the bio-cocktail generated by the use of her talent. For a moment she stood, barefoot, in the hallway, and tried to catch her breath while she gazed, stunned, at the unmoving man sprawled on the floor.

Harriet chortled, closed her amber hunting eyes, and fluffed her fur. The danger was past as far as she was concerned. Time to party.

But the danger was not past, Ravenna thought. It was barreling toward her. Full comprehension of what had just happened and the realization of what might happen next chilled her to the bone.

"Harriet, we've got a problem," she said, her voice shaky. "And if he's dead, it will be a much bigger problem."

She crouched beside Willis. The scent of a flowery cologne or aftershave made her wrinkle her nose. Ignoring the cloying fragrance, she checked for a pulse.

"Good news and bad news," she announced. "He's alive."

Harriet chortled and studied Willis with an intent expression. Ravenna followed her gaze and saw that Garrett's evening jacket had fallen open, revealing a pocket designed to carry a few necessities—a phone and a Lucky Quartz–branded pen.

"No, you can't take the pen, not even as a trophy. Talk about evidence that could land me in prison. Besides, you've already got a Lucky Quartz pen in your collection." She checked the time. "Oh, shit. We've got ten minutes, max, assuming Sweetwater is the right-on-time type. We'll have to take Willis down into the basement and dump him in the tunnels. There's no way to know how long he'll be out, but he's got tuned amber. He'll find his way back to the surface."

She tried to think of a way to maneuver Willis down the basement stairs. If she dragged him by his feet, his head would bounce on every concrete step. Even if he didn't die from the combined effects of whatever drug he had used and what she had just done to him with her talent, he would definitely be dead by the time she got him to the bottom of the stairs.

She did not have time to figure out how to maneuver Willis into the basement.

"I'll stash him in the hall closet," she told Harriet. "With luck he won't wake up until I get home from the reception. I can deal with him then."

She opened the closet door, bent down, wrapped a hand around each of Willis's ankles, and hauled with all of her might.

Nothing happened. He wasn't dead, but he was dead weight.

Sensing a new game, Harriet chortled, cheering her on.

"Shit," Ravenna whispered.

She tightened her grip, gritted her teeth, and tried again. This time Willis slid a few inches across the floor. Progress. If only she had a little more time.

Ethan spoke from the hallway behind her. "Can I be of assistance?"

CHAPTER TEN

Ravenna yelped in surprise. She dropped Willis's ankles, straightened, and spun around. Ethan was dressed for the evening in a sleek black evening jacket and trousers, white shirt, and black bow tie. Her high-heeled pumps dangled from the fingers of his left hand. He examined the scene in the hallway with deep interest but not horror. He didn't even look mildly shocked.

Harriet chortled and fluttered across the floor to greet him. Ethan leaned down and gave her a pat on the head.

"Looks like you two have been busy," Ethan commented.

Ravenna couldn't tell if he was talking to Harriet or her. She tried to think of something intelligent to say.

"You're early," she blurted.

Ethan checked his chunky, multifunction watch. "Six minutes. I apologize." He studied the scorch marks on the wall. "I thought I smelled smoke. Jeff mentioned that you were probably a fire witch."

Ravenna stared at him. "Uh."

"Is he dead?"

"No." She pulled herself together. "Unconscious."

"Things would be simpler if he were dead, but we can work with this," Ethan said.

His cool certainty and casual demeanor unnerved her as no amount of horror, shock, or accusation could have done. She was literally speechless. Maybe she was hallucinating. In an attempt to recover her composure, she squeezed her eyes shut and tightened her hands into fists. She took a deep breath and held it for a few beats. *Release.*

She opened her eyes and unclenched her fists. Nothing had changed except that Ethan was in the process of closing the front door. He returned to the hallway and surveyed the surroundings.

"Looks like you were going to stash him in the closet," he said. "But it would be better to dump him in the Underworld."

"Later," she said. Her heart was still racing. She took another deep breath. *Release.* "I was going to do that after the reception."

"Ditch him in the Underworld?"

"Yes." She cleared her throat. "There's a hole-in-the-wall entrance down in the basement. It's one of the reasons I bought this place. But I wasn't sure how to get him downstairs without, you know, killing him, and time was running out. And you're early, damn it."

Great. She was babbling.

"Again, I apologize for the six minutes, but maybe I can atone by taking care of Willis for you."

"Oh, shit." A fresh tide of unease threatened to drown her. "You know who he is?"

"Garrett Willis, owner of the Lucky Quartz casino and hotel. Rumored to have inherited the family talent for probability theory. Speaking of which, I'm assuming he didn't find his way to this end of Midnight Court by chance. Can I ask how the two of you came to be acquainted?"

"We were matched by the Banks matchmaking agency. He was my most recent failed date, number thirty-six."

"You've had thirty-six failed dates?" Ethan said, brows elevating a little. "Maybe you need to try another agency."

"Excuse me, but in case you haven't noticed, I'm in a situation here."

"Right. And if we don't get moving, we'll be late for the reception. I believe these are yours." He handed the heels to her. "I'll be back in a minute."

"Where are you—?"

She stopped talking, because he was already going out the front door. Harriet scurried after him, curious. They both reappeared a couple of minutes later. Ethan had an object in his hand.

"What is that?" she asked warily.

"The universal solution to ninety-seven percent of life's problems. Duct tape. Hey, Harriet."

Harriet rose on her hind paws. The tips of her ears peeked out from her dryer lint fur. There was an air of alert readiness about her. She was ready for the next game.

"Catch," Ethan said.

He tossed the roll of duct tape. Harriet caught it in her two front paws and chortled madly.

"If that stuff gets into her fur—" Ravenna said. "Never mind."

Priorities.

Ethan peeled off his black jacket and handed it to Ravenna. She couldn't think of anything else to do, so she took it. The jacket was warm from the heat of his body. The sensation was oddly reassuring. She wasn't dealing with the Willis situation on her own. She had help, evidently the nonjudgmental kind. That should probably worry her, but she had other problems at the moment.

Ethan tossed the unconscious Willis over his shoulder and looked at her. "Why don't you show me where the basement stairs are located?"

She stepped into the heels and led the way. When she reached the door in the middle of the hallway, she opened it and rezzed the lights. She gripped the railing and went down the steps into the two-hundred-year-old basement. The whisper of Underworld psi drifted in the atmosphere.

"I think he was stoned on something," she said.

Ethan followed her, carrying his burden as if Willis were a sack of dirty laundry. Excited by the prospect of an excursion into the tunnels, Harriet, clutching the roll of duct tape, scampered after them.

"What makes you think he was drugged up?" Ethan asked.

"It was as if he had undergone a personality transplant," she said. "On our date he was a perfect gentleman. Charming. We had a pleasant evening but that was the end of it. We both agreed we weren't a good match, at least not good enough for a Covenant Marriage. That was the last time I saw him. Tonight he showed up with the mag-rez. Evidently he's been stalking me for a while now."

"You had a stalker?" Ethan's tone was unnervingly neutral. "Why didn't you tell me?"

She reached the bottom of the steps and paused to look back at him, bewildered by the question. In the dim light it was impossible to see his face clearly, but she could read his mood.

"Why would I tell you?" she asked. "You're a client, not a close friend."

He didn't respond immediately. She realized the question had caught him off guard. When he reached the bottom of the steps, he spoke again.

"Have you told anyone?" he asked.

"Just my friend Sybil Banks."

"The proprietor of your matchmaking agency?"

"Right. We've talked about it, but neither of us knew what to do. The first thing I found on my doorstep was one of those little burner devices that chemists use to heat up the contents of a beaker or a test tube. The second was a chef's torch."

"Chefs use torches?"

"Sure, and so do home cooks. They make fancy desserts with them. The third item arrived yesterday. It was a barbecue grill fire starter. That was on my doorstep when I left for the office."

"No wonder you were a little tense during our meeting."

She shot him what she hoped was a withering look. "I was tense because you are a very difficult client. As I was saying, I was trying to figure out what, exactly, was going on. None of the gifts rose to the level of the sort of thing you can report to the police. All of the items were left on the doorstep. There was no indication that anyone had entered my home."

"And you knew that if you did go to the cops you might end up having to explain just why you found the items so intimidating."

"The last thing I wanted to do was tell the Illusion Town police that I have a talent for starting fires. Every time there's a case of arson I would pop up on their suspect list. The word would get out. I would have attracted the attention of all the wackos who are attracted to fire and fire witches."

"Okay, I get why you didn't go to the police."

"At least the mystery of who was leaving the fire stuff on my doorstep has been solved. Willis told me he was responsible."

"How did he find out about your talent?"

"I have no idea. But as you just said, he's a pretty strong talent. Maybe he figured it out."

"What made you think he would be a good match for you?"

"I had my doubts from the start," Ravenna admitted. "The casino business is a flashy, over-the-top world, and I am not the flashy, over-the-top type, but Sybil insisted I give Willis a try because I'd already had thirty-five failures. She thinks I'm being too choosy."

"Like me?" Ethan asked, a little too politely.

Ravenna let that go without comment. "Sybil suggested that I start dating out of my comfort zone."

"Which is exactly what you're doing with me," Ethan pointed out. "Have you considered that your matchmaker might be right?"

She was about to argue but thought better of it. Ethan was hauling her unconscious attacker into the tunnels in an effort to help her avoid the police and the possibility of being arrested for assaulting one of the pillars of the community. When you examined the situation from a certain point of view you could say that Ethan was being downright gallant, not to mention probably a lot more gracious and understanding than any of her previous thirty-six dates would have been under similar circumstances.

She owed Ethan Sweetwater. Big-time.

"It's possible my matchmaker is right," she said.

She knew she sounded grudging, but it was the best she could do. She was not in the mood to take dating advice from someone who was not a professional.

She led the way across the dingy basement and stopped in front of the old vault door that concealed the entrance to the Underworld. Tunnel energy leaked around the edges. She rezzed the lock.

"That door looks like it was installed a long time ago," Ethan said.

"The real estate agent told me that at some point in the past a previous owner had it put in as a security measure to protect against possible intruders entering the house from the tunnels."

"Smart. I've got a hole-in-the-wall in my basement, too. One of the reasons I bought the house. First thing I did was install a good vault door. You never know who might be wandering around the tunnels. The lock on yours is old tech, though. You should have it upgraded."

She frowned at the large, impressive lock. "Do you think so?"

"Trust me, you need a new one."

"Okay. I'll put it on my to-do list."

She stopped. So did Ethan.

"Amber check," Ethan said, automatically.

She didn't need the advice but she did not complain about it. Like everyone else who entered the largely uncharted maze, she never stepped foot inside the tunnels without making certain she had good, well-tuned amber. It was the only reliable way to navigate in the Underworld. To go into the tunnels without nav amber was a suicide walk. The local legends maintained that in the early days of Illusion Town, casino owners and mobsters had used the Underworld to dispose of rivals, enemies, and people who dared to cheat at the gaming tables.

She pulled open the vault door, revealing the glowing green fissure in the tunnel wall. A wave of energy wafted out. Excited, Harriet fluttered ahead into the radiant corridor on the other side. Every inch of the vast network of corridors and chambers was illuminated by the paranormal energy in the quartz the Aliens had used to construct the Underworld. As the saying went, the Aliens had vanished but they had left the lights on.

The luminous quartz had proven impervious to any tool or weapon the descendants of the colonists had thrown at it. But at some point in the distant past, great forces—perhaps the movement of tectonic plates, volcanic action, or a meteor strike—had succeeded in creating cracks, fissures, and ruptures in the otherwise indestructible stone.

Ravenna closed her eyes for a moment as the impact of what had just happened hit her.

"I almost killed one of the most powerful casino owners in town tonight," she said.

"You're looking at this from the wrong angle." Ethan shifted his burden and moved past her, maneuvering Willis through the human-sized opening. "It's the reverse. He almost killed you."

"Yes, I know, but who do you think the cops will believe, assuming he recovers his memories of tonight and decides to press charges? Willis is a big man in this town."

"Not necessarily for long," Ethan said.

He sounded dangerously optimistic. Almost cheerful. Very un-Ethan-like.

She followed him through the opening. "What does that mean?"

"We've got a couple of options," Ethan said. "Option one, we go old-school. Dump Willis down here and strip off his nav amber. Presto, the Willis problem goes away."

"You can't be serious." Shocked, she stopped in the middle of the corridor. "He'll never find his way back to the surface if you take his amber. Odds are he'll wander around here until he dies or goes mad, whichever comes first."

"Exactly," Ethan said. "Slick, right?"

He was several steps ahead of her now, striding briskly along the corridor. Harriet dashed alongside him, enthusiastic about the project.

"Wait." Ravenna hurried after them. "You don't mean that. We can't murder him. Not in cold blood."

"Nothing cold-blooded about it. Think of it as self-defense. Stalkers don't stop, Ravenna. As long as he's alive, he's a threat."

"Ethan, stop right now. I mean it."

"I had a feeling you were going to say that." Ethan came to a halt, then turned and looked at her. His predator eyes burned. "You know, for a fire witch you're not nearly as bloodthirsty as the legends would have one believe."

"I'm not a witch, damn it." She tightened her hands into small fists. "There are no witches, just certain talents that have been poorly understood over the centuries."

"Whatever."

Release, she thought. She took a breath and blew it out. She unfolded her hands.

"Release," she whispered.

"What?" Ethan asked.

"Never mind. There must be something else we can do to control Willis. You said there were a couple of options."

"Right. Option two won't be nearly as satisfying as option one, but if you're going to spend the rest of the evening nagging me about sending Willis into the Underworld minus his amber, I guess we'll go with the fallback."

She clenched her teeth. "I am not nagging you. I am attempting to talk some sense into you."

"Feels like the same thing."

She peered at him very closely. "You were never going to murder him, were you? Admit it."

"It would have been the simplest solution, but it's not without complications," he said. "Disappearing Willis into the tunnels would raise a lot of questions. Given that you were his last date at a matchmaking agency and the possibility that someone might have seen him making his way through the Dark Zone to Midnight Court, you would have popped up on the suspect list even without a mention of your talent."

"Don't remind me. So, uh, what is option two?"

"We dump him down here for a couple of hours while we're at the reception. We use the duct tape to make sure he doesn't come to and wander off. We come back later with Aunt Zora."

"Who is Aunt Zora? Or should I ask?"

"She's a hypnotist. Does a show at a small club off the Strip in the Emerald Zone. If anyone can erase Willis's obsession with you, it's Aunt Zora."

"A hypnotist," Ravenna said, more than a little stunned.

"Right."

"Powerful?"

"Off the charts," Ethan said.

Ravenna took a moment to process that news. It occurred to her that she was losing control of the situation. "Has anyone ever mentioned that you may not be entirely normal?"

"No offense, fire witch, but you don't have a lot of room talk."

She thought about that. "Fair point."

"Relax," Ethan said. "Personally, I'm feeling optimistic about our failure mode analysis and stress test date."

"You are?"

Ethan paused at the arched doorway of a glowing green chamber. "I don't know about you, but I've never had a date start out like this. I think it bodes well for our relationship."

"We don't have a relationship."

"We do now. I'm helping you deal with your Willis problem. I'm a witness and a coconspirator. I'd say that adds up to a relationship."

"I suppose it does," she admitted.

"Baby steps." He entered the chamber and dropped Willis on the floor. "Harriet, give me the duct tape. No, you can't have his pen. It's evidence. There will be fingerprints and psi prints on it."

Harriet offered the roll of duct tape. Ethan tore off a long strip and crouched beside Willis. He grimaced.

"You'd think a guy in Willis's position could afford a better grade of aftershave," he said.

CHAPTER ELEVEN

"What's going on, Ethan Sweetwater?" Ravenna asked.

He brought the Slider to a stop at the corner and looked at her, trying to get a fix on her mood. She had recovered from the drama in the front hall of the cottage with admirable speed and efficiency. Willis had tried to murder her, after all. Most people would be having a well-deserved panic attack. By rights, he deserved one himself. She could have been killed tonight. That knowledge was going to give him some very bad dreams.

But she was holding it together with grit and self-control. Those were exactly the characteristics required to handle a high-end talent like hers. He wondered just how powerful she was. It wasn't the sort of question you could ask in polite company. It bordered on asking a person if she was one of the monsters.

The dark green dress was made of some silky fabric that glided over her sleek curves. There was nothing showy or flashy about her, but there was an unmistakable vibe of power and simmering sensuality that suited her strong profile and compelling eyes. She looked amazing now but he would never forget the sight of her when he had arrived. There had still been a lot of hot energy in the air.

Fire witch. A thrill of satisfaction and certainty shivered across his senses. He accelerated gently through the intersection.

"What do you mean?" he asked. "We're on a date."

She shot him a stern look. "You know perfectly well what I mean. You ought to be shocked or appalled by what just happened back there in my house. At the very least you should be nervous. You are taking it all much too calmly."

"Now, see, that's where you're wrong. I'm not calm. I'm actually pretty rezzed. This reception is supposed to be a business affair. I wasn't looking forward to it. But now that I've got a date, I am no longer dreading the evening ahead."

She drummed her fingers on the seat. "Are you by any chance affiliated with some so-called casino security outfit?"

"You mean, am I an enforcer? Nope. I'm an independent engineer."

"Are you connected to one of the Guilds?"

"No, but I've done some work for the Guilds."

"Such as?"

"Usually the same kind of work I do for my other clients. They bring me specimens of unusual amber or quartz and request a rez analysis."

"What's a rez analysis?"

"They pay me to analyze and measure the potential resonating qualities of a stone. Those qualities will determine whether or not it has any useful tech applications."

There was a beat of silence.

"Usually?" Ravenna said.

"Yep."

"*Usually* strikes me as a sneaky word."

He whistled softly. "You're good, lady."

"I repeat my first question. What is going on tonight?"

"I told you tonight is a business affair. I'm doing a small favor for the new Guild boss."

"What sort of favor?"

"He wants me to keep an eye on the CEO of a major tech firm. See who he meets with."

Ravenna radiated disapproval. "You're involved in corporate espionage?"

"No." He eased the Slider into the heavy traffic of the Amber Zone Strip. "The Guild Council wants to know if the head of Spooner Technologies is engaged in illegal activities."

Over in the passenger seat the vibe of disapproval seemed to change to one of curiosity.

"So we're on an undercover mission tonight?" Ravenna asked.

"I am. But you're not involved in that end of things. You're my date."

"No, I am not your date." Ravenna's voice was suddenly laced with understanding. "I'm your cover. That's what this evening is all about, isn't it? You didn't need a date; you needed a cover."

"I know it looks that way, but—"

"It looks that way because it is that way. It's okay. Don't worry about it. But I think you owe me a little more information. Why did the new Guild boss ask you, in particular, to spy on this particular CEO?"

"Probably because I'm convenient. My last name is Sweetwater and I'm an engineer who specializes in exotic ambers and quartz, so I've got a legitimate professional reason to attend the convention. Also, I happen to live here in Illusion Town. Like I said, convenient."

"There's more to it than that." Ravenna slid him a speculative look. "You have some unique talent that Gabriel Jones thinks will be useful, don't you?"

"I keep telling you, I'm just a humble engineer."

"Don't give me that," Ravenna said. "You know about my talent. It's only fair for you to tell me about yours."

He had known this was coming. She had every right to ask the question. He had planned to tell her, but not so soon. The situation, however, had changed dramatically.

He considered his options while he turned off the main drag and drove down the lane that led to the big parking garage behind the casino. He never took the risk of putting the Slider with all its fancy tech in the hands of valet parking.

"In addition to being a pretty good engineer, I come from a long line of hunter talents," he said.

"I've never heard of a hunter talent."

She sounded deeply suspicious.

"Probably because it's not one that developed here on Harmony," he explained. "The Sweetwaters were hunters back on the Old World. It was a handy skill set at one time but modern technology makes it mostly useless."

"The ability to start fires is not a terribly useful talent in the modern world, either. Also it scares the daylights out of people."

He smiled, satisfied. "You don't scare me, Ravenna Chastain."

"I can see that. What kind of abilities does the hunter talent give you?"

"Fast reflexes. My night vision is excellent. But mostly I'm just very good at figuring out how prey will respond."

"Prey? Do you hunt wildlife? Because I don't approve of hunting for sport."

"There's no sport in that kind of hunting, not as far as the Sweetwaters are concerned."

"So what do you hunt, Mr. Sweetwater?"

The conversation was entering dangerous territory. He drove into the garage and parked in a space that was as far away from other vehicles as possible. He shut down the Slider's powerful engine and turned in the seat to face Ravenna. In the weak glare of the garage lights, her eyes shimmered with mysteries.

"In case you haven't heard, my family is in the amber mining business these days," he said evenly.

"Yes, you did mention that on the questionnaire you filled out for my agency. It was about the only blank you filled in properly. The lack of information is probably one of the reasons I wasn't able to come up with a great match for you. I knew it was going to be a problem."

"In that case, why did you take me on as a client?"

She gave him a chilly smile. "Figured the Sweetwater name would be enough to market you."

"Ouch. Okay, I had that coming. Is that the real reason you agreed to a date with me? Because of the Sweetwater name?"

"No, I agreed to this date as a way to keep you from suing Ottoway and because you're going to escort me to my grandparents' anniversary party. We have a deal. Now, about my question. If the Sweetwaters don't hunt animals here on Harmony, can I assume they hunt people?"

"Occasionally." He realized he was holding his breath. "As a favor to the Guild Council or Arcane. In this case both. This is a surveillance mission, nothing more. Are you okay with that?"

"I think so, yes."

He allowed himself to breathe again.

"Because you've done some profiling work for the FBPI?" he said.

"Yes, and because I'm now in the business of matchmaking. Same skill set. You could say that I've got a type of hunter talent, too."

He smiled. "Something in common."

"We're using each other, aren't we?"

"Yes, but I think we should refrain from judging each other, don't you?"

"Okay."

CHAPTER TWELVE

The vast ballroom of the Amber Palace glowed, thanks to walls covered in mirrors and amber. Massive crystal chandeliers lit the room in a glamorous light. There was a lot of amber and crystal jewelry in the crowded room. Much of it was tuned, infusing the atmosphere with a subtle buzz.

Ravenna surveyed the throng of expensively dressed and obviously successful business executives.

"How do you intend to hunt Taggert Spooner?" she asked. "Assuming we can find him in this crowd."

She and Ethan were standing on the edge of the constantly shifting throng, glasses of champagne in hand. She was feeling more balanced now. Back in control. The conversation in the parking garage had gone a long way toward clarifying the nature of her relationship with Ethan. It was simple, really. They were using each other. What they had was a strategic alliance. For some obscure reason that came as a somewhat depressing realization, but it gave her what felt like a firm grip on reality.

"Spooner won't be hard to find," Ethan said. "He's one of the VIPs in the room. Very Important People like to be seen. As for what I do once I find him, the answer is, not much. I just need to get close to him for a short time."

"Why?"

"A man in his position will be wearing signature amber, not the generic kind. It will be tuned to his unique frequency. If I get within a few feet I'll be able to lock it into my tracker."

"You can grab his sig amber frequency?"

"If I can get within range."

"I didn't realize that sort of tech was on the market," she said.

"It's not. I'm still testing it."

"You invented this tech?"

"I invented the kind I'm using tonight," Ethan said. "There are others working on similar technology. Spooner Labs, for example."

"I see. I have to tell you I'm impressed."

"I'm a pretty good engineer, Ravenna." Ethan moved, setting his untouched champagne on a nearby table. "I see Spooner. He's on the other side of the room. Time to circulate."

"Sure."

In spite of the bizarre way in which the evening was unfolding, she was intrigued. Rezzed. She could tell Ethan was energized as well. *Probably the hunter side of him,* she thought. What was her excuse? Until tonight she had not realized that a part of her missed her criminal profiling work. She did not want to return to it, at least not full-time, but she had to admit it had added a certain zest to life, a certain sense of satisfaction.

"Ravenna, dear, how nice to see you here tonight."

Startled, Ravenna stopped and turned to see a familiar face. She smiled at the middle-aged woman.

"Ms. Avery," she said. "It's great to see you again. I forgot you and your husband were in the telecommunications business."

"And I had no idea you were interested in amber technology," Beverly Avery said.

"I'm not." Ravenna smiled. "Well, no more so than the average person. Mr. Sweetwater here is an amber engineer, however. Ethan, this is Beverly Avery. Her daughter and her fiancé were Ottoway clients."

"Avery Connections," Ethan said. He smiled. "A pleasure to meet you."

"Happy to meet you, too," Beverly murmured. She studied Ethan with not-so-subtle curiosity. "My husband, Paul, mentioned that one of the Sweetwaters had opened a small analysis business here in town."

"I decided to run away from home and start my own lab," Ethan said. "You know how it is when it comes to family businesses."

"Of course." Beverly chuckled and patted his arm. "You can run but you can't hide, not from family."

"I have been reminded of that on several occasions since I arrived in town," Ethan said. "Setting up shop here in Illusion Town may have been a strategic mistake. My relatives seem to think I can get them discounted tickets for the sold-out shows and special deals on hotel suites."

Beverly winked. "Which you can do, of course, because the hotels and shows are always happy to do favors for locals, especially one with the last name of Sweetwater."

"How are Carla and Jake doing?" Ravenna said, anxious to change the subject.

"Fabulously, thanks to you. I don't know how you came up with the idea to match Jake and my daughter. I never would have thought they had anything in common. But as soon as I saw them together, I knew they would be happy. You'll get an invitation to the wedding soon."

"Thank you," Ravenna said. "I'll look forward to it."

Beverly gave Ethan a sly glance and then turned back to Ravenna. "Can I assume the professional matchmaker has finally met her own match?"

Ravenna felt herself flush. "Ethan and I are just"—she broke off, groping for the right word—"acquaintances."

"We're still getting to know each other," Ethan said easily. "This is our first date. I thought she ought to see a slice of the amber business."

Ravenna blinked, astonished by the adroit way he had dealt with the awkward inquiry. Who knew Ethan had a smooth side? Maybe it went with his gentleman-assassin look, a form of natural camouflage that let him get close to the target.

"Very wise." Beverly favored Ethan with an approving smile. "But for what it's worth, something tells me things are starting off well with the two of you. There's some good energy around you."

Ravenna thought about Garrett Willis lying unconscious and bound hand and foot in an Underworld chamber.

"Good energy?" she said. "Really?"

"Absolutely." Beverly glanced across the room. "Paul is looking for me. Probably wants to introduce me to another one of his business associates. You two run along and have fun tonight."

Ravenna watched Beverly plunge into the crowd. "'Fun.' Yep. That certainly captures the mood of the evening."

"Don't know about you, but I'm having a swell time," Ethan said. He checked his watch. "I need to get closer to Spooner. I'm still out of range."

"Do you think you might be arrested for grabbing his personal amber frequency? Asking for a friend who might get arrested if you do."

"Relax. You only get arrested if they catch you."

"Thanks for clarifying."

They moved through the crowd in a seemingly casual manner, drifting gradually closer to the tall, distinguished man chatting with a small circle of people who were clearly his peers.

"Powerful CEOs have a certain vibe, don't they?" Ravenna whispered. "They always seem to know that, whatever happens, the limo will be waiting."

"It's a reasonable assumption for them to make," Ethan said. "Spooner and those five people talking to him represent a large chunk of the total amber and quartz tech markets in the four city-states. They've all got government contracts."

Ravenna frowned. "Do you know them personally?"

"Never met any of them in my life. I've always made it a point to stay in the lab and out of the CEO suite at Amber, Inc. My brother Cruz knows all of those people but I don't. I did my homework, though. I can identify Spooner and the others."

They were very close to Spooner and his companions. Ravenna heightened her senses and immediately picked up the small shivers of power coming off the group. Even in a room full of people—many of whom possessed some serious talent—Spooner and the people with him stood out when you were in close proximity.

Ethan looked down at his watch again as if checking the time. "We're almost within range. Damn. There are a lot of tuned rocks in this room. I need to get a little closer to isolate Spooner's frequency."

They maneuvered their way to within a few feet of Spooner, who had his back to them.

"Damn," Ethan whispered very softly.

He abruptly steered Ravenna away from Spooner and the others.

"What's wrong?" she asked.

"So much for that plan. His sig frequency is locked. He's good."

"Now what?"

"Now we hang out here for a little while. There are some old Amber, Inc., customers in the room, including a couple of my grandfather's buddies from his prospecting days. If I don't say hello, I'll be in trouble. When I'm finished we'll slip away, swing by Aunt Zora's club, pick her up, and see what she can do about Willis's little obsession with you."

"What about Spooner?"

"I've got a plan B. I'll take care of it later tonight. Willis is our first priority."

"You make this utterly weird situation sound almost normal."

"What can I tell you? It's a gift."

CHAPTER THIRTEEN

"I haven't done any work this challenging in ages." Zora Sweetwater smiled at Ravenna. "I must tell you it's rather exciting."

"But you have done something like this before, right?" Ravenna asked.

Ethan had contacted his aunt from the Amber Palace to ask for her help. Zora had been waiting at the stage door of the nightclub. She was still in her Zora the Mysterious costume—a long, glamorous silver gown that glittered with a massive amount of sparkling crystals and matching elbow-length gloves. She had explained that she was between acts and, considering how long it would take to drive to the Dark Zone, hypnotize Willis, and drive back to the theater, there simply wouldn't be time to take the outfit and the makeup off and then put them on again for the late-night show.

Now that the time had come, Ravenna was more anxious than ever about the scheme.

"It would be really bad if Willis developed total amnesia or had some kind of psychotic break and wound up in a para-psych hospital," she said. "He's a well-known man in this town. The Willises are a powerful family. There would be questions, lots of them. If the police investigate, they would find out I had a date with Willis recently. Who knows where that would lead?"

"Don't worry." Zora waved an elegantly gloved hand. "I've had some experience with this sort of thing. I occasionally consult for the FBPI."

Ravenna's spirits rose. "Really? I used to do some profiling for the Bureau."

"Did you?" Zora smiled approvingly. "And now you're a matchmaker. How interesting. But it makes sense that profiling and matchmaking would require the same sort of talent."

That was somewhat reassuring. Still. Ravenna looked at Ethan.

"Relax," he said. "By the time Aunt Zora is finished with Willis, it will be like the whole stalking thing never happened."

"And if it doesn't work?" Ravenna asked. "Do we have an option number three?"

"No need for a third plan," Ethan said. "We'll just go back to option number one."

Ravenna swallowed hard. "That would be the one where we send Willis into the tunnels minus his nav amber."

"That one," Ethan said, clearly untroubled by the prospect. "But stop worrying. Aunt Zora can handle this."

The three of them were standing over the still-unconscious Willis. They were not the only ones present. Harriet had appeared and, not surprisingly, taken an immediate liking to Zora. She was currently gazing up at Ethan's aunt with adoring eyes, entranced by Zora's glittering evening gown, sparkling chandelier earrings, and dazzling necklace.

"Please make this work," Ravenna pleaded.

"Piece of cake," Zora said.

She studied Willis, her eyes dark and intent. Ravenna felt energy shift in the atmosphere. She had known immediately upon meeting her that Zora was a strong talent, but down here in the catacombs the heavy psi heightened the intensity of paranormal abilities of any kind. There was no question but that Zora was a woman of power. The question was whether she could finesse the tweaking of Willis's memory.

"Hmm," Zora said.

"What's wrong?" Ravenna asked anxiously.

"Have you had much experience using your talent on people, Ravenna?"

"No. Absolutely not. Well, there was a situation several months ago, but no one died, if that's what you mean."

"I didn't mean to alarm you," Zora said. "Willis certainly isn't dying, but there is something strange about some of his wavelengths."

"You can see his aura?"

"That's part of my talent," Zora explained. "I not only perceive auras in great detail, I can adjust them to some extent, at least temporarily. But in this case some of the wavelengths appear to be frozen. I was just wondering if that is a side effect of your own talent."

"Frozen," Ravenna repeated, numbed at the realization that she might be responsible. "Oh, shit. I just don't know."

"What about drugs?" Ethan said. He looked at Ravenna. "You said you thought he was on something when he arrived at your house tonight."

Ravenna brightened. "That's right." She looked at Zora. "Willis was definitely not acting like himself, at least not the version my matchmaker and I both saw. I'm almost positive he was on drugs. Would that cause the frozen effect?"

"Definitely." Zora nodded, satisfied. "All right, let me see what I can do."

The energy in the chamber grew stronger.

"Garrett Willis, can you hear me?" Zora asked.

"I can hear you," he said.

Ravenna was shocked. Willis appeared to be unconscious, and yet he had responded to the question as if he was in a trance. She looked at Ethan.

"I told you, she's good," he said quietly.

"You will listen to me," Zora said to Willis, "and you will do exactly as I instruct."

"Yes," Willis said.

Ravenna dared to hope the outrageous plan might work.

"Your intuition and your talent tell you that Ravenna Chastain is not a threat to you or the family business. She is a very nice person. You had a pleasant date with her but the two of you agreed that you are not a good match for a Covenant Marriage. You are not interested in her. You have no desire to see her again. Do you understand?"

"I understand," Willis said.

"You will not leave any more packages on her doorstep. You will not contact her in any way. Do you understand?"

"Yes."

"Tonight you took a cab to the Shadow Zone," Zora continued. "You went to several bars and got very drunk. When you wake up you will remember only that you spent the night getting stoned in the Shadow Zone. Do you understand?"

"I understand," Willis said.

"You will now go back into a deep sleep," Zora said. "You will not wake up until dawn."

Willis seemed to go even more limp than he had been earlier.

"That should do it, at least for now," Zora said. She looked at Ravenna. "I could tell from his aura that the hypnotic suggestions took hold, but memory is a tricky thing. I'm good, but there are limits to what I can do."

"I realize that," Ravenna said. "I really appreciate this."

"You're quite welcome, my dear. Any friend of Ethan's, et cetera, et cetera."

Ravenna looked at Willis. "Now what?"

"Now I take out the trash," Ethan said. He hauled Willis up off the floor and slung him over his shoulder. "Do me a favor. If you acquire another stalker, try to make sure he's a few pounds lighter."

Ravenna groped for a response. Words failed her, so she looked at Zora.

"Thank you," she said.

"No trouble at all," Zora said. "Would love to stay and chat but I'm afraid I must be on my way. The late-night show starts soon. It's been a pleasure to meet you, Ravenna."

"Nice to meet you, too," Ravenna said.

She scooped up Harriet, checked to make sure no pens had been purloined, and led the way back to the jagged hole-in-the-wall. It had been a very bizarre evening, but it was the way in which Ethan and his aunt were handling the situation that was the most disconcerting thing. The two Sweetwaters acted as if it were perfectly routine to help a fire witch tidy up after she had flamed one of the most powerful men in the city.

She reminded herself that she was new in Illusion Town. Evidently the rules were a little different here. Or maybe the Sweetwaters operated under their own rules.

When they reached the surface, Ethan dropped the unconscious Willis into the trunk of the Slider. He assisted Zora into the passenger seat and then returned to the front door, where Ravenna stood, Harriet in her arms.

"Sorry to have to rush off like this," he said. "I think the stress test went off well, don't you? Unfortunately, there isn't time for you to give me your analysis."

Ravenna went blank. "Analysis?"

"You were going to observe my dating skills and suggest ways in which I could improve, remember?"

"Right." She pulled herself together. "Things got a little off track tonight."

"Yes, they did, so what do you say we reschedule and try again tomorrow night?"

"You want to risk another date with me?"

"Are you kidding? This has been the most interesting evening I've had in ages. In fact, I think it's safe to say that it was different from every other date I've ever had."

"You make it sound like that's a good thing."

"It is, as far as I'm concerned. How did it go from your perspective?"

"I can truthfully say I have never had a date like this one."

"So, how about we do it again but without some of the special effects?"

"I don't believe you are for real, Ethan Sweetwater."

"I'll try to prove it. Dinner tomorrow night?"

She smiled. "Without the special effects?"

"That's the plan, but I'm adaptable."

"Yes, you are. All right. Tomorrow night."

"I'll make reservations. Pick you up at six."

Before she could say anything else, he was heading back to the Slider. He got behind the wheel. A moment later the sleek vehicle cruised out of the driveway and disappeared.

She stood in the doorway a moment longer, letting the evening energy of the Dark Zone envelop her. In spite of its name, the DZ was never truly dark at night. The radiant ruins of the Dead City bathed the haphazardly constructed lanes and alleys of the old quarter in a green chiaroscuro. The paranormal radiation emitted by the ancient quartz walls infused the atmosphere.

"Do you think I'm dating a mob man, Harriet? I know Zora said she does some work for the Bureau, but that doesn't mean the Sweetwaters aren't a crime family that just happens to be in the amber business."

Harriet chortled.

"Here's the thing. If the Sweetwaters actually are a crime family that just happens to be in the amber business, I might have a very big problem. I accepted their help, see? I let them clean up the Willis situation for me. They now know my biggest secret. Okay, pretty much my only secret. But do you realize what this means?"

Harriet chortled farewell and took off into the bushes.

"Sure, go back to the party, wherever it is tonight," Ravenna said. "Don't worry about me and my problems. Who cares if I am now seriously in debt to the mob? What can possibly go wrong?"

CHAPTER FOURTEEN

"What a charming young woman," Zora said. "A fire witch, you say? And a former FBPI profiler? She's perfect for you. She'll fit into the family very nicely. Congratulations. It's time you got serious about settling down. Your grandparents will be thrilled. So will your parents, of course."

"Don't get too excited," Ethan said. He eased the Slider to a stop in front of the stage door. "Ravenna and I are still getting to know each other. Tonight was our first date. As you can see, things got complicated."

"Marriage is always complicated for the Sweetwaters." Zora unbuckled her seat belt. "But I've got a good feeling about Ravenna Chastain."

"Glad to hear that." Ethan got out of the Slider and rounded the front of the car to open Zora's door. "Thanks for everything tonight. I appreciate the help."

"Anytime." Zora slipped out of the passenger seat. "I just hope my hypnotic suggestion sticks. I'm sure it will for a while, but as I told

Ravenna, memories are unpredictable, especially when they are rooted in an obsession. It would have been more sensible to send Willis on a long walk into the tunnels."

"The Sweetwaters are not in the business of making the monsters disappear anymore, remember?"

"That doesn't mean the monsters have gone out of business."

"I know." He escorted Zora to the stage door and opened it for her. "Thanks again." He leaned down and gave her a quick kiss on the cheek. "I owe you."

"Nonsense, I enjoyed myself," Zora said. "Besides, you're family. I'll look forward to seeing Ravenna again under more agreeable circumstances."

She swept through the doorway. Ethan went back to the Slider and got into the car. Two more stops and then he could go home, crawl into bed, and spend some time contemplating the possibilities of his next date with the fire witch.

He smiled and rezzed the engine.

The Shadow Zone was always shrouded in fog, but the mist was usually heaviest at night. The lights of the sleazy casinos, bars, and adult entertainment venues glowed eerily in the psi-laced vapor. The experts were not sure how to explain the perpetual gloom of the zone, but many were convinced it was the result of the unknown monumental forces that had devastated the Dead City eons earlier.

Whatever the cause of the atmosphere, it provided the ideal setting for the shady business transactions that went down in the narrow lanes and alleys of the Shadow Zone.

Ethan cruised past a flashy wedding parlor offering Marriages of Convenience officiated over by Elvis, turned a corner at the end of a lane lined with motels that rented rooms by the hour, and chose an alley at random. Security cameras were not much of a problem in the Shadow Zone, but he checked his sensor just to make sure. The small bit of tuned amber embedded in the wristband of his watch was still dark, indicating there was no working surveillance tech in the vicinity.

He got out of the Slider and opened the trunk.

"I hope this is the last time I have to haul you around, Willis. You are not getting any lighter."

He picked up the sleeping man and dumped him into a large, half-empty trash bin. He arranged a couple of flattened cardboard boxes on top of Willis to conceal him. If Willis got lucky, no one would notice him until he woke up. If he was unlucky, he would wake up without his designer watch and very expensive ring.

Ethan paused long enough to lock onto the frequency of Willis's sig amber.

"Just in case I ever need to find you," he said.

He went back to the Slider, drove sedately out of the Shadow Zone, and turned the corner at the end of one side of the Dead City Wall.

And just like that, the fog vanished in the rearview mirror. The bright lights of the glittering Amber Zone casinos and hotels illuminated the night. The Strip extended the entire length of one side of the high, octagonal Wall that enclosed the glowing ruins of the Dead City.

He made his second stop inside the garage of the big hotel where Spooner was staying.

When he was finished with that chore, he drove to the far end of the Strip and turned the corner into the Dark Zone. There were lights here, too, but they glowed in the windows of houses, apartments, and small shops, not in massive casino towers. There were several gaming venues in the DZ but they were boutique operations designed to attract the locals. The DZ was a neighborhood in the truest sense of the word—not a major business district that depended on tourism.

Not everyone was comfortable living in the DZ—there was a lot of psi in the atmosphere, enough to render most navigation equipment unreliable—and the energy that radiated from the Dead City was particularly strong. At night the maze of narrow streets and lanes and alleys was filled with acid-green shadows. It was unwise to take a stroll through the DZ in the dark unless you had an excellent sense of direction. His was world-class. It was an aspect of his talent.

He turned onto Ruin Gate Lane and drove all the way to the end, where it was blocked by the glowing Wall. He paused to rez the high gates that guarded his home and then pulled into the driveway.

When the mag-steel barrier closed behind him, he drove through the luminous gardens, checking to make sure the hidden security devices responded with the correct pings, and brought the Slider to a halt at his front door.

He sat quietly for a moment, wondering if Ravenna would like the house. It was one of the larger homes in the old neighborhood. The two-story structure was old. It dated back to the Colonial era and it needed work. Some of the windows had been boarded up.

It was a lot more house than a single man needed, but he had bought it because of the gardens that surrounded it on all sides. They had been sadly overgrown and choked with weeds—an urban jungle that suited the long-neglected house—but he had been entranced by the energy of the plants.

His newfound passion was something of a mystery. He had never considered himself a gardener. He appreciated an interesting or attractive display of foliage as much as the next person, but he had never felt compelled to invest in a lot of expensive garden equipment. Now, though, the shed at the back of the house was crammed with tools and he had a subscription to every gardening magazine he could find.

Early on he had realized he wanted to specialize in exotic, psi-luminous plants. He seemed to have an affinity for them, just as he did for rez-amber and quartz. At night his collection glowed, fluoresced, and sparkled in the green shadows. He was particularly pleased with the curtains of orchids.

He got out of the Slider, rezzed the front door, and walked into the mostly empty house. He had devoted himself to the gardens but he had not bothered with more than the bare essentials of furniture. He was dating seriously now. He had to pay attention to his interior decor.

Ravenna had a properly furnished home. The cottage on Midnight Court was filled with warm and inviting colors. He hadn't had a lot of time to note details because of the Willis problem, but he remembered a comfy-looking sofa, a large reading chair, and carpets with an abstract design.

He surveyed the sparse furnishings and bare walls of his own home with a critical eye. Ravenna probably wouldn't think much of his place. But maybe she would enjoy his little horticultural wonderland.

He checked his watch. Garrett Willis was still in the trash bin. A good night's work. He could go to bed and think about the next date with the fire witch.

CHAPTER FIFTEEN

Taggert Spooner took out his phone and crossed the hotel suite to the wall of windows. He rezzed the familiar code and contemplated the bright lights of the casinos while he waited for Melody Palantine to answer. It would not take long. It never did.

Palantine was the most capable administrative assistant he had ever had. Available any time of the day or night, she was a magician on the rez-net. She could find anyone online. Even more useful was her knack for manipulating people. She had an intuitive ability to figure out what they wanted most and then offer to give it to them. If she ever decided to become a professional con artist, she would be brilliantly successful.

Unfortunately, she was also the most ambitious administrative assistant he'd ever had. He was not yet certain of her agenda—he suspected she was angling to get into upper management and closer to the Vortex project—but until he knew exactly what she wanted, he had to be careful. He was the only one who knew all of the secrets of Vortex.

"Good evening, sir," she said. "How is the conference going?"

"The same way these things always go," he said. "Boring but somewhat productive. I managed to corner Heston and Booth tonight at the opening reception. You were right about both of them, by the way. They want in on the Lodestar Project and they're willing to pay to play. We can use them."

"Congratulations, sir. That's excellent news."

"Credit where it's due. It was your idea to bring them in on Lodestar."

"Thank you, sir."

"But we do not want another failure like the Illusion Town project a few weeks ago, do we?" he said, keeping his tone silky soft.

There was a beat of silence.

"No, sir," Melody said.

He smiled, satisfied with the tension in her voice. There was no *we* involved and they both knew it. He had let her run with the Illusion Town project and it had collapsed, thanks to the new Guild boss, Gabriel Jones, and a low-rent weather channeler named Lucy Bell. Once in a while you had to remind people of their mistakes. It kept them sharp. It also made them think twice about plotting behind the boss's back.

"Anything I need to know before I get some sleep?" he asked.

"No, sir. Everything is under control here."

"In that case, I'll say good night."

"Yes, sir."

He ended the call and stood looking out at the ruins while he considered the problem of Melody Palantine. True, she had her own as-yet-unknown agenda, but for now their interests were aligned. They were both one hundred percent invested in the same goal—to make sure Spooner Technologies remained a major player in the amber and quartz tech world.

When the time came, he would terminate Melody Palantine, but until then he was following the oldest rule of management: *Keep your friends close and your enemies closer.*

Palantine was a potential problem, one that could be dealt with in the future. He had a more immediate concern. He went to the small hotel safe and rezzed the code. He hadn't wanted to leave the stone in his room while he was at the reception but there had been no choice. While it would have fit into the inside pocket of his jacket, he hadn't dared take the risk of carrying it into a room full of psychically gifted engineers and techs.

He opened the door of the safe, reached inside, and picked up the small crystal. It was cut into the shape of a little pyramid. Just holding it in his hand rezzed his senses. The vibe of some unknown power whispered in the atmosphere. He didn't know what the crystal could do or how to resonate with the frequency locked inside, but he knew it was incredibly valuable.

He tightened his grip on the pyramid and got a euphoric rush. After a moment he went back to the window and looked out at the night. He had lied to Palantine. He had no intention of going to bed yet. He did not need much sleep now. He was getting stronger by the day, mentally and physically preparing to fulfill his legacy.

He would succeed where his ancestors on Earth had failed. He would make Vortex a reality and he would control it utterly.

CHAPTER SIXTEEN

Melody Palantine resisted the urge to hurl her phone at the nearest wall.

"Bastard," she whispered. "Fucking *bastard*."

Spooner was lying to her. That was not exactly news. She was well aware he did not trust her. She didn't trust him, either. They worked well together because they needed each other.

The lack of mutual trust was not a problem as far as she was concerned, but lately Spooner appeared to be changing. That was worrisome. Spooner had become more secretive than ever in recent weeks. The word *paranoid* came to mind.

Initially she had wondered if he was planning to fire her because of the Illusion Town project disaster, but he had not taken any action to terminate her. That had been a relief, of course. She did not know all of Spooner's secrets, but she knew some of them, more than enough to get her killed if he decided he no longer needed her.

It wasn't only the increased tendency toward secrecy that alarmed her. For as long as she had known him, he had been a model of ice-cold control. He certainly had a temper but he wielded it like a stiletto. His temper was always, *always* under control.

Lately, however, she had witnessed him screaming at underlings. On at least one occasion he had hung up on an R and D manager and smashed an expensive vase against a wall.

An unpredictable Spooner was a dangerous Spooner.

She shot up out of the chair and worked to suppress the surge of rage and panic threatening to choke her. Wrapping her arms around herself, she prowled the living room of her apartment and summoned her mantra.

"You have a destiny. You have a destiny. You have a destiny."

When she had herself back under control she returned to her desk and took out her other phone, the one she never used for anything except to advance her private project.

She was aware that Taggert Spooner spied on her, just as he monitored the handful of other people at Spooner Tech who had some knowledge of the company's ultrasecret lab, code-named Vortex. She made sure to give him plenty to look at on her primary phone—an active search history, email, personal business, social media—enough to make him think he knew everything about her private life.

She was certain he was still unaware of the special project phone. She had set up a smorgasbord of traps and alarms. Spooner was very good when it came to sophisticated technology. He had, after all, launched his high-flying company with one of his own inventions. But when it came to navigating the rez-net, she was light-years ahead of him.

Her talent was not limited to locating and manipulating data—she had a talent for locating and manipulating people, as well. And in the end it always came down to people. The ability was an aspect of one of her three talents.

She was a true triple. Theoretically she should be dead or incarcerated in the locked ward of a para-psych hospital by now. Most triple talents did not survive long into adulthood. The few who did were invariably highly unstable.

The experts claimed the human brain was not capable of handling the heavy load of sensory input generated by multiple talents. It was parapsychology dogma, an assumption that had been made generations ago, back when it became obvious something in the environment on Harmony was releasing and enhancing the latent psychic senses in the colonists.

Most people could manage one talent, the experts said. A few strong individuals could handle two, but that was the upper limit. Even dual talents made others uneasy. The result was that those who commanded two psychic talents were careful to keep a low profile.

Triple talents like her—those who survived, at any rate—took even more precautions. In her case, no one but her mother had ever known about her three psychic abilities. Her mother was dead. Her father had been an indie quartz prospector who had spent his life chasing the dream of a big strike in the Underworld. He had vanished into the tunnels shortly after she was born, never to be seen again.

So, yes, most normal people born with multiple talents would have been dead or insane by now. But she was not normal. She was descended from Vincent Lee Vance, the powerful triple talent who, a hundred years earlier, had almost succeeded in conquering the Federation of City-States.

Like Vance, she was quartz-solid stable. She had inherited not only his powerful talents but his ability to control them.

Furthermore, she understood what Vance had failed to grasp. In the modern world there was no need to engage in an armed rebellion to establish an empire. Vance had taken that approach and failed spectacularly.

The secret of true power lay in controlling the technology and vital resources that enabled modern civilization to exist.

Taggert Spooner understood that, as well. He was the president and CEO of Spooner Tech, so, for the moment, he held power over her. But when the time came, she would be the one who took control of Vortex.

She had a destiny to fulfill. Spooner had a role to play in it. He just didn't know that yet.

Chapter Seventeen

"So, any advice for me on how to improve my dating style?" Ethan asked.

Ravenna looked at him across the short expanse of the intimate, candlelit table. It was impossible to tell if he was joking or entirely serious.

She had spent the day in a state of restless tension. It had taken a supreme effort to focus on work. One moment she found herself fretting over all the things that could go wrong if Garrett Willis regained his memory. In the next she obsessed over what to wear for a date with a man who might have mob connections. And then there was the very real possibility the Illusion Town police would storm into the office at any moment and arrest her.

At the end of the day, when she realized she was not going to be handcuffed at work and dragged ignominiously out of the office, she had gone home and made the hard decisions about attire. Harriet had, as usual, supervised and offered commentary.

After trying on all five black dresses, she had gone with the snug little sheath sprinkled with a scattering of black crystals. She had added a tiny black evening bag on a long gold chain. Harriet had seemed quite excited when she selected a pair of obsidian-and-amber earrings and a matching bracelet to go with the outfit.

Ethan wore a steel-gray blazer over a black pullover and black trousers. Gentleman-assassin evening casual, probably.

He had chosen a chic, cozy establishment in the Dark Zone. As was usually the case in the DZ, it was easier to walk than drive through the twisty streets and try to find parking in the narrow lanes and alleys. He had met her at her front door on foot and they had strolled to the restaurant. Harriet had accompanied them for a few blocks, riding on Ethan's shoulder, and then she'd nipped off to disappear into the softly glowing night.

The menu promised *A culinary experience featuring Old World classics interpreted through the lens of contemporary Harmonic sensibilities*, whatever that meant. But the seafood stew, roasted vegetables, and crusty bread were excellent.

Ravenna had been surprised to find herself starting to relax during dinner. Ethan had asked her questions about the matchmaking business and how the talent worked. He had seemed genuinely interested in her answers. She, in turn, had asked him why he had struck out on his own instead of taking a position in the family business. He had explained the decision in a single, concise sentence: *I love my brother, but I can't work for him or anyone else.*

All in all, things had been going remarkably well, Ravenna thought. Until now.

She dipped her spoon into the rich fish stew. "I think it's safe to say your dating style is . . . unique."

"So as my matchmaker, you need to identify a niche market and sell me into it, right?"

"We at Ottoway try not to describe our professional work in crass marketing terms. It makes the process of finding the right person sound too much like a business transaction."

Ethan nodded in understanding. "It does take away the romantic aspect, doesn't it? Hypothetically speaking, what does the profile of my ideal soul mate look like?"

"Hypothetically speaking, I have absolutely no idea. Back at the start I was sure I could find the right person for you. Like I said, I was over-optimistic."

Ethan slathered herbed butter on a chunk of bread and made a tsk-tsk sound. "And you call yourself a matchmaker."

"In fairness, you didn't give me a lot of information to work with."

"You are supposed to use your talent, not a lot of questions about hobbies and lifestyle."

"You might be interested to know that you are my first failure." She put down the spoon and reached for her wineglass. "That wouldn't be the biggest disaster in the world for me—no matchmaker gets it right one hundred percent of the time. But unfortunately, the Sweetwater name makes you a potentially career-ending failure."

He had the grace to wince. "Sorry about that."

"If I don't find you a good match, I will be put on probation."

"I appreciate your situation but I am not going to accept a bad match just to save your career. I'm happy to help you dispose of an inconvenient stalker, but I have to draw the line somewhere."

She took a sip of wine and lowered the glass. "I spent the whole day wondering if the cops were going to arrest me."

Ethan frowned, apparently surprised by that admission. "I'm sorry you were under so much stress. You should have called me and said you were worried. I could have reassured you."

"How?"

"The Sweetwater name does have some practical uses. Willis has clout in this town, but that's as far as his reach goes. My family's reach is a lot longer and more powerful, and the folks who run this city are well aware of that."

"I see." Ravenna swirled the wine in her glass. "You mean if I got arrested you would have pulled some strings to keep me out of jail?"

"Sure. Don't forget, I'm as deep in this thing as you are. So is Aunt Zora."

Out of nowhere a rush of guilt rolled over her. "You're right. I hadn't thought about it in those terms. Thanks to me you're both involved in what probably constitutes a felony. My fault. I shouldn't have let you help me deal with Willis. I should have taken care of things on my own." A thought struck her. "If you hadn't arrived six minutes early—"

"Oh, so now it's my fault?"

"In a way."

"Stop right there." Ethan raised a hand, palm out. "Aunt Zora and I knew exactly what we were doing. It was our choice to give you a hand with Willis. Don't worry about it. We can take care of ourselves. Let's get back to the matchmaking business. You admitted you have no clue how to match me. What about yourself?"

"Me?"

"How would you define your ideal match?"

"I have no idea," Ravenna said.

Ethan had been about to eat some of the roasted vegetables. He stopped and set the fork down with great precision. His eyes flashed with curiosity.

"You're serious," he said.

"Of course." She tore off a hunk of bread and reached for the butter knife. "Everyone in my business knows that matchmakers are never able to spot the best match for themselves. We hire professionals, same as everyone else. That's why I'm registered with the competition."

"Huh." Ethan picked up the fork and went back to the roasted vegetables. "Is it hard to identify your own match because you can't be objective? Can't get enough distance from your own emotions?"

"Maybe. Or maybe we don't want to take the risk of trusting our own emotions. No one knows for sure. It's just a fact."

"Think back to that first day in your office," Ethan said. "What made you so optimistic about matching me?"

"My intuition. But everyone knows you can't always rely on intuition. I think the problem is that I just didn't have enough data." She waved a spoon at him. "Your fault."

"What more do you need to know about me?"

"Seriously? I need to understand why you were able to walk in on a scene like the one in my hallway last night and act as if the problem was no more complicated than taking out the trash. I'd like to know why you didn't even flinch when you found out I was a fire witch. Why your aunt didn't have a problem with rearranging the memories of one of the most powerful men in town." She paused. "And why you marked so many questions *N/A* on the Ottoway questionnaire."

"Right," Ethan said. He drank some wine and lowered the glass. "I think I see the problem."

Ravenna leaned forward and lowered her voice. "Tell me the truth. Are the Sweetwaters a mob family?"

"Define *mob*."

"I'm serious."

"So am I," Ethan said. "We make our money in strictly legal ways these days, but I admit we have a complicated history. The short version is that back on the Old World we were in the monster-hunting business."

"Your turn. Define *monster*."

"Taking down monsters here on Harmony keeps law enforcement busy, but on Earth it was next to impossible for the cops to deal with psychic criminals. The general population didn't even believe there were bad guys who could rob, murder, and deceive their victims by using paranormal talents. They were rare in the population, anyway, because para-normal abilities were uncommon. The monsters were not what you'd call a huge problem, but they still did a lot of damage."

It dawned on her that she was starting to take a more relaxed view of Ethan. Probably the wine.

"I think I see where you're going here," she said.

"At some point the Sweetwaters, who happened to have a pretty strong para-psych profile even on Earth, saw what you might call an opportunity. They went into the private security business. Very private."

"Hunting monsters?"

"Yep. According to the family archives, we never had more than a couple of clients at any one time. Arcane is our oldest and most loyal customer. We did a lot of work for Jones and Jones, the organization's psychic investigation agency. Sometimes we were hired by a couple of clandestine government outfits as well."

"But here on Harmony you're in the amber business."

Ethan ate the last of his stew and set the spoon down. "That's how we make our money, yes."

"But you still do favors for Arcane."

"And occasionally the Guild Council. Got a problem with that?" Ethan watched her intently. Behind the lenses of his glasses his eyes were even more unreadable than usual. "Because I can't pretend we're out of the monster-hunting hobby entirely."

"Hobby." She processed that description for a moment. "No, I don't have a problem with it. I've done a little monster hunting too."

"Your profiling work."

"Right."

"Something else in common," Ethan suggested.

"Yes," she said, warming to the notion. She leaned across the table and lowered her voice again. "Some people would consider me to be one of the monsters."

Ethan looked amused. "Is that right?"

"They say there's a light side and a dark side to every talent," she said. "But I gotta tell you, the fire witch thing is mostly dark, as far as I can tell. Sure, it's handy for making popcorn and fireworks, but that's about it."

His eyes glinted. "Popcorn and fireworks? Doesn't sound like a dark talent to me. Sounds cool."

"Are you kidding? It's been a nightmare. Pretty much ruined my social life, and now it's making it impossible to find a decent match for a Covenant Marriage."

"Are you sure?"

She gave him a steely smile. "My fire talent has cost me at least four serious relationships over the years. Two men panicked when I told them about it. A third was a researcher who got excited and wanted to run experiments on me in his lab. The fourth and most recent one didn't have any trouble at all with my fire talent. In fact, he didn't seem to care about it. In hindsight, that should have been a clue, I suppose."

Ethan's eyes sharpened. "Tell me about that one."

She frowned. "You want to know about Dawson? Why?"

"I get the feeling he's the one who caused you to be so cautious."

"You may be right," she admitted. "He's the one who made me finally accept the fact that I can't trust my own judgment."

"Talk to me."

She eyed him warily. "Generally speaking, it's a bad idea to talk about past relationships on a date."

"This isn't a real date, remember? The rules are different tonight."

She wasn't so sure about that logic, but she decided to go with it. "Before I moved to Illusion Town I lived in Cadence. I registered with a matchmaking agency there. That's how Dawson and I met. He was a strong talent himself. For a while I thought he just might be Mr. Perfect. Things seemed to be going well between us. Getting serious. I decided to tell him about my fire talent."

"How did he handle the news?" Ethan asked.

"As if it was no big deal. I was so relieved I leaped to the conclusion that he really was the right one for me. It took me a while to realize he saw me as a business asset. He wanted to use my other talent, the one I had put down on the questionnaire."

Ethan got a knowing look. "Your profiling ability."

"Dawson owns a large company. He thought I would make a great addition to his staff, and as his wife, I'd be someone he could be certain would be loyal to him."

"A strong profiling talent would definitely be an asset in the business world," Ethan said.

"He intended to use me to assess his competitors and his management team to identify their strengths and weaknesses. Like any high-level CEO, he craves business intel."

Ethan nodded in understanding. "Sounds like he's a strategy talent. Probably a very good chess player."

"Yep. Brilliant, in fact."

"Did he suggest marriage?"

"Oh, yes. But when I finally realized I was being played, I terminated the relationship. There was a heated argument. He viewed a Covenant Marriage as, essentially, a business transaction. He couldn't understand why I was not interested in being a permanent member of his management team."

"When did you figure out that he wanted to marry you for your profiling talent?" Ethan asked.

"After we attended a major social event where I was introduced to his associates. In the car on the way home, he asked me for my take on two of them. He wanted to know if they were strong talents. If I could detect any weaknesses. I was flattered at first. Then I began to realize what was going on. As far as he was concerned, the evening had been a test of my ability. I got mad."

"Yeah?" Ethan looked intrigued. "What happened in the car?"

"I told him I didn't like being used. He explained to me in great detail that I was allowing my emotions to override logic. He claimed we made a great *team*. He lectured me at length on the subject of my failure to see the big picture. I listened for a while because I was trapped in the car. But when we stopped at an intersection, I opened the door and got out."

"That was it? You just got out of the car?"

"Well, I found a cab and went home. Never heard from him again. I think he was not only annoyed, he was embarrassed."

"Huh."

"Why? What were you expecting?"

Ethan shrugged. "Fire. An explosion. Something hot."

"Seriously? You think I should have used my fire talent to make a scene in the back of a limo?"

"In my family we're cold-blooded about business, but we do high drama when it comes to love."

She stared at him for a beat, aghast. "Seriously?"

"Seriously."

He said it as if it were merely a fact, like saying a talent for amber engineering ran in the family.

She collected herself. "As it turns out, there was no love involved in my relationship with Dawson. On my side the romance was a fantasy. On his side it was just another business deal he was trying to put together."

Ethan nodded, satisfied. "I'll bet you weren't exactly forthcoming on the questionnaire you filled out for the Banks agency."

She wrinkled her nose. "No. Sybil knows the truth, of course, but she was afraid putting it on the questionnaire would discourage too many potential matches."

"You need to take a different perspective," Ethan said. "It's not the talent that defines the monsters. It's what they do with it. Bad guys are bad guys, regardless of where they show up on the spectrum."

"I know, but—"

"Your talent isn't all dark or all light, and it's definitely not useless."

She drummed her fingers on the white tablecloth. "Maybe I should go into the popcorn business."

He reached across the table and put one warm, powerful hand on top of hers, stilling her fingers. "Pay attention, Ravenna. Your fire talent is a form of self-defense, like my fast reflexes and good eyesight."

"You've got good eyes? Why the glasses?"

"Guess."

She suddenly understood. "When people see the glasses they are more inclined to view you the way you want to be seen, as an engineer, not a potentially dangerous individual."

"That's the idea. My point is that, evolutionarily speaking, your psychic ability probably developed as protection against certain kinds of other dangerous talents. Nature is always engaged in an arms race. It makes sense that when lethal psychic abilities develop in a population, defenses against those talents will also appear."

She sat very still for a moment, aware of the heat and power in his hand. "I hadn't thought of it that way. Still, it doesn't change my fundamental problem. I'm very tough to match."

He took his hand off hers and sat back. "Like me."

"I suppose so. I'll mention your insight to Sybil Banks. Maybe that will help her reassess potential matches for me."

Irritation flashed briefly in his eyes. "What about me? Think you'll be able to do a better job of matching me now that you know the family secret?"

"No. Unfortunately that just makes it a gazillion times harder. Talk about trying to find a niche market." A thought struck her. "By any chance did you mention your old family business to any of those nine dates I arranged for you?'

"Of course not. I may have poor dating skills, but I'm not stupid."

"Why tell me?"

Ethan's smile was slow, sexy, and satisfied. "Because you've got your own big secret. Figured you'd understand."

Chapter Eighteen

They lingered over coffee and liqueurs and a small tray of exotic cheeses. At the end of the meal they walked out into the luminous night and started to make their way back toward Midnight Court.

A wistful sensation settled on Ravenna. She was reluctant to see the evening end. In spite of the weird manner in which the relationship with Ethan had begun, and the fact that she had spent hours wondering if she would be arrested at work, and regardless of the Sweetwater family's unusual history, she wished the date were real. She remembered the after-action reports from the nine agency dates she had arranged for Ethan.

"Is this when you tell me you have to rush back to your lab to check on the analysis of some rare and exotic amber?" she asked.

"Can I assume that was one of complaints lodged against me by some of the dates you fixed me up with?"

"All nine told me that's how you ended the evening."

"I was going to try a different approach tonight."

"What would that be?" she asked.

"I'd like to suggest a detour that would take us to my place."

She had not seen that coming. She decided to play it as if she really was trying to offer helpful advice.

"Are you going to invite me in for a nightcap while you show me your amber collection?" she asked. "Because if that's the plan, I need to tell you that you are moving too fast for a Covenant Marriage date. That approach is fine for a hookup, but when it comes to a serious date, you should not rush things."

"Okay."

"When you're on an agency date, you aren't looking for a one-night stand or a Marriage of Convenience. You don't want to give the wrong impression."

"So it's too soon to give you a tour of my garden?"

"Your garden?" She hesitated, once again thrown off-balance. "That's a much better idea. A stroll through a garden sounds like a pleasant way to end an agency date. Romantic but restrained."

"I think I'm getting the hang of this matchmaking-date thing," Ethan said. "My place is at the end of Ruin Gate Lane. Let's take Lost Alley. It's a shortcut."

The balmy night, infused with a soft, senses-tingling buzz and green shadows, enveloped them as they walked through the DZ. Ravenna knew Ruin Gate Lane was an upscale neighborhood, but that was all she knew about it. The real estate agent had made it clear at the outset that the houses in the area were not within her budget.

At some point along the way a comfortable silence descended. Ethan did not attempt to take her hand, but they were very close to each other, so close their shoulders brushed occasionally. When that happened she got a thrilling little zing of awareness. She always enjoyed strolling through the DZ at night, but having Ethan beside her added a layer of intimacy that was new and unexpectedly compelling. She could have walked like this for hours.

She did not feel the need to keep talking. Apparently Ethan didn't, either. They ambled through the maze of narrow streets and passages until they reached Ruin Gate Lane. Here the modest houses, apartment buildings, and storefronts gave way to estates protected by mag-steel gates and high stone walls.

She looked around with interest. "I've spent a lot of time wandering through the DZ since moving here," she said. "But I've never walked down this lane. Nice territory."

"I like the energy and the privacy," Ethan said.

At the end of the winding lane he stopped and rezzed a lock. The heavy gates swung open, revealing a driveway that curled through a luminous garden. The energy of the flowers, ferns, and plants flowed over Ravenna in a wave, delighting all of her senses.

She stopped, entranced. "This is incredible."

"Think so?" Ethan asked.

"Beautiful," Ravenna whispered. "A fairy-tale garden."

She was aware of the big gates closing behind her, but she ignored them. Enthralled by the exotic wonderland that was Ethan's garden, she moved off the narrow drive and started along a path that meandered through a forest of tree-sized ferns that fluoresced a paranormal shade of green.

Ethan followed a few steps behind, not crowding her. "I've been working on the garden since I moved in about a year ago. It's a long way from finished."

She heard the pride and satisfaction in his voice and smiled. "A garden is never truly finished, is it? My grandmother says gardens are living works of art that are constantly in the process of changing and evolving."

"She's right. Does she garden?"

"It's her passion." Ravenna paused, mesmerized by a curtain of psi-hot orchids. "Got a feeling the two of you would have a lot to talk about."

"Do you think it would be okay to end a serious agency match date here?"

She glanced at him. He was watching her with a smoldering intensity that sent a sparkling rain of sensual awareness sleeting across her senses. Was he going to kiss her?

"Yes," she said. She caught her breath. "Yes, I think this garden makes a wonderful ending for a serious—"

"Shit." Ethan glanced at his watch. "He would pick now."

It took her a beat to figure out what was going on. "Are you talking about Taggert Spooner?"

"Yep." He took her arm and steered her to the Slider. "Let's go."

"All right, but I thought you said you weren't able to get a fix on Spooner's frequency. How do you know he's moving?"

"When I realized he had blocked his sig amber I went old-school. I got a fix on the tracking device the rental company put on his car."

"Is that legal?"

"I've never actually asked that question."

They reached the Slider. He released her arm. She slipped into the passenger seat. He loped around to the driver's side. By the time she got her seat belt fastened, the powerful vehicle was in motion, shooting down the driveway. The heavy gates were already swinging open.

Ethan glanced at his watch as he drove out of the garden. "Looks like Spooner's heading for the Shadow Zone."

She was intensely aware of the energy in the atmosphere of the front seat. Ethan was rezzed. The hunter in him had surfaced. She knew that sort of energy. She had picked up similar vibes from the members of the FBPI task force team.

"You know," she said, "there might not be anything sinister about Spooner's visit to the Shadow Zone. It's popular with tourists who are looking for the old-fashioned Illusion Town experience. It's got lots of atmosphere."

"It's also got a lot of fog and minimal security, which makes it an excellent location for a meeting with someone you'd rather not be seen with."

"Good point," she said.

Ethan piloted the Slider through the narrow streets and pulled into her driveway a short time later. She got her door open before the vehicle stopped, then jumped out and looked back at him.

"Go," she said. "I can get myself through the front door of my own home."

"I'll call you," he said, putting the car in gear.

She smiled. "I'll bet you say that to all your dates."

"Damn it, Ravenna—"

"Just teasing. Go on. Do what you have to do."

She closed the door and stepped back to watch him race off into the night.

A set of blinding headlights appeared at the other end of the driveway. A big vehicle drove toward the house, effectively blocking the way out.

Her first thought was that someone who didn't know the DZ had taken a wrong turn and wound up in her front yard. Before she could sort out what was happening, she realized that Ethan had slammed on the brakes and was leaping out of the Slider.

"Open the door," he ordered.

She obeyed without thinking. Whirling, she turned and rezzed the lock. She had the door open by the time Ethan reached her. They plunged into the hall.

Ethan slammed the door, set the lock, and turned to look at her. "Feels like a hit team. Downstairs. Now. We'll go into the tunnels. Odds will be better there."

Outside, vehicle doors slammed open. Ravenna ran for the basement door, Ethan hard on her heels. She got the door open and started down the steps. Ethan paused long enough to bolt the door, and then he followed her.

She raced across the basement to the vault door that sealed the entrance to the tunnels.

"Amber check," Ethan snapped.

She focused briefly and got a reassuring ping from her earrings and bracelet.

"I'm good," she said.

She rezzed the lock. The vault door swung open.

"Go," Ethan said.

She went through the fissure in the quartz wall and into the glowing Underworld.

CHAPTER NINETEEN

You couldn't trust anyone in the mining business, but sometimes you had to roll the dice.

Travers Bowen huddled in the alley behind the abandoned, boarded-up warehouse. It wasn't cold—it was never really cold in the Shadow Zone—but he was shivering from the combined effects of adrenaline, anticipation, and fear. He was almost afraid to believe his good luck. The years of fruitless prospecting in the Underworld had finally paid off. Glass House was the discovery of a lifetime.

The moment he realized exactly what he had found, he had also understood the danger involved, hence the fear that sparked beneath the excitement. He knew the only safe thing to do with Glass House was unload it as quickly as possible. That meant he had to sell it to one of the big corporations and he had to do it fast.

Bowen had been in the prospecting business long enough to know he was in mortal danger. There were a lot of people who would cheerfully slit his throat in exchange for the coordinates to Glass House. The big outfits, like Sweetwater and Coppersmith, could afford private security. They also had the money to deal with the paperwork involved in filing and protecting a rich claim like Glass House.

He was a one-man operation. He took plenty of precautions, but he could not protect himself indefinitely against the ruthless raiders and pirates who operated in the Underworld.

It wasn't that he trusted the CEOs of the big companies any more than he did the small-time operators. You didn't get to be the guy in charge of a large outfit by playing by all the rules. But there were two things in favor of dealing with a big firm. The first was that the head of a large corporation had access to the kind of cash he was looking for. The second was that it seemed unlikely a CEO would resort to violence—not because of inhibitions about using such tactics, but because murder tended to draw the attention of the police, and that, in turn, led to bad publicity. A CEO had to protect the brand.

There were only a handful of corporations who could afford to buy what he was selling. It would have been great to set up an auction, but that approach would have been equivalent to suicide. Auctions were too risky for small-time independents like him because it was impossible to keep them entirely secret. Too many people invariably got wind of what was going down. There were always leaks and rumors in the rough-and-tumble environment of Underworld mining.

In the end he had been forced to choose between Coppersmith Mining; Amber, Inc.; Spooner Technologies; and a couple of other players in the hard-rock tech market. He had opted to approach Spooner Tech because word in the mining world was the company would pay top dollar, no questions asked, for any specimen that looked like Alien engineering.

He had known from the start there were going to be a lot of questions about his find—the kind of questions that could easily lead to having the government step in and take charge on the grounds the discovery was too dangerous and too powerful to be left in the hands of the private sector. Glass House definitely came under the heading of Strategic Importance. The Feds would be very interested.

It wasn't that he cared if the government took control of the stones. The problem was that he was pretty sure he would get stiffed in the process. Sure, the Federation of City-States would give him some compensation, but it wouldn't amount to anywhere near what he could make by selling to a company like Spooner Tech.

The transaction that was going to be concluded tonight had been a delicate process. He had sent a single crystal anonymously to Taggert Spooner along with a note explaining it was merely a small sample. He had also included the number of the anonymous bank account he had opened.

The following day an impressive sum of money had been deposited in the account. Tomorrow morning there would be a lot more. He was about to become one of the richest men in Illusion Town. Make that one of the wealthiest people in the Federation of City-States.

He put his hand into the deep pocket of his battered leather jacket and touched the small crystal pyramid for good luck. Energy pulsed, fortifying his resolve. No need to mention to the buyer that he was keeping one little specimen as a souvenir.

The psi-infused fog that swirled through the Shadow Zone seemed heavier than usual tonight, more oppressive, but he told himself that was a good thing. It offered plenty of cover. The location he had chosen for the meeting was in a neighborhood of boarded-up storefronts and defunct nightclubs. The nearest operating casinos and clubs were several blocks away, close to the Dead City Wall. In this part of the zone there were no inconvenient passersby on the sidewalk. No random cars cruising the street.

He checked the time. Spooner was a few minutes late. Maybe he had gotten lost. The corporate man was from out of town. He didn't know his way around. The thought elicited another little flicker of panic. How long should he wait?

Out on the street headlights glowed briefly in the fog and then winked out. A car stopped. Bowen breathed a sigh of relief. Spooner was here.

A moment later a figure appeared at the entrance of the alley, silhouetted in the paranormal radiance that infused the fog. Another wave of anxiety swept through Bowen. This was it. The deal was going down. He released the pyramid and took his hand out of his pocket.

He put his other hand into the pocket on the opposite side of the jacket. His fingers closed around the small mag-rez.

"Spooner?" he said.

"Yes." Spooner moved toward him. "And you are?"

Bowen relaxed a little when he realized Spooner's hands were in plain sight.

"You don't need to know my name," he said.

"How can I be sure you won't cheat me?" Spooner asked. "Maybe give me phony coordinates and then turn around and sell Glass House to my competition."

"We both know I need to make this deal happen as soon as possible."

"You're a highly motivated seller. I understand. If there are even a few more crystals like the one you sent to me, that cache is worth every penny you're asking."

"It's not just a cache of crystals, Spooner. It's an incredible place. So much power. I don't know how to describe it. Not just another Underworld ruin. I think it's an Alien lab of some kind. That little pyramid I gave you is just a tiny sliver of what's in Glass House."

No need to tell Spooner he had found the crystal and the one in his pocket lying on the floor in the tunnel, and that there was a massive crystal gate protecting Glass House.

"An Alien lab?" Spooner said. He sounded astonished. "Are you sure?"

"That's my guess."

Spooner's eyes heated. Bowen felt energy shiver in the atmosphere. The man had some serious talent, he thought. Probably for strategy. Most successful CEOs were variations of strategy talents.

"Can't wait to see what I bought," Spooner said. "I'll take the coordinates now."

Spooner's hands were still in plain sight but shards of ice trickled down Bowen's spine. He tightened his grip on the mag-rez in his pocket.

"No coordinates until I see the money in my account," he said.

"I assume you have your phone with you. Check your account."

"You already made the transfer?"

"Of course. I trust you for the reason you mentioned earlier. You need to unload Glass House."

Bowen kept his grip on the mag-rez and used his other hand to unclip his phone from his belt. He rezzed the anonymous account. For a moment he just stared at the numbers, unable to believe his eyes. A giddy euphoria jittered through him.

"Here you go," he said. He clipped the phone back on his belt and reached inside the jacket for the locator. He tossed it to Spooner.

"I locked in the coordinates," he said.

Spooner caught the locator and rezzed it. He studied the numbers on the screen for a moment. "This is in an uncharted sector beneath Illusion Town."

"Course it is. If it had been in a mapped sector it would have been discovered by now. I'm telling you there's a whole Alien lab down there, Spooner. Untouched by human hands. Wait until you see what you just bought."

Spooner's eyes got hotter. "I'm looking forward to it."

Ice-cold energy surged in the atmosphere. Waves of darkness struck Bowen. His heart skittered. His vision blurred. His whole body chilled as if he had been plunged into a giant freezer. He struggled to get the mag-rez out of his pocket but he didn't have the strength. He sagged to his knees, more confused than terrified.

"The money," he managed. "You paid—"

"Don't worry about my money," Spooner said. "It was never actually in your account. It was an illusion. It's amazing what you can do when it comes to online banking these days. I'm pretty good with tech."

You can't trust anyone in the mining business, Bowen thought. He took one more shivering breath and then there was nothing.

Spooner suppressed the hot excitement that accompanied the use of his new talent. He could kill without leaving a trace. He had not had many opportunities to savor the rush. Sure, he'd run a few experiments using test subjects he'd found in the darkest alleys of Frequency—street people and drifters no one would ever miss—but tonight was the first time he had done it for the payoff of a lifetime. It was an incredible sensation.

He crouched beside the dead man and went through his clothes. According to the items in the wallet, the old prospector's name was Bowen. Spooner continued, stripping the body of anything that would provide a quick ID. The goal was to make sure that when the corpse was discovered no one would conclude that anything out of the ordinary had gone down in the alley. An aging, failed indie prospector had died of a heart attack in the depths of the Shadow Zone. Not the first time that kind of thing had happened. Certainly not worth a police investigation. In the unlikely event an autopsy was performed, there would be nothing unusual to find.

There was a small green pyramid crystal in one of the prospector's pockets, a mag-rez in the other. Spooner took both and got to his feet.

He went back to the rental car and paused to check the update from the Concierge. The team was operational, moving in on the target. Yes, there would be some collateral damage, but nothing that couldn't be handled. She was just a matchmaker.

In the old days—last month—he would have tried very hard to avoid taking out a member of the Sweetwater clan. He would have told himself it was unwise to do something that was fraught with the risk of attracting the attention of such a powerful family. But now that his para-psych profile was so much stronger, he was far more adept at calculating risks. His talent for strategy had been enhanced even as the new talent took hold.

When he had spotted Ethan at the reception, his enhanced intuition had kicked into a high-rez state. Theoretically there was nothing unusual about a Sweetwater showing up on the opening night of the convention. Amber, Inc., was a major player in the mining and tech world. But when the resonating stone in his tie clasp signaled a device in close proximity was attempting to lock onto his sig frequency and he had looked around and seen Ethan Sweetwater, he had known he had a problem. He did not believe in coincidences.

Sweetwater might not be involved in the family business, but he was a Sweetwater, and by all accounts he was a high-level engineering talent. The combination was cause for concern.

He had immediately used his own tracking device to try to snag Sweetwater's frequency. Not surprisingly, it had been blocked. The Sweetwaters were very, very good with amber tech.

But there had been no problem grabbing the frequency of the amber that the woman was wearing. It was clear she and Sweetwater were a couple. Tracking her was the next best thing to tracking Sweetwater.

Spooner fired up the rental and drove sedately through the Shadow Zone. He had hired the untraceable two-person hit team from the same broker he had used occasionally in the past. The Concierge was as anonymous as it got on the rez-net, a ghost.

Under normal circumstances he would have had Melody Palantine make the arrangements, but he had not mentioned this project to Melody.

She would have been horrified, not by the prospect of hiring a freelance contract hit team, but by the risk involved in taking out a Sweetwater. At the very least she would have demanded an explanation for the move, and he was not ready to bring her in on Glass House.

Tonight he was more convinced than ever that the future of Vortex—his future—was riding on Bowen's incredible discovery. Eventually Palantine and a handful of others would have to be involved in Glass House, but he wanted to get a handle on it first. He needed to assess the true potential of what he had acquired tonight. Only then could he make plans.

Sure, taking out a Sweetwater was risky, but this was a hands-off third-party arrangement. There was nothing that could be traced back to him.

He touched the pyramid crystal that he had found on Bowen. The shiver of power hit him like the jolt of a high-rez drug. He smiled, satisfied. It had been a good night's work so far, but it wasn't over yet. He needed to get down into the tunnels and see Glass House for himself.

Chapter Twenty

Sound, like everything else in the psi-laden atmosphere of the Underworld, often played tricks on the senses, but there was no mistaking the footsteps Ethan heard pounding on the floor above the basement an instant before he got the vault door closed.

"They're inside the house," he said. "They'll find the hole-in-the-wall and realize we made it into the tunnels. That should be enough to discourage them. But just in case they get through that old lock of yours and decide to take a look around, let's not hang out here where we can be seen if they get the door open."

"All we have to do is disappear around a corner," Ravenna said. She stepped out of her heels and bent down to pick them up. "Once we're out of sight they won't be able to track us."

"We're going to stash you somewhere and then I'm going to come back here and see if I can grab one or both of those guys. I want some answers."

Ravenna gave him an uncertain look. "I don't think that's a good idea. We don't know how many of them there are, and they probably have pistols."

"Which don't work down here," Ethan pointed out. "Let's go."

They hurried toward the nearest intersection. A sleeked-out dust bunny, all four eyes showing, appeared from around a corner and raced toward Ravenna.

"Harriet," Ravenna said. She scooped her up and tucked her under her arm without breaking stride. "How did you know we were in trouble? Never mind."

Apparently satisfied that Ravenna was no longer in immediate danger, Harriet fluffed up, closed her amber hunting eyes, and chortled a cheery greeting.

"She's obviously got a psychic bond with you," Ethan said. "Makes sense."

Ravenna shot him a curious look. "It does?"

"According to the legends, a witch often has a familiar, right?"

"That is not amusing, Sweetwater."

"I apologize."

They reached a vast rotunda and paused to give themselves a few beats to orient their senses. A half dozen glowing corridors branched off the circular chamber. The currents of energy flowing in from the six hallways created a small, invisible whirlpool in the center of the rotunda.

Ethan chose a corridor at random and they entered it. At the first arched doorway he stopped and motioned Ravenna and Harriet into a small antechamber.

"Stay here," he said. "I'll be right back."

"I really don't think this is a good idea," Ravenna said.

"In spite of appearances, I do know what I'm doing," he said. He reached inside his jacket and produced a miniature flamer.

She glanced at the weapon, startled. "You brought that on a fake date?"

"Sorry. I'm a Sweetwater. Family tradition."

"Never mind. If you're going up against a hit team, you need backup. I've got some talent, remember?"

"Yes, but I don't want to have to worry about you while I'm dealing with those guys. Stay here."

Sensing action, Harriet wriggled out from under Ravenna's arm, scrambled up onto her shoulder, and then vaulted the short distance to Ethan's shoulder.

Ethan knew another hunter when he saw one. "I'll take Harriet as backup."

He was braced for an argument but Ravenna did not give him one.

"Be careful," she said. "Both of you."

He moved out of the chamber and started back across the rotunda, using his amber to retrace his steps.

He was about to enter the passageway that led to the hole-in-the-wall in Ravenna's basement when Harriet growled a warning.

He took the warning seriously and immediately changed course. He moved into the nearest hallway. A moment later he heard a man's voice. It was distorted by the currents of psi but audible.

"Got a fix. The intersection up ahead. Looks like they've stopped moving. This won't be a problem."

Seconds later two men dressed in khaki and leather pounded out of the hallway and stopped at the entrance to the rotunda. Ethan did a quick calculation. They had pistols but the weapons were holstered. Each gripped a flamer instead. They had come prepared to pursue their targets into the Underworld, and they knew how to operate in that environment.

A couple of ex-Guild men gone rogue, he decided. There were a lot of freelancers working the gray market of private security these days, a by-product of the changes going on in management at the top of the Ghost Hunters Guilds. When you cleaned up, the garbage had to get dumped somewhere. In this case, a lot of it was landing on the streets.

"First hallway on the left," the one who was monitoring the locator announced. "Shouldn't be a problem. They just came from a restaurant. Sweetwater is a tech guy. He won't be carrying."

They headed toward the passageway that led to the small chamber where Ravenna was concealed. Ethan felt Harriet quiver in anticipation, preparing to spring.

"Not yet," Ethan said.

He spoke quietly. Harriet seemed to get the message. She stayed put. But, ever unpredictable, the churning paranormal currents in the rotunda sent the words echoing across around the space.

"What the fuck?" the man with the locator yelped.

He whipped around to confront the threat. His companion did the same. They both fired. Narrow bolts of amber-generated energy resembling spears of lightning flashed from the barrels of the flamers. They struck the quartz wall at the entrance to the corridor that shielded Ethan, not leaving so much as a scorch mark.

He moved quickly, relying on his hunter talent reflexes to lean around the edge of the opening and fire his flamer. The energy bolt struck the man with the locator. He convulsed once, dropped his own flamer, and collapsed.

Startled, the second man fired twice in an attempt to cover himself while he grabbed the locator. But he was unnerved and off-balance. The shots went wild.

Ethan took advantage of the opening and fired once more. The second man went down hard, unconscious. Harriet, sensing the danger had passed, chortled gleefully, hopped down to the floor, and scurried across the rotunda to investigate the two unmoving men.

Ethan followed. He crouched to confiscate the flamers and then began a quick search of the assailants. Ravenna appeared just as he was recovering the locator.

"Are you okay?" she asked.

"Yes," he said.

"How did they track you to my place and then into the tunnels?"

"They weren't tracking me." He stood and examined the locators. "They were following you."

"Me?" Startled, she crossed the rotunda to look at the screen. "You're right. But why would they track me? I'm just a matchmaker."

Ethan gave that a moment's thought and then nodded once, satisfied he knew what had happened.

"They followed you because they couldn't track me," he said. "My frequency is blocked. Spooner must have spotted us at the reception last night. He assumed we were a couple. He locked onto your amber when he couldn't get mine. He concluded that if these guys followed you, they would find me. He was right."

"It's hard to believe a high-flying CEO like Taggert Spooner would hire people to kill you. I mean, sure, I understand corporate espionage, but this is over the top. He has to know he's taking a huge risk. He could get arrested for attempted murder—of a Sweetwater, no less. Talk about reckless."

"Obviously he thinks the stakes are worth it," Ethan said. "I don't know what's going on here. I need time to think. But right now we've got other priorities."

"Like calling the cops?"

"Not the cops. Here, take this." He handed her one of the flamers. "If either one of them so much as twitches, use it. Don't worry, you won't kill anyone. It's set on stun."

"All right, but where are you going?"

"Back to the surface to make a phone call and grab some duct tape."

"Duct tape again?" Ravenna said. She held up a hand. "Never mind. I'll watch these two while you're gone."

He hesitated. "You do know how to fire a flamer, right?"

"How hard can it be?" She gave him a flashy smile. "It's like a camera, right? You just point and shoot."

"Ravenna—"

"Yes, of course I know how to use a flamer. Once upon a time I was a profiler on an FBPI task force, remember? Collins, the guy in charge, made me go through basic weapons and self-defense training. Also, I've got Harriet. Stop fretting. I think I've already proven I can take care of myself."

She was right. He was letting emotion get in the way of logic.

"I'll be right back," he said.

He raced down the hallway to the hole-in-the-wall. The vault door stood open. He crossed the basement and took out his phone as he went up the stairs. He rezzed Gabriel Jones's private number.

"This is Jones. What's wrong?"

"That favor we talked about?"

"You're calling it in already?"

"Afraid so."

He explained what he needed, hung up, and went outside to grab the roll of duct tape from the trunk of the Slider. He was heading back into the cottage when he got another ping on his watch. Spooner was leaving the Shadow Zone.

Ravenna was waiting, flamer at the ready, when he returned to the rotunda. Harriet was on the floor playing with a pen.

"She found it in the pocket of one of the hit men," Ravenna explained. "It's from a club called the Night Dive."

"Interesting," Ethan said. He set about using the duct tape to secure the unconscious men. "That constitutes a lead. With luck, Jones can run it down."

"Jones? The local Guild boss?"

"Right." Ethan got to his feet. "He's sending a couple of his men to collect these two and keep them under wraps at Guild headquarters. I don't have time to question them. Don't know exactly what questions to ask, anyway. I'm just the tech guy."

Ravenna looked uneasy. "What are you planning to do?"

"You and I are going to disappear for a while. We'll use the tunnels to get to the Shadow Zone."

"Why?"

"Because Spooner spent some time there tonight. He's on his way back to his hotel now, but I want to see if I can figure out what he was doing or who he saw while he was on that side of town."

"You're planning to walk to the Shadow Zone through the tunnels? That is going to be a long hike."

"My sled is parked under my house. We'll use it. But first you're going to have to leave all of your tuned amber here."

She was properly horrified. He was asking her to violate the number one rule of safety in the Underworld.

"Are you serious?" she asked.

"These two were tracking it, Ravenna. We have to assume Spooner knows where you are right now. That is not good. We need to buy some time. There's a strong possibility that if you ditch your amber down here, he will assume, at least for a while, that his hit team was successful. Don't worry, I'll give you some of my amber."

Grim understanding shadowed her eyes. "You said yours was locked."

"It is. You won't be able to navigate with it, but I can use it to locate you."

"Better than nothing." She brightened. "Besides, I've got Harriet. In a worst-case scenario she would lead me back to the surface."

Harriet chortled at the sound of her name and waved her new pen.

"I think you're right," Ethan said. He held out his hand. "Harriet, can I borrow your pen? Jones and his people will make good use of it."

Apparently getting the message, Harriet gave him the pen. He set it on the floor beside one of the attackers. Harriet went very still, watching closely. It was clear she did not approve of leaving her new acquisition behind.

"It's important, Harriet," Ravenna said.

Harriet made a grumbling sound but she did not try to recover the pen. She muttered, clearly alarmed, however, when Ravenna stripped off her earrings, bracelet, and watch and set everything down on the floor.

"She seems to understand my amber is important to me," she said to Ethan.

He studied the dust bunny for a moment. "Yes, she does."

"It's okay, Harriet," Ravenna said. "Those things are dangerous for me tonight. We have to leave them here."

Harriet muttered some more but she did not make any effort to retrieve the amber jewelry.

Ethan used his locator like a wand, checking to make sure Ravenna hadn't missed a piece. Nothing pinged.

Satisfied, he took off his amber-and-gold signet ring and handed it to her. "Hang on to this until we can get you some generically tuned amber."

She closed her fingers around the ring. He sensed her rez a little energy, testing the lock. A deep knowing whispered through him. He would always recognize her vibe. It was as unique to her as her scent. Like one of his own high-tech trackers, he had locked onto her frequency.

"You're right," she said. "I can't use it to navigate, but better than nothing." She dropped the ring into the little evening bag slung across her body. "One more thing. Before we go anywhere, I need to grab my sneakers. I keep a pair in the basement next to the hole-in-the-wall door. I can't move very fast in heels."

He wanted to argue about the delay, but she was right. "Whatever you do, stay close to me. I can find you as long as you've got the ring, but I don't want to have to go looking for you."

"Right." She gave him a steely smile. "What a waste of time that would be. Mustn't delay the top-priority investigation."

"Damn it, that's not what I meant."

"Forget it. Let's get my sneakers."

They went back to the hole-in-the-wall. Ravenna retrieved the sneakers from the basement and brought them back out into the tunnel. She stepped into them and then crouched to tie the laces. The hem of the short, flirty little black dress rode high on her thighs.

"That's better," she said, straightening. "I'm ready."

He realized he had been staring at her thighs. He had to stay focused. "Let's go," he said.

CHAPTER TWENTY-ONE

Harriet took up her favorite position on the sled, the dash-board. The light breeze created by the motion of the vehicle plastered her fur back against her small frame. She chortled every time they rounded a corner.

"She likes to go fast," Ravenna explained.

"So do I," Ethan said. "Sometimes. Other times I like to take it slow."

Ravenna got a ping of feminine intuition. She could have sworn his words carried a hint of sexual nuance. Probably just her imagination, she decided.

Ethan was at the wheel. She was sitting beside him. The sled was gliding through the tunnel at top speed, which wasn't saying much. Still, they were moving a lot faster than they could have on foot.

"What happened to your shoes?" he asked.

"What?" She realized he was looking at her soot-stained sneakers. She cringed. "Nothing. They're just dirty."

"It looks like they were scorched." Ethan kept his attention on his driving, checking the sled's built-in locator. "In a fire."

There wasn't much point in keeping her new hobby a secret, not from Ethan. The fake date was over. They were chasing a bad guy. That sort of thing tended to seriously change a relationship.

"I've been spending a little time in the Fire Zone," she said.

"Yeah?"

"I'm still new in town," she said. "I was curious about it."

Ethan's mouth kicked up a little at the corner. "Given the nature of your second talent, that's not surprising."

"No, I suppose it isn't, but I don't think most people would understand. They might conclude I was somewhat obsessed with fire."

"Probably. I've done a little off-the-books exploring in the Underworld myself," Ethan said. "Don't worry, your secret is safe with me."

"Thanks."

"You know, I see this as a critical stage in our relationship."

"Our fake relationship?"

"Whatever." Ethan drove the sled down a hallway lined with arched doorways and radiant green chambers. "The point is, I feel a level of trust is developing between us."

"Probably because a couple of goons tried to murder us tonight. That sort of thing can result in a bonding experience."

"Do you think so?"

"I'm sure the feeling is temporary."

"Who knows? But on the plus side, I feel like I'm learning a lot of stuff that will be useful when you finally find the right match for me."

"I don't think that's going to happen, Ethan."

"I have faith in your talents." He glanced at the locator and brought the sled to a halt. "Looks like there's an exit near here. This is as close as we can get to the location where Spooner made his stop in the Shadow Zone."

They got out of the sled. Harriet hopped onto Ethan's shoulder and chortled enthusiastically.

"Since I've met Harriet I have come to realize life is simple for a dust bunny," Ravenna said. "Hours of games, snacks, and adventures, interrupted by moments of acute danger."

"We could probably learn a lot from dust bunnies," Ethan said.

They found the exit from the tunnels that had been detected by the locator. Ethan grabbed a small backpack from the cargo bay of the sled and slung it over one shoulder.

The hole-in-the-wall proved to be a narrow fissure in the quartz that opened onto the unlit basement of an abandoned warehouse. Ethan took a slim flashlight out of the pack and rezzed it. The beam splashed across an assortment of old card tables, broken stools, and antique slot machines. What was left of a long mirrored bar stood in the back of the room. There was a small stage in the corner.

With an exuberant chortle Harriet plunged into what was probably a dust bunny's idea of an amusement park. She vanished almost immediately.

"Looks like an old unlicensed gambling den," Ethan said. "The hole-in-the-wall probably served as a handy exit in the event the place was raided by the cops."

There was a glass-and-steel spiral staircase in the middle of the room. The once-transparent treads were coated with decades of dust.

"That must be the way out," Ravenna said.

Ethan speared the staircase with the light. "Looks like it's still in good shape. I'll give it a try."

He threaded a path through the clutter and put a cautious foot on the bottom step. The metal squeaked but the glass tread held.

"It feels solid," he said. "I'll go first."

He went up the stairs. There was nothing more than a couple of squeaks from the steel frame. When he reached the landing he paused to sweep the light around. "This place was abandoned a long time ago. Come on up."

Ravenna put a sneaker-clad foot on the stairs. "Harriet, we're leaving."

There was an answering chortle. Harriet appeared out of the darkness and bounced up the glass stairs. Ravenna followed her. When they reached the top, Ethan led the way through the empty warehouse to a door that sagged on rusty hinges.

When he got the door open, they stepped out into an alley seething with luminous fog. Ethan paused to check the locator one last time.

"We're close," he said. "The car stopped not far from here. He parked on the street for a few minutes. Not long."

They started toward the far end of the alley. When Harriet growled a warning, they stopped. The beam of Ethan's flashlight fell on the dead man.

Chapter Twenty-Two

"You don't think this is a coincidence, do you?" Ravenna said.

"No." Ethan crouched beside the body, his hunter's intuition rezzed to the max. "I don't see any obvious signs of violence, but he hasn't been dead long. We're close to where Spooner was parked earlier. There has to be a connection."

"Do you think this man is the person Spooner came to Illusion Town to meet?"

"At this point I think that's a good bet," Ethan said. He began the unpleasant process of going through the dead man's clothes.

"What are you looking for?" Ravenna asked.

Her voice was unnaturally thin and faint. He reminded himself she had already been through a lot tonight and now they had stumbled onto a probable homicide.

"I'm looking for anything that will tell me who this man is," he said. "Are you all right? Let me know if you think you're going to faint or get sick."

"I am not going to faint or get sick."

Her voice sounded stronger now. He got the impression she was annoyed, but he had no time to deal with her emotions. He had to figure out what was going on and get her to safety.

"Good," he said. He did not look up from his work. "Glad to hear it."

He unfastened the dead man's scuffed leather jacket and exposed a faded denim work shirt.

"He was living rough," Ravenna ventured after a moment. "He hasn't shaved in a while. His clothes are old. Not shabby or ill fitting—just old, as if he bought them a long time ago and wore them for years. Same with his boots."

"Whoever he is, he's dressed like someone who spent a lot of time in the Underworld." Ethan sat back on his heels and considered the body, paying attention to detail. "Not a Guild man. Looks more like an independent ruin rat. A guy who surfaced once in a while to do a little gambling and drinking here in the Shadow Zone and then headed back down into the tunnels in hopes of striking it rich."

"If he was a ruin rat he would have had a lot of tuned amber on him," Ravenna pointed out.

"Amber that we might have been able to use to identify him. Whoever did this stripped him of anything that could tell us who he is or where he comes from. No wallet, no watch, no receipts, no keys—nothing. The cops will probably be able to identify him eventually, but not for a while, which means the trail will grow very cold."

"He wasn't a young man," Ravenna said.

"No," Ethan said. "He wasn't. I'd say he's about Big Jake's age."

"Who is Big Jake?"

"Jake Sweetwater, my grandfather. He was a prospector who got lucky. Founded Amber, Inc."

"He's retired now, isn't he?"

"In theory. But that doesn't stop him from trying to tell Cruz how to run the company."

"Why are we talking about your grandfather?" Ravenna asked.

"Because I remember the stories he used to tell us grandkids when we were growing up," Ethan said. He began wrestling the leather jacket off the body. "The indies have it tough down below. They work alone in a dangerous environment. In addition to pirates and raiders, they have to worry about getting disoriented by energy rivers and storms."

"So does everyone else who goes into the Underworld without a trained team. Why is that important tonight?"

"I'm not sure it is important. Give me a minute."

He set the jacket aside and went to work removing the dead man's shirt. When that was done he sat back again and studied what he had uncovered.

The tattoo started high on the left shoulder and ran all the way down the arm. The artwork was elaborate, a fairy-tale castle made of glass or clear crystal. Elaborately decorated letters and numbers appeared in the windows.

Ethan rezzed the camera on his phone and took several photos. Ravenna, with Harriet clutched in one arm, watched him, saying nothing.

When he was finished he got to his feet. "Let's get out of here."

"Fine by me," Ravenna said. "But where are we going?"

"We need to disappear for a while but we can't go back into the tunnels, at least not yet." He led the way toward the far end of the alley. "I've got to stay on the surface so I can make some phone calls."

"Got a suggestion?"

"We'll find a place to spend the rest of the night. There is no more anonymous location than a Shadow Zone motel that rents rooms by the hour. No forms to fill out, no identification required. Cash works just fine. No questions asked."

"Please tell me that observation is not based on personal experience."

"That observation is not based on personal experience," he said in dutiful tones.

She shot him a suspicious look but evidently decided not to confront him on the matter.

"Are you sure about the anonymity of one of those by-the-hour operations?" she asked, clearly uneasy. "Ms. Ottoway will be very annoyed if word gets out that one of her matchmakers was seen checking into a hot-sheet motel in the Shadow Zone."

"Trust me, the front desk staff won't recognize you and wouldn't care who you were even if they did happen to catch your name. But if it makes you more comfortable, we'll pick a place with outside stairs. You can wait in the parking lot while I check in. That way you won't have to walk through the lobby."

"Are you sure that will work?"

"Trust me, most of the motels in this part of town feature outside entrances."

"You really do know a lot about the hospitality establishments around here."

So much for trying to lighten the mood, he thought.

"I'm joking," he said. "I'm an engineer. I observe stuff."

Chapter Twenty-Three

The Rendezvous Inn (*Ask About Our Honeymoon Special*) was situated directly across the street from the Starlite Wedding Chapel (*Home of the Marriage of Convenience of Your Dreams*). The flashing stars on the sign in front of the chapel pulsed relentlessly in the fog, illuminating the interior of room 210 in throbbing rays of ghostly light.

Ravenna went to stand at the window. Harriet hopped up onto the sill and joined her in a survey of the fog-shrouded street.

"Atmospheric," Ravenna said.

"What?" Ethan said.

She turned around. He was sitting at the small table. He did not look up from his phone. Focused.

"Never mind," she said. "It's not important."

And it wasn't, she thought. What mattered was that they found a way to clean up the mess in which they found themselves. Ethan was working the problem. She should stop distracting him.

He put the phone on speaker. A man with a deep growl of a voice answered Ethan's call.

"You've got Jake Sweetwater. Ethan? What the hell are you doing calling at this time of night? Your grandmother and I went to bed hours ago. Are you in trouble?"

"Sorry to wake you up, Jake," Ethan said. "No, I'm not in trouble. Not exactly."

"You're in trouble."

It was a statement, not a question. Jake Sweetwater didn't sound particularly concerned. Intrigued, perhaps.

"I could use some help with a little project I'm working on," Ethan said.

Ravenna raised her brows at the words *little project* but she did not offer a comment. Not that Ethan would have paid attention to it. He was concentrating one hundred percent on the conversation with his grandfather.

"What's up?" Jake asked.

The new intensity in the older man's voice told Ravenna he was now as focused as Ethan. Like grandfather, like grandson. Probably a family trait.

"Remember those stories you used to tell us kids about your days as an indie prospector?" Ethan asked. "How the thing that miners feared the most was making the find of a lifetime and then losing the memory because they blundered into a psi storm or some other paranormal hazard that caused them to develop amnesia?"

"Or wipe out the coordinates on a locator," Jake said. "Some of those Underworld psi storms were strong enough to destroy data stored in the first generation of locators. Losing the coordinates of a big find and dealing with pirates have always been the two biggest problems for an indie. Well, aside from the possibility of getting lost in the tunnels, of course. Why?"

"You said that in the old days if a prospector got lucky with a major strike, the first rule was to get back to the surface as soon as possible and record the location in a secure place."

"Right."

"You mentioned that some of the indies went so far as to get the co-ordinates tattooed on themselves."

"The theory was that if you lost the coordinates for one reason or another, you would have a permanent record right there on your skin. I've still got the coordinates of the first Amber, Inc., mine on my arm. You don't hear about prospectors doing that anymore. Locator technology is more reliable these days. Easier to make a backup when you get to the surface and lock it with a code."

"You also said the tattoos were often in code, too."

"That's right. Something that only the prospector would be able to understand and interpret. I think that's one of the reasons the practice fell out of favor. It takes work to devise your own personal code."

"Like a password for a computer."

"Exactly. What's going on?"

"I'm doing a favor for the local Guild boss and the Guild Council."

"Sounds interesting," Jake said.

"It started out as a straight-up surveillance operation, but as of tonight there's a dead man involved."

"Don't tell me you need my help to get rid of an inconvenient body. You're an adult."

Ravenna froze and closed her eyes. *Mob family, all right. And that's the godfather on the other end of the connection. How did a nice girl like me end up in a tacky Shadow Zone motel room with a mob man? What would Mom say? What would Grandmother say?*

She opened her eyes, because Ethan was talking again.

"I don't need to get rid of the guy," he said to Jake. "I need information on him. I found him dead in an alley tonight. No signs of violence but I'm pretty sure he was murdered."

"By someone with talent?"

"Or some kind of new tech. I think I know who killed him. But that problem can wait until later. What I'm getting at is that it looks like the dead man was an indie prospector. One of his arms has been seriously inked. I get the feeling it isn't just decoration."

"Any reason to think he may have wanted to conceal the location of an Underworld strike?"

"Yes. If I'm right, he was murdered to be kept quiet. There was no ID on him. Just the ink. I took pictures. Can I send them to you? I would appreciate it if you would take a look and let me know if I'm going down a dust bunny hole with my current theory."

"Sure, I'll be glad to take a look. No guarantees, though."

"I understand."

"Old prospectors aren't the only ones who used tats to make sure they could locate something in the Underworld they didn't want anyone to find," Jake mused. "Back in the day I took down a couple of serial killers who had the locations of their body dumps tattooed in code."

"Yeah?"

"The good news is that when you're talking Underworld coordinates, it always comes down to numbers and a tuned amber compass. That limits how much you can hide in a tattoo design."

"Thanks, Jake. I'll send the photos as soon as we hang up."

"By the way, your Aunt Zora called with the good news."

Ravenna froze for the second time. She stared at Ethan, horrified.

Ethan must have sensed her scrutiny, because he shot her an uneasy glance before he turned back to the phone.

"Good news?" he said. He sounded cautious. Very, very cautious.

"Yep." Jake chuckled. "She said it looks like you finally found a match using one of those Covenant Marriage agencies. Got to admit, I've never thought that was the way to go, not for a Sweetwater. As your grandmother likes to say, we usually do things with a lot more drama. But first time for everything, I reckon."

Ethan tightened his grip on the phone. "Uh, Jake—"

"A fire witch, huh? Good choice. From the sound of it she'll fit right in with the Sweetwater family."

I'm doomed, Ravenna thought. *My career as a matchmaker is finished. I am totally screwed.*

Stunned, she dropped onto the side of the bed. She needed to sit down, and the bed was the only available option, because Ethan was using the room's one and only chair.

"The situation is a little more complicated than Aunt Zora made it sound," Ethan said firmly. He spoke to the phone but he was watching Ravenna with a wary expression. "I don't have time to talk about it right now. I need to send you those photos. This is time-sensitive material. Call as soon as you have any info for me."

"Will do. This will be interesting. Haven't done any hunting in a while."

"Thanks." Ethan ended the call, took a deep breath, and looked at Ravenna. "Sorry about that. I didn't think this was the time to try to explain the whole fake-date thing."

"Probably not," Ravenna said. She kept her tone neutral.

"Let's worry about it later," Ethan said. "Right now we have other priorities."

"True," she admitted.

Harriet popped out from under the bed, chortling with excitement. She waved a small glittering object and hopped up onto the windowsill.

"What have you got there?" Ravenna asked.

Harriet graciously offered her find—an amber earring. Ravenna took it, rezzed her senses, and smiled when she felt the vibe.

"It's tuned," she announced. "A standard, generic frequency. I can use it."

Ethan looked at Harriet. "Good job, pal."

Ravenna remembered the signet ring. She opened her evening bag. The amber-and-gold object gleamed. She took it out, wondering why she was suddenly reluctant to return it. It wasn't as if she could use it.

"I won't need this now," she said.

"Right." He took the ring and slid it on his finger.

"It's a very nice ring," she said.

"My father gave to me."

"I see. Special."

"Yes," he said. He watched her with an expression that sent a flutter of awareness through her. "You're welcome to borrow it anytime."

She went blank. "Why would I do that?"

"I dunno. Maybe so that I could find you if you ever got lost?"

She had no idea how to take that. Was he flirting with her ever so slightly?

"Would you want to find me?" she asked.

Ethan smiled a slow, wicked smile. "Oh, yeah."

The crystalline tension was shattered when Harriet bounced a little and scurried toward the door. Ravenna did not know whether to be relieved or disappointed by the distraction.

"She wants to go outside," Ravenna said. "She probably detected some friends in the vicinity."

She opened the door and checked the walkway that ran in front of the second-floor room.

"All clear," she said.

Harriet chortled a cheerful goodbye and fluttered outside. She scuttled down the stairs and disappeared into the fog.

"I'm going to make one more call," Ethan said. He was already reaching for his phone.

If there had been a moment, Ravenna thought, it had passed.

She closed the door. "Who is it this time?"

"Gabriel Jones. By now he will have had a chance to chat with that pair we left for him to pick up in the tunnels."

"Right. Things seem to be moving very quickly. Did you mean it when you told your grandfather that decoding the dead man's tattoos is time sensitive?"

"That's what my gut is telling me. If Spooner did meet that man in the alley and got the location of a major discovery out of him, he'll want to file the claim as quickly as possible. Until the legal side of things is taken care of, it's open season on whatever the prospector found."

"Whoever claims it first will own it."

"Right."

Ethan made the call. Gabriel Jones answered midway through the first ring. Ethan put the phone on speaker again.

"I haven't got much for you," Gabriel said. "The two you left for us are awake and talking but they're not saying anything we need to know. They maintain they work for a private security firm, and they've got the ID to prove it. In this town that covers a lot of territory. They claim the situation at Ms. Chastain's home was a case of mistaken identity. They were given the wrong address. Their story is they were hired to collect a gambling debt for one of the small operators in the Amber Zone but they can't give us a name because their jobs always come through an anonymous broker."

"Pure ghost shit," Ethan said. "Except for the anonymous broker bit. That is probably true."

"Agreed. We're working that angle, but brokers who survive in that business are very, very good when it comes to staying out of sight on the dark rez-net."

"How long can you keep the pair you picked up under wraps?"

"As long as you want," Gabriel said. "The Illusion Town Guild is dedicated to serving the fine, upstanding citizens of this community."

"Who told you to say that?"

"My administrative assistant. I believe I mentioned that Aiden is quite keen on rebranding the Guild. Apparently the organization's image has suffered somewhat in recent years."

"Try recent decades. He's got a lot of work ahead of him. But thanks for hanging on to those two. In exchange, I've got an update. I'll give you the details later, but the bottom line is I'm certain Spooner killed a man in the Shadow Zone tonight. It went down in an alley. Looks like natural causes but it was murder. The body was stripped of ID. If Spooner got the coordinates of a major discovery, he'll want to verify it and file a claim."

"Any way to connect Spooner to the murder?"

"Not yet."

"Then there are no grounds for an arrest. Spooner is a high-profile CEO. The Guild can't haul him in on a murder charge without some evidence."

"I know."

"Where are you now?"

"In the Shadow Zone. Ms. Chastain is with me. I may have a lead on the location of whatever it was the dead man found down in the tunnels. My grandfather is working on some photos of the tattoos on the body. There's a possibility they might be coded coordinates."

"I've heard stories about prospectors and others with something to hide having coordinates tattooed on themselves in a private code," Gabriel said.

"It's a lead, but it may be a dead end. I'll let you know if anything comes of it."

"Thanks."

Ethan ended the call and looked at Ravenna. "That's all we can do. The rest is up to Jones, Arcane, and my grandfather."

"Are you sure we have to stay out of sight?" Ravenna asked.

"I don't think you're in the line of fire now, but I don't want to take any chances."

"What about my job? Ms. Ottoway will be very upset if I don't show up for work in the morning."

"There's a good chance this will all be finished within the next few hours."

"I suppose I can call in sick first thing in the morning if absolutely necessary. It's never a good idea to do that when you're the new hire, but if I tell Ms. Ottoway that I'm working on your case, she might let me slide."

"The prospector must have felt the discovery was so dangerous he was willing to risk an off-the-books deal with Spooner rather than go the standard auction route. One thing is clear—it's no longer our problem. We've done all we can from our end."

Ravenna smiled. She couldn't help it. "Love the *we*."

Ethan's eyes darkened. "I realize it's my fault you got dragged into this situation."

"Hey, we're even. I more or less dragged you into the Garrett Willis problem."

"I told you not to worry about that. I was happy to do you a favor."

She raised her brows. "Why?"

"You're going to analyze my poor dating skills and come up with useful advice. By now you must have some notion of how I could improve my technique."

She looked at him. "Are you serious?"

He had the nerve to look hurt.

"Damn right, I'm serious," he said.

She blinked. "In my professional opinion, I don't think you need to worry about upgrading your dating game. You're a natural."

"I sense sarcasm."

She gave him her most dazzling smile. "Let's review our evening. We got chased into the Underworld by a couple of hired thugs. We discovered a dead body in an alley. Now we are spending the night in a tacky motel in the sleaziest part of town. And, oh, right, we have a charming view of a quickie Marriage of Convenience wedding chapel directly across the street. You really know how to show a date a good time, Sweetwater. Yep, doesn't get any more romantic than this."

He looked around the room as if seeing it for the first time. Frowning, he turned back to her. "To be fair, I feel I was not set up for success tonight."

The laughter bubbled up inside her and burst forth. She knew it was triggered by a combination of stress and an adrenaline overload. She was probably having some sort of meltdown. Maybe she was sliding into hysteria. Whatever the case, she could not stop. She laughed until the tears welled up and spilled over.

She leaped off the bed, rushed into the small bathroom, grabbed some tissues and wiped her eyes.

Ethan came to stand in the doorway. "I'm really sorry about tonight. This is my fault. I never should have let you get involved in this thing—"

"Oh, shut up."

She tossed the tissue aside, moved toward him, and wrapped her arms around his neck. She went up on her toes, but he was still too tall. Impatient now, she pulled his head down to hers and kissed him with all of the adrenaline-generated heat and energy churning inside her.

It was not a tender, romantic kiss. She recognized it for what it was— a kiss ignited by a bio-cocktail of supercharged emotions generated by a brush with death, and the sizzling physical attraction she had been trying to suppress from the moment she met Ethan Sweetwater. This kiss was all thrills and chills. No love involved.

If Ethan did not respond, she would rip free of the embrace and lock herself in the bathroom for the rest of the night. That way she would not have to spend the next few hours in the presence of the most frustrating, infuriating, compelling man she had ever met.

But Ethan did respond. That changed everything.

CHAPTER TWENTY-FOUR

Ethan's mouth locked down on hers with an intensity that shocked her senses and sent them sparking and flashing. She could not read all of his emotions—maybe they were as chaotic as her own—but there was no mistaking the hot energy driving his response.

He pulled her close and tight. She was shatteringly aware of his fierce erection. He was hard all over. Sensual tension charged the atmosphere. There was no doubt he wanted her.

The knowledge that she had such a strong effect on him was exhilarating. She was old enough and smart enough to know that the physical evidence of desire signaled lust, not love, but it was more than enough for tonight.

He groaned, raised his head, and lifted her up off the floor. She gripped his shoulders to steady herself and wrapped her legs around his hips. Fabric ripped. She knew she had done some major damage to the narrow skirt of the little black dress, but she didn't care.

She managed to free her mouth. "For the record, there is nothing wrong with your kissing technique."

He gripped her bottom to hold her in place, turned, and carried her toward the bed. "Your technique is damn good, too."

She considered informing him she had never kissed anyone else with so much energy, but he was standing her on her feet and she got distracted. He turned her around and lowered the zipper of the dress so that the upper half crumpled around her waist.

He spun her back around so that she was facing him and used both hands to ease the garment over her hips. It fell to the floor, leaving her in the dainty bra, silky panties—and sneakers. She had time enough to reflect on the awkward fashion statement, and then Ethan was sitting her down on the edge of bed.

"I'm no Prince Charming," he said, "but I can handle a pair of sneakers."

She wanted to laugh—a real laugh this time, not the wild laughter of a moment ago. A laugh of pure delight spiced with sensual anticipation. But she was so consumed with sensations now it was all she could do to breathe.

He crouched and untied the laces of the sneakers. She kicked off the shoes, extended her arms behind her, and flattened her palms on the bed. She leaned back and watched him unbuckle his leather belt. His eyes were molten amber.

She could no longer resist the intoxicating fire in her blood. The pleasure of knowing her talent didn't scare him or even make him nervous pushed her to the edge. She succumbed to the impulse to exercise her psychic side.

She pulled a little talent and created a shower of fireworks. Ethan paused in the act of unfastening his shirt and watched the sparkling rain of paranormal fire wink in and out of existence.

He smiled a slow, wicked smile. "That's just for openers. Things are about to get a whole lot hotter tonight."

She returned the smile, savoring the prospect of uninhibited sex with a man who wasn't intimidated by a fire witch. A man who didn't want to conduct experiments on her. A man who wasn't trying to use her to secure personal data on his business rivals.

Ethan's phone buzzed. He stilled. So did she.

CHAPTER TWENTY-FIVE

His first impulse was to ignore the damn phone. Ethan looked at the offending device. It buzzed again.

"Shit," he said.

Ravenna smiled. Not the sultry, inviting smile of a moment ago—more a rueful-acknowledgment-of-reality smile.

"Priorities," she said. Amusement, regret, and understanding infused her voice and illuminated her eyes. "You and Jones and your grandfather are trying to catch a bad guy. We both know you have to answer the phone."

"Yeah. Damn it."

He stalked to the table, scooped up the phone, glanced at the screen, and took the call.

And just like that, he was refocused on the mission.

"Got something for me already, Jake?" he asked.

Out of the corner of his eye he watched Ravenna lean down from the bed to recover the sexy black dress. He reminded himself she had been a profiler for the FBPI. She knew something about tracking bad guys. He put the phone on speaker so she could listen to the other side of the conversation.

"It didn't take long to work out the code," Jake said. "Whoever he was, he was not very creative. Maybe he was in a hurry or worried that if he overcomplicated the ink art he wouldn't be able to decipher it himself if it became necessary. Whatever, I've got the coordinates."

"Any idea what he found?" Ethan asked.

"If I'm right, your dead prospector found Glass House, or thinks he found it."

"What is Glass House?" Ethan asked.

"That's just it—no one knows." Jake's voice was infused with controlled excitement. "It's a legend. If it exists—and that's a big if—it may be a cache of Alien tech. Or not. I spent a lot of years in the Underworld. Tracked down my share of legends. I never came across any proof that Glass House existed, but if it does, you can't put a price on it. And it would be dangerous as hell."

"Better give me those coordinates."

Jake rattled off the details. Ethan studied them.

"Looks like the location is in an unmapped sector under Illusion Town," he said.

"Makes sense," Jake said. "Prospectors usually work the unexplored sectors."

Ethan heard the trace of wistfulness in his grandfather's voice and smiled. You could take an old prospector out of the Underworld but you couldn't take the Underworld out of the old prospector.

"It's possible the dead man didn't find anything of value," Ethan said. "He might have figured he could sell a fake mine to Spooner and get away with fraud."

"Wouldn't be the first time someone tried to run that con," Jake said.

"It's also possible the so-called discovery is nothing but fool's quartz or maybe the product of a hallucination. Some indies spend way too much time down below. They get burned. Start imagining things."

"Maybe," Ethan said. "But one thing's for sure, I have to get these coordinates to Jones. He needs to find out what this is all about. Thanks for the help."

"Anytime. Deciphering the code brought back a lot of memories. Sometimes I miss the old days."

"Don't tell Grandmother. I've got to go. Goodbye, Jake."

"Let me know how things turn out."

"I will," Ethan promised.

"And tell Ms. Chastain that your grandmother is looking forward to meeting her."

Ethan looked at Ravenna, who was on her feet, shimmying into the slip of a dress.

"You're on speaker, Jake," he warned.

"Well, in that case, delighted to meet you, Ms. Chastain," Jake said.

"A pleasure, Mr. Sweetwater," Ravenna said politely.

"We'll have to get together soon," Jake said.

"Goodbye, Jake," Ethan said firmly. He ended the connection and called Gabriel Jones. Once again Jones picked up immediately.

"What have you got?" he asked.

"Some interesting coordinates. They may lead to a dead end."

"We need to find out, one way or the other. Let me have them."

Ethan read off the data.

"Thanks," Gabriel said. "I've got a team standing by. We'll head down now. With luck we can get there before Spooner does, assuming he's on his way."

"Ms. Chastain and I are going to stay out of sight until you figure out what we're dealing with."

"I'll call you as soon as I get back to the surface."

"Thanks."

Ethan heard a tap-tap-tap at the window just as he ended the call. He turned and saw the ragged silhouette of a dust bunny on the other side of the glass. Harriet was fully fluffed and using one of her six paws to make her presence known.

"How in the world did she make it all the way up to the second floor?" Ravenna asked. "Never mind. She's a dust bunny. They know how to get around."

Ravenna raised the window and picked up Harriet. The buzzy, psi-laced fog drifted into the room.

"Where have you been?" she asked. She frowned. "That looks like pie crust on your fur. And maybe some ketchup?"

Harriet chortled a cheerful greeting and offered a small round object to Ravenna. She took it and examined it. "Uh-oh."

"What is it?" Ethan asked.

She looked up, clearly worried. "It's a five-dollar poker chip from the Golden Amber Casino."

Harriet lost interest in the chip. She bounced up onto the foot of the bed, flopped down on a pillow, and closed her eyes.

"Who knew dust bunnies played poker?" Ethan said. "Look on the bright side."

"There's a bright side?"

"I doubt if the casino's security staff will bother chasing after Harriet for a five-dollar chip."

"I don't think the missing chip is the problem," Ravenna said. "According to the logo, the Golden Amber is the home of the 'Famous All-You-Can-Eat Buffet.'"

"So what if Harriet swiped a slice of pie or a couple of fries? We're not talking about major crimes."

Ravenna appeared uncertain for a moment, but she finally relaxed. "I suppose you're right." She turned back to the window and contemplated the flashing lights of the wedding chapel. "About what happened just before your grandfather called—"

His talent allowed him to read the subtle body language of someone who was getting ready to attack or to flee, but he was lousy at picking up more complicated emotions. No, that wasn't strictly true. He could tell that a person was in the grip of strong emotions—he just didn't know what to do about it.

It was obvious that Ravenna was regretting the hot kiss that, if not for the phone call, would have led to some very hot sex. But he did not have a clue how to handle those regrets. The only thing he was regretting was the fact that she wished the flash of passion had not happened.

One thing was crystal clear. It didn't take a psychologist to know the sizzling sensual energy in the atmosphere had changed dramatically, at least as far as Ravenna was concerned. Talk about ruining the mood. Time to be mature.

"Don't worry," he said. He tucked in his shirt and buckled the belt. "Probably would have been a bad idea anyway."

"It was my fault," she said earnestly, still looking out into the fog. "But you're right. It would have been a very bad idea."

"I said it *probably* would have been a bad idea. We'll never know, because it didn't happen." He paused. "Not exactly."

"Whatever. A matchmaker should never sleep with a client. At Ottoway that alone is grounds for termination. Sleeping with a high-profile client like you would be an even bigger disaster. Not only would I be fired, I probably wouldn't be able to find a position with any of the elite matchmaking agencies in the city-states. I would end up working at one of those sleazy escort agencies that offers to set up short-term Marriages of Convenience."

"I'm starting to think I should feel insulted," Ethan said.

"Nothing personal."

"I'm not so sure about that."

She swung around to face him. "It's extremely unfortunate that your aunt and your grandfather got the wrong impression of our relationship."

He shoved his fingers through his hair. "I'll get it all sorted."

"I would appreciate that," she said. She paused. "I want to apologize for my unprofessional conduct. I do realize I sent mixed signals."

"Do me a favor and change the damn subject." He shut his eyes. Great. Now he was snapping at her. He opened his eyes. "Okay, now I need to apologize. This conversation is deteriorating rapidly, isn't it?"

She gave him a shaky smile. "Yes, it is. Stress, probably."

"Right." He glanced at the bed and then he checked the time. "There's no point trying to get any rest."

"No," she said. "I would not want to trust those sheets, anyway."

Harriet made a little huffing noise and snuggled deeper into the pillow.

Ravenna sat down on the edge of the bed, crossed her legs, and fixed Ethan with a sincerely determined expression. "What subject would you like to discuss?"

Ethan tried not to look at the skin revealed by the tear in the little black dress. He dropped into the chair, leaned back, and stretched out his legs. He stacked one foot on top of the other.

"Tell me about your big career change," he said. "How in green hell do you go from being a criminal profiler to a matchmaker?"

She frowned, evidently surprised by the question. "It's a long story. Do you really want to hear it?"

"We've got time to kill," he said. "Yes, I'd really like to know how you wound up here in Illusion Town."

"The skill sets involved in matchmaking and criminal profiling are quite similar. As it happens, there's a long history of both professions in my family. The tradition goes back to Earth. One of my ancestors, Sierra Raines, was the first person on the family tree to display the talent in a major way. She became a matchmaker. But a lot of her descendants who inherited the ability took up profiling instead. When I started out, I liked the thought of helping to bring bad guys to justice, so I followed that path first. I worked for a private firm that did jobs for various law enforcement agencies."

"My nephew said word in the Bureau is that you were one of the best."

"That's good to know," she said. "I'm glad I left with my reputation intact. But truth be told I'm a lot happier in the matchmaking profession. At least I was until recently."

"You can't possibly get it right every time," he said. "People are just too complicated."

She exhaled deeply. "That's true."

"I see the parallels in the two career paths," he said. "Go ahead, tell me why you made the shift."

"I liked aspects of profiling," she said. "It felt like important work. I was making a contribution to society. But there is a lot of death and darkness attached to the job."

"I know." Ethan laced his fingers behind his head. "Why do you think the Sweetwaters got out of the old family business?"

"You mean, mostly out," Ravenna said.

"Mostly out," he agreed. "Like my grandfather says, over time, hunting human monsters takes a toll on the soul."

Ravenna exhaled softly. "So does profiling—at least that's what it felt like to me. When I got out of college, profiling seemed like an intriguing intellectual puzzle, a challenge with very high stakes. Then I started getting emotionally involved. I began to obsess on the job. To get the profile right I had to go into the dark places of the monsters' minds, sometimes for weeks or even months. The process affected my sleep. My dreams. I started having nightmares about getting trapped in those dark places."

"I understand. These days when the Sweetwaters do favors for Arcane or the Guilds it's with the understanding that when it's time for the end game, we get out of the way and let regular law enforcement take over. We're hunters, Ravenna, not hired assassins."

She surprised him with a wry smile. "Maybe you should have made that clear on the Ottoway questionnaire. It would have made it so much easier to find a match for you."

He looked at her.

She raised her eyes to the ceiling. "I'm joking, Sweetwater."

"I believe we are talking about you, not me," he said. "I want to hear the rest of your career transition story."

"Well, let's see. Last year I was assigned full-time to an FBPI task force. I didn't feel I was accepted as a full member of the team. I was very good at my job, but my boss, Collins, and the other agents treated me as if I was a cross between the office mascot and a handy computer. All they had to do was bring me coffee and feed me a lot of raw data. I was supposed to spit out the answers on demand."

"And when the case was closed?"

"Sometimes I got a pat on the head. Sometimes I got propositioned. Sometimes everyone forgot about me altogether until the next time. I was just part of the office furniture."

"So it was your dissatisfaction with your job that made you decide to quit?"

"Well, that and the fact that Harriet and I nearly got flatlined by a delusional psychopath named Clarence Fitch. He fancied himself a witch hunter. He flatlined three women before we caught up with him."

Ethan watched her closely. "Jeff told me you were the profiler on the task force that took down Fitch, but he didn't tell me you nearly got flatlined."

"That's because Collins did a very great job of making the team look good. Your nephew was a last-minute addition. After the takedown he was immediately yanked off the task force and assigned to another project. He didn't attend the debriefings, so he doesn't know that Collins was careful to keep me out of the final report."

"Because it was his fault you got into trouble?"

"Not entirely," Ravenna said. "I have to accept some responsibility. I made the classic mistake of volunteering to act as bait."

"Never a good idea."

"The idea was that the task force would monitor me and move in if and when Fitch's goons tried to grab me. There were a couple of major snafus. The result was that I got kidnapped and locked in a cage in the Underworld. I was scheduled to be the guest of honor at a little ceremony that was supposed to conclude with me getting flatlined by Fitch. The team was late. Took a wrong turn in the tunnels. I had to rescue myself, with Harriet's help."

"Shit," Ethan whispered.

Ravenna smiled at the sleeping dust bunny. "It wasn't all bad. That's how Harriet and I met."

Ethan studied her. "Why did you volunteer to act as bait?"

"Because I knew exactly how to make myself look like a witch online, of course. That was where Fitch did his hunting—his own kind of profiling—online. I made sure he found me."

"I get it." Ethan thought for a moment. "You said Fitch is delusional. Did he really believe he was on a mission to hunt witches?"

"I'm convinced of it. He was—is—a powerful talent. One of the monsters. They've got him on drugs to keep him from using his psychic senses. He's in a locked ward at a high-security para-psych hospital for the criminally insane. In fact, that's where he spent most of his adult life. He escaped last year and was free long enough to set himself up in the witch hunting business."

"What about his followers? Also delusional?"

"Depends how you define *delusional*," Ravenna said. "From what I could tell they were typical cult recruits, the type who would follow any charismatic figure. Fitch just happened to be the one who came along. They are in jail now, but when they get out they will probably end up in thrall to some other psychopathic con artist."

"After that takedown you decided to go into the matchmaking business?"

"Yep."

"Think you'll ever go back to profiling?" he asked.

"No. It's not for me, not full-time at any rate. I can see that now. My only regret about leaving is that something didn't feel right about my last case."

"Jeff said the witch hunter case was a big success."

"It was." Ravenna brightened. "What's more, my dad told me that thanks to a Chastain aura balancer, the doctors were able to unfreeze the paranormal senses of the three women Fitch had flatlined."

"I hadn't heard that. Great news."

"Yes, it is."

Ethan studied her in the pulsing glow of the wedding chapel lights. "So why aren't you satisfied with the conclusion of the case?"

"According to my profile of him, Fitch was delusional and charismatic, but he was not organized. He was in and out of asylums throughout his youth and wound up in one permanently when he became an adult. He could not cope with the details of normal life. He was scary because of his talent but he was also disordered. So much so that he couldn't finish school or drive a car or pay his bills. He could not tell the difference between reality and his delusions."

"Why doesn't that information fit with your profile?"

Ravenna looked at him, her eyes shadowed. "Not only did Fitch engineer his escape, he managed to get his cult up and running in a matter of weeks. His Order of the Guardians was small, but well organized. Efficient. Disciplined."

"Do you think one of the other cult members was managing things for him?"

"Maybe."

"Did you advise the task force of your theory?"

"I told Collins that I didn't think we had a complete picture of the cult. He said it didn't matter because everyone involved was going to be locked up." Ravenna moved a hand in a short arc. "He's right. They're all in prison or, in the case of Fitch, an asylum."

"Good to know," Ethan said. "You never told me how you saved Harriet and yourself when the task force was delayed."

"I gave them a working demonstration of the dangers of messing with a fire witch."

"Sweet." Ethan smiled. "I'd like to have seen that."

Energy shifted in the atmosphere. Ravenna's eyes heated. Ethan felt the burn deep inside.

"You're really not afraid of me, are you?" Ravenna asked. She sounded intrigued, curious, not quite believing but wanting to believe.

"I like fireworks," Ethan said.

CHAPTER TWENTY-SIX

It was a trap and he had almost walked straight into it. Two more steps and he would have been dead or, worse, lost in an endless Alien nightmare. The faint shadows just inside the chamber were the only clue to the dangerous pool of paranormal energy that seethed near the entrance.

The only reason he was still alive and still sane was because of his powerful new para-psych profile. Thanks to the Vortex machine, his senses were more acute.

Taggert Spooner backed away from the arched doorway and stared into the glowing quartz chamber. The initial flash of panic was subsiding. In its place was a white-hot fury. The prospector had cheated him.

He turned away from the chamber and its deadly trap. He should have made certain the old bastard had given him the right coordinates before icing him. Now the one person who could tell him where the pyramid crystals had come from was dead.

The rage was playing havoc with his senses. Strong emotions were always enhanced by the powerful currents of energy in the Underworld. He flattened one hand against the quartz wall to steady himself. After a moment his head cleared. He tried to think, to plan. It was true he had a new high-rez talent—he was an icer who could kill—but he was still a strategy talent. That was the ability that had enabled him to build his business empire. He needed to use that skill set now.

It wasn't easy to lower the temperature of the rage churning through him. He took his hand off the wall and clenched it into a tight fist. He wished he could kill the old bastard again, much more slowly this time.

The thought sent a shudder through him but his strategy talent was telling him he should have verified the discovery before getting rid of the one person who had the information he needed. Bowen had spent a lifetime in the Underworld. Mining was a business that fostered paranoia. It made sense that Bowen had hedged his bets. He hadn't trusted computers or his phone. He had wanted to be certain the money was actually in his account before he turned over the real coordinates.

Or maybe Bowen had been foolish enough to try to sell the location twice. Maybe the other buyer was Amber, Inc.

That possibility sent another flash of rage across his senses. This time the churning fury threatened to spin out of control. Maybe the bastard had lied from the beginning.

Spooner reached into his jacket and took out the two pyramid stones. No question there was a lot of energy trapped inside each. He put them back into the pocket of his jacket and started toward the hole-in-the-wall he had used to enter the tunnels. One thing was certain—he wasn't going to get the answers from a dead man. The trip to Illusion Town had been a waste of time. He'd been conned.

The only good news was that he had been smart enough to handle the entire project on his own. Melody Palantine did not know about the arrangement to meet Bowen. She would never know about the failed project. It was very important that Palantine did not detect any weakness in him.

A part of him understood it was time to cut his losses. Yes, he had been played by the old prospector, but shit happened in business. Win some, lose some. As they said in Illusion Town, you had to know when to walk away from the table.

He had no option. He had to abandon Glass House. But that did not mean he had to forgo revenge. He knew exactly who to blame for the disaster—Ethan Sweetwater.

CHAPTER TWENTY-SEVEN

The call from Gabriel Jones came just as a foggy dawn illuminated the Shadow Zone. Ravenna was in the small bathroom, washing her face and trying to pin her hair into a knot. She had considered taking a shower, but one look at the grungy tile work and stained shower curtain had convinced her to wait until she got home. She cracked open the door so she could hear the conversation via the speaker on Ethan's phone.

"I don't know exactly what in green hell we've got," Gabriel Jones said, "but it is now duly registered as the Glass House Antiquity and the legal owner is the Federation of City-States. Of interest to everyone involved, there was no sign of Spooner in the vicinity. All we know for sure is that he didn't try to register the claim."

"The prospector gave him the wrong coordinates," Ethan said.

"Looks like it."

"Where are you now?"

"Just got back to my office here at headquarters," Gabriel said. "The team is securing Glass House until the Feds get their people here."

"Tell me about Glass House."

"Hard to describe. You'll have to see it for yourself. There's a wall of solid, transparent crystal, a gate of some kind, but we have no idea how to get through it, and no one wants to rush the job. Too risky. Looks like another maze of tunnels on the other side, but they're made of glass or crystal, not the green quartz the Aliens used in most of the Underworld."

"What do you think it is?"

"Best guess at this point is that it's a lab of some sort or a power generator, but who knows?"

"Sounds like an incredible find."

"And a dangerous one," Gabriel said. "No wonder the dead prospector wanted to unload it rather than risk filing the claim. The Feds will bring in the experts and decide how to move forward with exploration and development. That's not my job. The question is, what happened to Spooner?"

"Looks like he got double-crossed. He's a player. He knows when to walk away. He'll go back to his office in Frequency and act like nothing happened."

"Leaving the Illusion Town police with no way to tie him to the murder of the prospector or the attacks on you and Ms. Chastain."

"That's where it stands now," Ethan said. "Do you need anything else from me?"

"No, but thanks. The Guild appreciates the favor. So does Arcane. You can go back to trying to make a Covenant Marriage match."

"I'll do that, but I gotta tell you, solving your problem was easier."

The call ended. Ravenna concentrated on her hair. Ethan appeared at the crack in the bathroom doorway and watched her work in front of the small mirror. There was some heat in his eyes but she couldn't tell if it was because of her or because he had accomplished his mission.

"Did you catch all that?" he asked.

"Yes." She smiled. "Congratulations."

"The Feds have control of Glass House, but the way things look now, Spooner will go free. Unless something turns up in the way of evidence, the cops can't grab him for the prospector's death, and the Feds can't touch him for illegal research in his labs."

"He's the CEO of a successful tech company," Ravenna said. "He's smart, but sooner or later he'll screw up."

"The bottom line for us is that Spooner is someone else's problem now."

"That's a relief. If I move fast I may be able to keep my job for at least another day." She pushed the door wider. Ethan was forced to step back. She hurried past him, heading into the outer room to collect her evening bag and Harriet. "Let's go. I need to get back to my place so I can shower and change my clothes. With luck I will walk through the door of Otto-way Matchmakers right on time."

Ethan watched her with an unreadable expression. "What about breakfast? Don't you want coffee at least?"

"I don't have time." She slung the small bag crosswise over her shoulder and went to grab Harriet, who was perched on the table. "This is about my job, Ethan."

"Your job," he said evenly, "depends on you finding me the right match, remember?"

She scooped up Harriet. "I've been thinking about that. It occurs to me I know you a lot better now than I did before this whole mess started. I'll start reviewing my files again as soon as I get to my office. I may have overlooked some potential matches. Don't give up."

"I'm trying not to," he said.

She glanced at him, bewildered by his grim tone.

"What about your assessment of my dating technique?" he continued before she could figure out the shift in his mood.

"I'll get there." She went to the door. "Priorities, Ethan."

"Right. Priorities." He paced across the room, grabbed his jacket, and slung it over one shoulder. "Don't forget, we still have your grandparents' anniversary event. Given what we just went through, I'd say our relationship passed the stress test. We should be able to do a road trip together."

She thought about that. "You're right. Last night was definitely another bonding experience."

"Glad you thought so."

He sounded disgruntled again, but she did not have time to analyze his mood. Maybe he was not a morning person.

"Let's go," she said. She yanked the door open. "We've got to get to your sled."

Ethan followed her down the outside stairs and caught up with her on the sidewalk. "Relax, it's only six o'clock. We've got time."

Ravenna started to respond, but she stopped, frozen with horror. She stared at the headlines of the *Shadow Zone Insider* in the sidewalk stand.

Dust Bunny Mayhem at the Golden Amber.

Diners Amused While Management Panics.

A band of dust bunnies struck the Famous All-You-Can-Eat Buffet at the Golden Amber last night. They hit the line shortly after midnight. Diners laughed when the critters arrived and, apparently having seen the All-You-Can-Eat ads, proceeded to chow down in style. Eyewitnesses report the dessert section was the hardest hit.

There was a full-color photograph of a ravaged buffet. Five furry diners could be seen. The one with a half-eaten slice of indigo berry pie in her paws looked all too familiar.

"That's you, Harriet," Ravenna said. "Don't try to deny it."

Harriet chortled.

"I knew something bad happened last night," Ravenna muttered. She turned to Ethan, who was admiring the photo. "We need to get out of the Shadow Zone before someone recognizes Harriet."

Ethan looked at Harriet. "Hear that, pal? You're a wanted dust bunny."

Harriet chortled again, wriggled out from the crook of Ravenna's elbow, and hopped up onto Ethan's shoulder.

Ravenna started walking briskly, heading for the abandoned warehouse and the hole-in-the-wall that led to the sled.

"I need to take a more balanced attitude toward my dating life," she said. "I should practice serenity and gratitude. Open myself to new experiences. Meditate twice a day."

Ethan caught up with her. "Where's that coming from?"

"As I recall, that advice was given to me by date number twenty-three. Or maybe it was twenty-four. I'll have to check my little black book when I get home. His name was Derek, I think. He operates a couple of wellness spas here in town."

"You've got a little black book?" Ethan demanded.

"After the first half dozen dates, I realized I had to start making notes because I was losing track. I didn't want to take the risk of putting that sort of personal information online, so I bought the notebook. It happens to have a black cover."

"Thoughtful of you," Ethan said. His voice was very even now. "I take it the date with Derek was yet another failure."

"Turns out I'm not very good at changing my approach to dating. I was unable to open up to the possibilities he had in mind."

"Was sex involved?"

"Derek is convinced that sex between two well-matched individuals is a potentially transcendent experience that can clarify the emotions and establish a psychic bond. After a very nice dinner he suggested we go back to his place and test his theory."

"Anything to his theory?"

"Beats me," Ravenna said. "I declined to run the experiment and called a cab."

"Just answer one question for me," Ethan said. "Am I in your little black book?"

"Of course not. You're a client."

She did not notice the pen Harriet had managed to acquire until they were in the sled and headed back through the tunnels.

"Where did you get that?" she asked. Harriet gave her the pen. She read the words stamped on the barrel. "'Rendezvous Inn. Where Dreams Come True.'"

"Great," Ethan said. "A souvenir."

CHAPTER TWENTY-EIGHT

Ravenna walked into the offices of Ottoway Matchmakers at exactly two minutes to nine. She was so busy congratulating herself on having managed to save her job for at least another day that she did not immediately notice the subdued atmosphere.

It wasn't until she paused at the open door of Sarah Mulhouse's office that she realized something was terribly amiss.

"Good morning, Sarah," she said.

Harriet chortled her customary greeting and gazed, enraptured, at the small candy dish on Sarah's desk.

Sarah looked up and managed a wan smile. "Hi."

Alarm jolted through Ravenna. "What's wrong? Are you okay?"

"I'm fine," Sarah said quickly. She picked up a small chocolate wrapped in foil and offered it to Harriet. "Here you go."

Harriet bounced down from Ravenna's shoulder, scurried across the floor, and hopped up onto Sarah's desk. She accepted the chocolate with profound excitement and proceeded about the delicate business of un-wrapping it.

"Sarah?" Ravenna took a few steps into the office. "Do you want to talk about whatever it is that's bothering you?"

"I can't," Sarah squeaked. "You'll find out soon enough. I just want you to know that I think it's wrong. It's not your fault."

"What isn't my fault? Wait. Is this about the Sweetwater case?"

"Maybe. Sort of. Ottoway will explain."

"Damn," Ravenna said. "This doesn't sound good."

"It's not," Sarah said. She looked at Harriet. "I'm going to miss both of you."

"That sounds even worse." Ravenna went to the desk and picked up Harriet, who had managed to get rid of the foil and was now munching the chocolate. "Let's go, pal."

She headed back to the door with Harriet tucked under one arm. Sarah got out of her chair.

"I just want to say how sorry—" she began. And stopped.

"Whatever it is, it's not your fault," Ravenna said.

She marched down the hall to her office, opened the door, and rezzed the lights. She plunked Harriet down on the desk so that she could inspect her pen collection. She was in the process of hanging up her coat when Bernice Ottoway appeared at the entrance of the office. She had a folded newspaper in one hand.

"You have thirty minutes to pack up your personal possessions and leave the premises, Ms. Chastain. As of this morning you are no longer an employee of this firm."

Ravenna clutched her jacket. "What have I done?"

"You have done the unforgivable. You have besmirched the reputation of Ottoway Matchmakers."

"Just because I haven't closed the Sweetwater case?"

"For the last time, we don't close cases. We are not the police or the

FBPI. We are Ottoway. We launch perfectly matched couples upon the tranquil seas of a Covenant Marriage."

Harriet lost interest in her collection. Her second set of eyes opened. A soft growl rumbled through her. She wasn't sleeked out yet, but the signs were ominous.

Bernice yelped in alarm and took a hasty step back. "Control your dust bunny, Ms. Chastain. I should never have allowed you to bring her to work."

"You know the clients adore her." Ravenna touched Harriet lightly. "It's okay, Harriet."

Harriet did not appear convinced. She kept her attention on Bernice.

Ravenna decided to try reason. "Ms. Ottoway, in case you haven't noticed, it's not easy launching Sweetwater. It's going to require a lot of shoving just to get him away from the dock. But I haven't failed yet. Why are you firing me?"

"I can't believe you have to ask." Ms. Ottoway snapped open the newspaper and held it up with both hands. "This is why I'm forced to let you go."

Ravenna stared at the front page of the *Curtain*. The photo on the front page of the *Shadow Zone Insider* had been bad enough, but at least no one had known the identity of the dust bunny who had led the raid on the buffet. This picture, however, was on the front page of the biggest scandal sheet in the four city-states, and it showed Ethan, Harriet, and herself hurrying away from the Rendezvous Inn. Harriet was the only one who looked innocent. It was her default mode. As for Ethan, his hair was rumpled as if someone had been running her fingers through it. With his jacket nonchalantly hooked over one shoulder, his rumpled white shirt, and the unknotted tie draped around his neck, he looked like a man who was leaving a lover's bed.

She was in far worse shape. The long tear in the narrow skirt of her little black dress revealed a lot of bare leg, and her hair was in a chaotic twist, not an elegant chignon. She was the very picture of a woman who had spent the night engaged in illicit passion in a sleazy motel.

The shocking headline almost set fire to the newspaper.

Sweetwater Scion Spends Night with Elite Matchmaker Escort.

Has Ottoway Found a New Way to Service Clients?

Stunned, Ravenna could only stare at the newspaper. She groped for some way to explain the unexplainable and finally gave up.

"I understand," she managed finally. "I'll clear out my desk immediately. I'm so sorry, Ms. Ottoway."

"There you are," Ethan said from the doorway. "I hope I'm not too late. Have you already told Ms. Ottoway the good news?"

Harriet chortled a greeting and closed her hunting eyes. Ethan ambled past a frozen Bernice Ottoway and went to the desk to pat Harriet on the head.

Bernice unfroze. She lowered the paper and turned to stare at Ethan. "Mr. Sweetwater. I didn't realize you had an appointment today."

"I don't," Ethan said. "I just came by to tell Ravenna that I changed my mind about waiting to share our good news. Not much point now, is there? Not with those headlines in the *Curtain*."

Ravenna pulled herself together. "What good news?"

Ethan winked. "Ms. Ottoway deserves to be the first to know. After all, if it hadn't been for her, you and I might never have met, although I like to think that fate would have found a way."

"What good news are you talking about?" Ms. Ottoway said. Her eyes were blank with bewilderment. "Are you saying Ms. Chastain found a successful match for you?"

"That is exactly what happened," Ethan said. "She and I are hoping to be married."

Bernice Ottoway stared at him. So did Ravenna. Ethan appeared oblivious to the tension in the room. Either that or he simply did not give a damn about the stressful atmosphere. Ravenna's intuition told her the latter was the case. Ethan and Harriet had a lot in common, she decided. If the situation looked like it was under control, why sweat it?

"We planned to hold off announcing the news until after we told our families, but given the headline in the *Curtain*, there's not much point keeping it a secret, is there? You can be the first to congratulate us, Ms. Ottoway. Don't worry, we will make sure everyone knows."

"Knows what?" Bernice demanded.

Ethan smiled. "That Ravenna and I found each other the right way— the Ottoway."

Ravenna wondered why the floor did not simply open up under her feet and plunge her into some uncharted sector of the Underworld. That would have been so helpful. But stuff like that never happened when you really needed it to happen.

Ms. Ottoway blinked. "Oh." Comprehension struck. Her eyes suddenly sparkled with excitement. "Oh, my."

"Well, that's it for now." Ethan leaned over and gave Ravenna a quick, affectionate kiss on the nose and headed for the door. "Got to go. I just dropped by to thank you, Ms. Ottoway. I'll pick you up for lunch, Ravenna."

With a last pat on the head for Harriet, he was gone.

The engineer of the apocalypse.

CHAPTER TWENTY-NINE

"Don't get me wrong," Ravenna said. "I understand why you did it. You felt guilty for dragging me into the Spooner case. You were trying to be gallant. Noble. Good intentions and all that. But now we've got an even bigger problem. Surely you can see that."

"The way I see it, things are actually back under control," Ethan said. He dipped a chunk of battered-and-fried fish into a small container of hot sauce. "We would be in a much worse situation if I had not made an executive decision."

She opened her mouth to outline the full extent of the catastrophe he had wrought, but there were no words, not for such a monumental disaster. Flabbergasted, she munched a fry instead.

They were sitting at a picnic table in a park eating the take-out order of fish and chips that Ethan had provided. Harriet was perched on the table, working her way through a pile of fries. The day was pleasant, sunny, and warm in the way that only the desert can be warm in the spring—full of the promise of oppressive summer heat, but tourist-bureau perfect for now. Under any other circumstances she would have been savoring the day and enjoying the company of the man sitting on the other side of the table. But today she was consumed with the vision of oncoming disaster.

"Try looking at it this way," Ethan continued. "The problem isn't any bigger than it ever was. The only difference now is that it's more clearly defined."

She glared at him. "Spoken like an engineer."

"I am an engineer," he said around a mouthful of fish. "Look, you and I are still scheduled to do the fake date thing for your grandparents' anniversary, right?"

"Yes, but it was just a fake date, not a fake engagement. There's a difference."

"Technically we're not engaged. Not yet."

She stared at him in disbelief. "After those headlines in the *Curtain*, everyone—including both of our families, I might add—will assume we're engaged. It's practically an announcement."

"You will notice that there is no ring," Ethan said. It was as if he had just pointed out the answer to a mathematical equation. QED.

Once again she could not find the words, so she ate some of the crisp fish. She was amazed to discover she had an appetite, given the situation. True, she hadn't had time for breakfast. Still. Stress eating, probably.

"You're looking at this from a skewed perspective," Ethan said.

She narrowed her eyes. "That sounds like mansplaining."

"Just pointing out an obvious fact. So what if everyone thinks we're on the brink of announcing our engagement? Engagements can be terminated just as easily as a casual dating relationship."

"No," Ravenna said. "A formal engagement implies that a Covenant Marriage is expected and intended. Ending an engagement is a very big deal."

"Not really," Ethan said, munching a fry. "There are no legal consequences. Some minor social embarrassment, maybe, but no career-destroying repercussions. Besides, we won't actually be ending an engagement. We'll be terminating an almost engagement. After the shock wears off, everyone will say it was a good thing we figured out our mistake before it was too late."

Ravenna ate another fry and thought about that. He had a point. Maybe she was overreacting. Maybe the situation could be managed. Maybe.

"What about our families?" she said. "Right now our fake match is just local news, but it won't be long before my parents and yours hear about it."

"Zora called me already," Ethan admitted. "Wanted to know what was going on."

"What did you tell her?"

"The truth, more or less—that we hadn't made a formal announcement and that we were holding off until after I met your family. She understood."

"Huh. No formal announcement until after we meet each other's families." Ravenna gave that some thought. "Okay, I guess that line works. For now."

"Your enthusiasm is a little underwhelming, but never mind. One step at a time. Meanwhile, I have an update on Spooner."

Ravenna perked up. "What?"

"He's on his way back to his company's headquarters in Frequency."

"He's going to get away with the murder of that prospector, isn't he?"

"Looks like it. Arcane will keep an eye on him. Meanwhile, we know for sure he didn't get control of the Glass House Antiquity, and everyone involved seems to think that achievement is a very, very big deal."

"Still. Spooner is getting away with murder."

"Yeah."

CHAPTER THIRTY

"I'm trying not to look too far ahead, Sybil." Ravenna put the phone on speaker, set the device on the counter, opened a cupboard door, and took down a bottle of brandy. "I just want to get through this big family gathering thing before I decide what to do next."

"You're stalling for time."

"Well, sure. What would you do?"

"Stall," Sybil admitted.

It was almost eleven. Two hours earlier Harriet had disappeared into the green shadows of the Dark Zone for her nightly round of partying. Ravenna was in her nightgown, robe, and slippers. She had finished packing an hour ago. She knew she ought to get some rest. Ethan was picking her up early in the morning. It was a long drive to the Silver Lake resort. The anniversary gala, which would kick off with a barbecue in the late afternoon and conclude with a midnight ball, would be exhausting.

But she was too restless to sleep, so she was in the kitchen preparing to drink some therapeutic brandy. She needed to talk to someone. Fortunately, Sybil was a night person.

"I understand," Sybil said. "But we both know showing up at your grandparents' anniversary party with a Sweetwater who is a sort-of fiancé is going to be messy."

"Maybe not. Ethan seems to think we can make it work. Meanwhile, I'm trying to stick with the truth as much as possible. When my mother called this afternoon to ask what was going on, I told her Ethan and I are dating, which is true, more or less, but that we had only recently met and weren't comfortable making a formal announcement. I stressed there was no ring involved."

"Yet."

"Yet. I told her we wanted to be sure." Ravenna opened the bottle and poured a stiff shot of the brandy into a glass. "Mom said she understood."

"What about Ethan's family? How are they handling it?"

"I don't know. That's Ethan's problem. Fortunately no one from the Sweetwater clan has called to ask me if I'm an amber gold digger trying to seduce a Sweetwater heir into marriage."

"At least you're still employed."

Ravenna took a healthy swallow of the brandy and lowered the glass. "For now. And only because Ethan told my boss we were expecting to enter a CM."

"You make things sound so ominous."

"I've got a house of cards going here, Sybil. Sooner or later it's all going to come tumbling down."

"Maybe, but it doesn't have to be the end of the world when it does. I've been thinking. I can't afford to hire you. I'm still a one-person operation. But if you lose your job at Ottoway, you might consider going into business on your own."

"I've thought about that." Ravenna leaned back against the counter and sipped the brandy. "The basic problem is the start-up cost. I'd have to rent an office. It would take a while to build a reputation that would attract a high-end clientele. It might be a year before I would be able to make a decent living."

"What about sharing an office with me? I can't afford to pay you, but what about a partnership?"

"Are you serious? That is an extremely generous offer."

"Not really," Sybil said. "I can barely afford the rent as it is, but if you were bringing in some additional business and sharing expenses . . . Just something to think about."

"It's a very intriguing idea. Let's talk about it after I get back from Silver Lake, assuming I survive."

"You will do just fine. You're a fire witch. You've got skills."

"Useless skills. But thanks for the pep talk and the offer to share office space. I actually feel much better now."

"Good. Fake or real, enjoy dating Ethan Sweetwater while it lasts. It's obvious you're finding him a lot more interesting than the thirty-six dates in your little black book."

Ravenna thought about the events of the past forty-eight hours. "You have no idea. Good night, Sybil."

She ended the call, finished the brandy, set the alarm, and went to bed. She did not go to sleep until Harriet bounced up onto the quilt, bringing the scents of the night with her.

CHAPTER THIRTY-ONE

The whisper of a draft of night air stirred her restless dreams and sent a flash of electricity across her senses. Ravenna came awake with the sure and certain knowledge that something was terribly wrong.

A low growl sounded from the end of the bed. In the green shadows she could see Harriet's sleeked-out silhouette. All four eyes were open. She was no longer a cute fluff-ball. She was a hunter.

"Wait," Ravenna whispered.

Harriet blinked her hunting eyes but she did not dash recklessly off the bed. Once again she seemed to get the message that they were supposed to function as a team.

Ravenna sat up carefully and swung her feet to the floor. Out in the hall a floorboard creaked, sending another chill across her senses. Harriet growled again.

Ravenna stood, intending to close and lock the bedroom door. She was pretty sure that was what you were supposed to do when you suspected there was an intruder in the house. Stay in the bedroom, lock the door, and call the police. Worst-case scenario, she and Harriet could slip out the window.

She tiptoed across the room on bare feet, but she didn't move fast enough. A figure loomed in the doorway. In the radiance of the Dead City Wall streaming through the window, she could make out his features. Date number thirty-five. She was stunned.

"Clark?" she said. "What are you doing here?"

Clark Hatch raised a mag-rez gun. "I can't write a word and it's your fault. You stole my plot. You stole my characters. I've got a contract deadline coming up."

"Clark, you're hallucinating," she said. "Listen to me. You need to put down the gun."

"I have to kill you or I'll never be able to write again."

Harriet launched herself off the bed and streaked across the room. She vaulted up Clark's leg, going for the hand that held the gun.

Clark shrieked and stumbled back, swiping frantically at Harriet, who had her teeth sunk into Clark's forearm.

"Get it off." He dropped the pistol and shook his arm in a desperate attempt to dislodge Harriet. "Make it stop."

He flung his hand to one side. Harriet lost her grip and sailed across the room. She landed on the bed. Clark lunged for the gun. Ravenna kicked it out of the way and pulled hard on her talent.

Paranormal flames leaped around Clark. He jerked in reaction to the fierce energy, convulsed, and collapsed. He did not move. Ravenna cut her talent, rezzed a light, and studied the unconscious man.

"He seemed like a nice guy," she said to Harriet. "The second nice guy who has tried to murder me in the past week. He gave you a lovely pen. What is going on here? Is it me?"

Harriet was once again fluffed out. She chortled, satisfied the immediate threat was over. Ravenna took a few deep breaths and tried to think.

After a moment she moved to the bedside table, picked up the phone, and made the call.

Ethan answered midway through the first ring. "What's wrong?"

"I don't know," she said. "But something really weird is happening. I seem to be in need of trash removal service again."

"I'm on the way."

Chapter Thirty-Two

"We should probably stop meeting like this," Ethan said.

Ravenna folded her arms very tightly around her middle. "If that is supposed to be funny, your timing is extremely poor."

"Right," he said. "Sorry."

So much for trying to lighten the mood. He had felt the need to do something to ease her obvious distress, but clearly he had failed.

They were standing over Clark Hatch's unmoving body, which was sprawled across the threshold of Ravenna's bedroom doorway. There was a bandage over the teeth marks in Hatch's forearm, evidence of Harriet's attack.

Ethan smiled. *Go, Harriet.*

Ravenna had cleaned and covered the wound before he arrived. She was still in her robe and nightgown. Her hair was loose around her shoulders. As far as he could tell, she seemed more bewildered than panic-stricken by the fact that this was the second time she had been assaulted in her own home by a former agency date. Shock, probably.

"This is just so . . . bizarre," she said.

"I agree," he said.

"We ought to call the cops."

"Definitely." He looked at her. "So why didn't you? Why call me?"

She shook her head. "I don't want to get Clark in serious trouble, not yet at any rate."

"He's not Willis," Ethan pointed out. "Hatch may be a well-known author, but he doesn't have any special clout in this town. And this scene is pretty damning. The police are not going to doubt your version of events. The lock on the back door was broken. There will be prints on the pistol. Lots of evidence."

"The thing is, he's really a nice person."

Ethan looked at her. "Hatch? Seriously?"

"There is nothing in his background to suggest he would do something like this," Ravenna said, defensive now. "Sybil runs exhaustive online checks. I liked Clark. Harriet liked him, at least until tonight."

"You said Harriet liked Willis, too. Maybe dust bunnies aren't always real perceptive when it comes to judging humans."

Ravenna contemplated Hatch. "I think he was on something."

"Hatch?"

"Yes. When he came through the doorway he was hallucinating. He accused me of stealing his plot and his characters. He claimed he wouldn't be able to write again until I was dead."

"You said Willis seemed to think you were planning to destroy his casino empire."

"Both of them were acting very much out of character. Maybe there is some new drug in town."

"Got any reason to think either of them is into drugs?" Ethan asked.

"No," Ravenna admitted. "But something weird happened to Garrett Willis, and now it's happened to Clark. I'm sure of it."

"Maybe." Ethan glanced out the window. "It's almost dawn. If we're going to make it to your grandparents' anniversary in time for the big barbecue, we're going to have to get on the road in the next couple of hours. An investigation into Willis's and Hatch's behavior will need to wait until we get back from Silver Lake."

"What about Clark? We can't leave him here. He's going to wake up soon—at least I hope he is."

Ethan leaned down, grabbed one of Hatch's arms, and hauled him up over one shoulder. "Maybe you should revise your agency profile to specify that you prefer smaller, lighter men."

Ravenna shot him another glare. But behind the fierceness he could see the worry. It wasn't panic, not yet, but it wasn't good.

"Relax," he said. "We'll get this figured out when we get back from Silver Lake."

"Thanks," she said. "It's very nice of you to help me again."

"No problem." He caught a whiff of an unpleasant floral scent and grimaced. "Hatch is apparently using the same bad aftershave that Willis favors."

"I noticed. What are you going to do with Clark?"

"He and I are going to drop by Aunt Zora's house. She can do her memory-erasing thing on him and then I'll dump him on his own doorstep. Which reminds me—got an address?"

"Yes." Ravenna picked up her phone. "I'll get it for you. Ethan?"

"Don't worry, I'm not going to send him into the tunnels without amber."

"I know you won't. It's just that this is the second time this has happened, and I can't help but wonder—"

"What?"

"Well, I wasn't completely truthful when I filled out the question-naire for the Banks agency."

"I am, of course, shocked to hear that."

"The point is, maybe my lack of honesty on the questionnaire is one of the reasons this is happening. I'd like to think Willis and Hatch were under the influence of drugs, but what if I'm the problem?"

"What are you trying to say?" he asked.

"I'm starting to think that maybe it's not these two very nice men who have suddenly gone bonkers. Maybe I have a vibe that destabilizes the auras of certain males."

"I gotta tell you, that's a bit of a stretch."

"I'm serious."

"Speaking for myself, I find your vibe damned exciting. I might even go so far as to say you are one hot fire witch."

She narrowed her eyes. "Get out of here before I set your trousers on fire."

"On my way."

CHAPTER THIRTY-THREE

"I've been thinking about how to tell my family the truth about our fake match," Ravenna said. "I don't want to spoil my grandparents' big celebration by dropping the news on them before the festivities. I've decided it would be best to wait until tomorrow morning. I'll inform Mom and Dad privately when we're ready to leave. They can tell my grandparents."

"It's your family, your call," Ethan said.

He was at the controls of the Slider, wraparound, mirrored sunglasses veiling his eyes. He drove with the ease and smooth coordination with which he did everything else. She wondered if he danced with the same sensual, masculine grace. There would be dancing at her grandparents' party that night. She and Ethan would have to take the floor at least once. It would look odd if they didn't.

She put on her own sunglasses and focused on the view through the windshield for a while. They had left the Connerville truck stop two hours ago, passing a series of warning signs: *Do Not Attempt to Cross Desert After Dark, No Services Until Grimley Pass, Don't Forget Extra Water, No Cell Service Until Grimley Pass, Do Not Stop in the Hot Zone.*

They were now well into the vast expanse of the Mirage Desert. The imposing heights of the Silver Mountain range were still just a smudge on the horizon. There was very little traffic. Most of the handful of vehicles they passed were huge tractor-trailer rigs driven by long-haul truckers.

Harriet was perched on the back of the seat, munching a pretzel and enjoying the ride. Like Ethan, she appeared unconcerned about the stressful situation that awaited them at Silver Lake. Well, she would be unconcerned, wouldn't she? Ravenna thought. Harriet was a dust bunny. But why was Ethan so unfazed?

"We're probably going to have to dance tonight," she blurted out before stopping to think.

"I'll try not to step on your toes," Ethan said.

Yep. Unfazed.

"Does it strike you that our lives have gotten quite weird lately?" she asked.

"Never a dull moment."

"I'm serious."

"So am I. And speaking of serious, when we return to Illusion Town, we're going to have to deal with the fact that two men recently tried to murder you. Do we mention the problem to your family?"

"No, absolutely not, at least not at this stage. They approved of my career change but they were not in favor of my move to Illusion Town. If they find out what has been happening to me, they will insist that I come back to Cadence."

Ethan glanced at her, his eyes unreadable behind the lenses of the sunglasses. "Why did you decide to fire up your matchmaking career in Illusion Town?"

"I like the energy there."

Ethan smiled. "I like it, too."

"There's another reason why I'm comfortable in Illusion Town. The locals don't ask a lot of personal questions. It's understood everyone has secrets."

"I agree. Speaking of secrets, you said your matchmaker knows about your affinity for fire?"

"Yes. She tries to factor it in when she selects a date."

"And yet two of the thirty-six matches she has come up with so far have proven to be high-risk individuals," Ethan said.

Ravenna thought about that for a moment. "Maybe they lied on their profiles, too."

"Tricky business, this matchmaking stuff."

"Yes, it is, but I'm a professional. Don't try it at home." Ravenna glanced at the picnic basket in the back seat. "Want some road food?"

"Sounds good."

She unfastened her seat belt, leaned over the seat, and picked up the basket. Harriet chortled enthusiastically.

Ravenna got the basket into the front seat, sat back, and put on the seat belt. She opened the basket. Harriet peered over her shoulder, surveyed the selections available, and chose an energy bar.

The warning sign at the edge of the highway came up just as Ravenna was opening a bag of chips for Ethan and herself.

WARNING
MIRAGE LAKE AND NIGHTMARE CAVE AHEAD
YOU ARE ENTERING A HOT ZONE
DO NOT STOP FOR NEXT THIRTY MILES

"Oh, wow," Ravenna said. She munched some chips and held the bag out to Ethan. "I've been looking forward to seeing Mirage Lake. I read about it online when I realized I would be driving this road to Silver Lake."

"Don't get too excited." Ethan fished out a couple of chips. "I drove out here to take a look shortly after I moved to Illusion Town. There's not much to see during the day. Like the sign says, it's just a mirage. But there's a lot of hot energy in that area. It really heats up at night."

She looked at him, her brows lifting. "You went through the hot zone at night?"

"I was curious."

Ravenna cleared her throat. "The signs clearly say no one should drive through here at night. They also say no one should stop in this zone for the next thirty miles."

"I know," Ethan said. "I can read."

She wrinkled her nose. "Well? What was it like?"

"Interesting. I think both the mirage and the cave are being fed by some Underworld source of intense paranormal energy. A vein of some unknown quartz, maybe."

"Or an Underworld volcano?"

"That's a possibility," he agreed. "Don't eat all the chips."

"Help yourself." She held the bag out to him again. "Did you actually go inside Nightmare Cave?"

"I ducked in and had a look around. There's a lot of energy in there. It's manageable if you've got enough talent to handle it, but it's not fun."

"How bad was it?"

"Let's just say I didn't stay long."

She started to ask another question, but what looked like a sapphire-blue lake began to coalesce in the distance.

"That's amazing," she said. "It looks so real."

The closer they got to the shimmering mirage, the more difficult it was to focus on it. The vision of incredibly blue water was constantly shifting. Every time she thought she could make out the surface of a real lake, it faded back into raw desert.

"The energy in the area is somehow producing the mirage," Ethan said. "At night it generates thunderstorms and serious winds."

She glanced at him. "How long did you stay in this zone after dark?"

"The whole night. Not by choice, though. Turns out the sign is right. You can't drive this section of the highway after dark."

"You mean it's illegal to drive it after dark."

"No, I mean it can't be done, at least not with current technology. The energy in the storms rendered the Slider's engine inoperable. I spent the night in the car. The next morning I had to retune the ignition amber and the fuel bars. Luckily I always carry an emergency starter kit."

"But you were okay inside the car?"

Ethan patted the dashboard with affectionate pride. "This is a very good car. Needed a new paint job, though."

Chapter Thirty-Four

Late that afternoon Ravenna got the first of what proved to be a deluge of unsubtle hints that her grand plan for finessing the social situation at the anniversary celebration was on shaky ground. She was lounging against the railing of the hotel veranda, drinking tea and doing her best to deflect probing questions from several inquisitive cousins, when she spotted Ethan and her grandmother returning from a tour of the gardens.

She had been growing increasingly anxious, because the pair had been gone for nearly an hour. That seemed like way too much time to spend on a simple garden tour. Now the sight of them strolling along the path, deep in animated conversation, sent an ominous premonition jolting across her senses. She could not overhear what was being said, but it was obvious the two had hit it off.

Even from this distance it was clear Adelaide Chastain wasn't just being her usual gracious self—she was delighted with Ethan's company.

As for Ethan, it didn't look like he was simply trying to be charming. He appeared to be deeply engaged in the conversation.

As they drew closer to the veranda, it became possible to hear some of the conversation.

". . . I discovered my moon orchids do better when they are exposed to the energy of shadow ferns," Adelaide Chastain enthused. "There seems to be a symbiotic relationship that causes both to thrive."

"Thanks for the suggestion," Ethan said. "I don't have any shadow ferns in my garden, but I'll start looking for some as soon as I get back to Illusion Town."

"You don't want the standard variety you usually find at the commercial nurseries. They don't have the right vibe. When I get home I'll send you some from my garden. I'm sure they will do well in Illusion Town. There's plenty of energy in the atmosphere and the ground there."

"My house is right up against the Dead City Wall, so my plants get a lot of heat. Have you tried using a few chunks of green amber near your roses?"

"No, but one of the people in my garden club mentioned she's experimenting with green amber."

"I've had good luck with it," Ethan said. "I'll send a few rocks to you."

"Thank you, that would be lovely." Adelaide caught sight of Ravenna. "Oh, there you are, dear. Ethan and I have had the most interesting tour of the grounds. Several unique specimens here. The energy in these mountains produces some amazing plants."

Ravenna pasted on a smile. "I'm glad you two found something to talk about."

"Ms. Chastain gave me some great tips for my herbs," Ethan said.

"How nice." Ravenna kept the smile in place with an effort.

"Your grandfather is looking forward to chatting with Ethan about that Old World antique that has been sitting in the living room at home for years," Adelaide said. "No one knows what it is or what it was designed to do, but it definitely has a paranormal provenance. Maybe Ethan could take a look at it when he comes for the holidays."

"Ethan's expertise is in rez-amber and quartz, not Old World antiques," Ravenna said. It was scary enough that Adelaide and Ethan had bonded over their shared passion for gardening. It would be catastrophic if Mark Chastain developed a similar rapport with a fake future grandson-in-law.

"You know how it is with engineers," Ethan said. "We love gadgets of all kinds, and Old World paranormal engineering is fascinating. I'd like to get a look at that antique."

The hum of a small engine drew everyone's attention. A golf cart whizzed around the corner of the lobby. Brix, one of Ravenna's nephews, was at the throttle. The little vehicle was crammed with an assortment of young relatives.

Harriet was on the dashboard. She chortled when she saw Ravenna.

Brix spotted Ethan and brought the golf cart to a halt. "Mr. Sweetwater, we're taking Harriet down to the lake for a swim. Want to come with us?"

"Sure," Ethan said. "Let me grab my swim trunks and a towel."

He came up the veranda steps and paused to give Ravenna a quick, proprietary kiss on the cheek.

"See you at the barbecue," he said.

He disappeared into the lobby.

Adelaide beamed at Ravenna. "What a charming young man. Congratulations, dear. Ethan is perfect."

I'm doomed, Ravenna thought.

In spite of forebodings and premonitions, Ravenna clung to a few wispy scraps of hope throughout the barbecue, even though it had become clear her parents were as thrilled with Ethan as her grandparents.

"It's impressive that he's determined to step away from Amber, Inc., and build his own business," Dean Chastain remarked during the interlude between the barbecue and the ball. "It would have been very easy for Ethan to remain embedded in the family business. I admire a man who has the grit to take a few chances and find his own way."

Natalie Chastain smiled at Ravenna. "It's obvious the two of you have a lot in common."

"Well—" Ravenna began.

"I must say I'm a lot less worried about you living in Illusion Town now that I've met Ethan," Natalie continued. "At first I was so afraid you'd meet some sleazy nightclub owner or a professional gambler. When you told me you were bringing home the man involved in the Kavanagh affair, I was even more worried. But Ethan's grandfather told your grandfather the truth about that scandal, so we were all reassured."

Ravenna froze. "Jake Sweetwater called Granddad?"

"Oh, yes," Natalie said cheerfully. "Those two have known each other for decades. Their friendship goes back to the days when they were both prospectors in the Underworld. And now that I've met Ethan, I'm no longer concerned. It's obvious that you found yourself a nice, solid engineer like your father."

"Well—" Ravenna said.

She didn't finish the sentence, because she could not think of anything to say. The observation was true. Her father was an engineer. So was Ethan.

"Your brothers like him, too," Natalie said. She looked toward the barbecue grills and smiled.

Ravenna followed her gaze and saw Ethan standing with her siblings, Jon and Harry. All three men held cans of beer. They were talking in an enthusiastic, animated manner.

Of course they were all getting along splendidly. Jon and Harry were engineers, too.

I'm psychic, Ravenna thought. *Why in green hell didn't I see this coming?*

She looked around for the one creature who might offer comfort and support in this time of crisis.

But Harriet was at the children's table, and it was evident she was having a very good time. Ravenna watched, her mood darkening by the second, as the crowd of youngsters finished their meals and jumped up from the table. One of the kids grabbed an enthusiastic Harriet. They all headed for the nearby play area.

Harriet and her newfound buddies disappeared into the bounce house.

"Looks like the dust bunny is having a good time," Natalie remarked.

"Yes, it does," Ravenna said. "What could possibly go wrong?"

The answer to that question arrived a short time later when the bounce house mysteriously came untethered and began to float up into the air. Shrieks of delight and a lot of chortling could be heard.

Ethan, Jon, Harry, and several other men went to the rescue. They grabbed the trailing ropes and quickly secured the bounce house. Harriet and the kids leaped out, wildly excited by the adventure. They headed for the small carousel.

It was, Ravenna reflected, going to be a very long night.

Chapter Thirty-Five

The slender thread of hope that had sustained her through the barbecue began to shred further that evening at the midnight ball.

Her grandparents were seated on the dais, their siblings flanking them on either side. She and Ethan were seated at one of the large round tables together with her parents and her brothers and their wives. They were all sipping champagne and munching on elegant, bite-sized desserts, assorted cheeses, and canapés from the late-night buffet.

She did not have to worry about making tense conversation. No one wanted to talk to her. Everyone at the table was focused on Ethan.

There were questions about his schooling, his hobbies, his engineering work, and his theories on the future uses of rez-amber now that technology was finding more applications for resonating quartz.

He handled the not-so-subtle inquisition with a friendly aplomb that would have been impressive if it had been a real meet-the-family occasion. He wore his tux, with its elegantly knotted bow tie, black jacket, and trousers, with a cool attitude that managed to convey a compelling mix of sophistication and danger.

But he talked like an engineer.

"The primary engineering obstacle with rez quartz is that we haven't found a way to install a generic frequency," Ethan said in response to a question from Dean. "There's definitely the potential for a lot of power in some of those rocks, but at this point only certain kinds of high-end talents can resonate with very specific types of quartz. That puts severe limits on the commercial applications. There are a lot of unknowns."

Ravenna ate a small chocolate-and-coffee-flavored tart, feeling very much alone even as she sat with her family. Harriet, the little traitor, had once again vanished with a herd of young people.

By the time the dancing started, Ravenna was walking the very narrow line that separated anxiety from outright panic. There was a round of applause as Adelaide and Mark Chastain ended their solo waltz. Other couples drifted onto the floor. Ethan got to his feet, turned to Ravenna, and held out his hand.

"Dance with me?" he asked.

Everyone at the table smiled. There was really only one right answer to the question—and deep down Ravenna knew she wanted to give it.

"Yes," she said.

He wrapped her fingers in his and led her through the maze of tables to the dance floor. The band was playing a slow, romantic ballad. Ethan took her into his arms, and she discovered she had been right when she had speculated about his dancing prowess. Of course he danced with controlled, masculine grace. She, on the other hand, moved like a clockwork toy.

"Relax," he said. "Everything is going just as you planned."

"No, it's not," she whispered. "Everyone in my family loves you."

"I like your relatives, too. Is that a bad thing?"

"Yes. No. I don't know. It's going to make everything harder in the morning. Bringing you here was a huge mistake. I don't know what made me believe it was a good idea."

"You're overthinking this, Ravenna. Everything is going to be fine—"

Ethan broke off because the band abruptly stopped playing. The dancers halted and turned toward the dais. Ravenna saw that the master of ceremonies, Uncle Hampton, was rapping a spoon sharply against a large crystal goblet.

"Family and friends, we are here tonight to celebrate the marriage of Adelaide and Mark Chastain," he intoned.

Another round of applause rolled across the crowd.

"But I have been asked to announce a very special toast to two people who are about to take the most important step of their lives together. Mark? Will you do the honors?"

Ravenna froze.

Her grandfather rose to deliver the toast. He searched the dance floor and smiled when he spotted Ravenna and Ethan.

"Ethan Sweetwater," he said, the words reverberating around the room. "Adelaide and I understand there has not yet been a formal announcement. We realize this is because you and Ravenna did not want to steal the show tonight. But secrets like this have a way of getting out. I had a call from your grandfather last night."

"Oh, shit," Ravenna whispered.

Ethan squeezed her hand. "We can do this."

"After that conversation, Adelaide and I decided to take the initiative and let you know that we are looking forward to welcoming you into the family."

The crowd cheered. Ethan clamped an arm around Ravenna's shoulder and pulled her close against him.

"It will be okay," he whispered.

"No. No it won't be okay. It's a disaster."

"I hate to have to say this, but I feel I must. It's for your own good. Do. Not. Panic."

"Too late." She stepped out from the protection of his arm and raised her voice to a shout. "Stop it. Stop it right now. Everyone, listen to me."

A stunned hush fell on the room. From out of nowhere, Harriet appeared. She scurried across the floor, weaving a path through the crowd, and leaped up into Ravenna's arms.

"There has been a terrible mistake," Ravenna said. "And it's all my fault. I'm sorry. I never meant to make everyone think Ethan and I are on the verge of getting engaged. Okay, maybe I did. In a way. But it's gone too far. The truth is, Ethan is here tonight, pretending to be my date, because he is doing me a favor."

There was a collective gasp from the crowd. It was followed by more stunned silence.

"Not exactly a favor," Ethan said into the stillness.

"Right," Ravenna said. Her throat was getting raw. "Not exactly a favor. I pressured him to come with me to this event because I didn't want to show up alone. But it was his fault, because he was threatening to sue if he didn't get another date, and then some people chased Ethan and me into the tunnels because Ethan was doing a favor for the local Guild. But it was okay, because he took care of everything. Made it all go away. Damn, it's so complicated. He's a client, so I shouldn't be dating him at all. And I'm not, not really."

She burst into tears. Horrified, she whirled around. Clutching Harriet under one arm, she grabbed a fistful of the long blue skirts of her gown and tried to run toward the door. The high heels betrayed her after two steps. She stumbled and would have gone down, but Ethan, moving with startling speed, deftly caught her and steadied her.

In full panic mode now, she kicked off the heels. The crowd parted before her. She freed herself from Ethan's grasp and fled the ballroom. She ran out through the open doors, into the luminous gardens. Into the night.

CHAPTER THIRTY-SIX

She stopped running when she reached the gazebo overlooking the lake. She stepped inside and sank down onto one of the padded benches. Harriet wriggled out from under her arm, perched on the railing, and made soothing dust bunny sounds.

"I am strong. I am in control," Ravenna said to the night.

It wasn't the night that answered. It was Ethan.

"I know," he said. "But I repeat, you are overthinking this."

She turned her head and watched him make his way along the path. Her stilettos dangled from the fingers of his left hand. She remembered the night he had arrived six minutes early for their first date and found her trying to stuff Garrett Willis into a hall closet.

She managed a rueful smile.

Evidently sensing she could turn the situation over to Ethan, Harriet chortled and fluttered away into the night.

Ethan sat down beside Ravenna, not quite touching her.

"I should have known you would come after me," she said.

"Who else? We're in this together. Matchmaker and client."

"On a fake meet-the-family date. I can't imagine what made me think this would work. One thing is for sure, it's a complete fiasco now. I lost it back there in the ballroom. Total meltdown."

"You panicked," he agreed.

She winced. "You didn't have to confirm my conclusions."

"I was just giving you a straight-up failure mode analysis," Ethan said.

She looked at him in disbelief. "Let me make one thing perfectly clear: I am not in the mood for a pep talk that involves engineering speak."

"Okay. What would you rather talk about?"

"Me." She straightened a little. "I want to talk about me."

"Got it. Let's start with a question. Why are you being so hard on yourself?"

"Are you joking? What happened back there in the ballroom was nothing short of a totally humiliating disaster."

"Depends on your point of view," he said.

"Really?" she said. She was starting to get mad now. So much for regaining control. "And just how do you view that embarrassing scene?"

"As a riveting example of high drama."

She stared at him, aghast. "*High drama?* I didn't think engineers did high drama."

"I'm not only an engineer, I'm a Sweetwater."

"So?"

"I told you, Sweetwaters are good with high drama when it comes to romance and passion. Check with my brother if you don't believe me. Or ask anyone else in the family."

She blinked a couple of times, nonplussed. "That's . . . interesting."

"You want interesting? I'll give you interesting. Based on my failure mode analysis, I'd say your family and the crowd back there in the ballroom are also good with high drama, at least when it involves you."

"But I embarrassed my grandparents."

"They didn't seem to mind. Last time I looked, your grandmother was smiling and your parents didn't appear to be at all worried."

"That doesn't make any sense," she said.

"It does if you consider the possibility they think that dramatic scene was an indication you and I are a lot more emotionally involved than client and matchmaker ought to be."

"Well, crap."

"Way to stroke my ego. I have to tell you, it's already taken quite a beating."

"Sorry," she muttered.

"Don't apologize. Just tell me if you think it might be true," Ethan said.

"True that we are a lot more emotionally involved than a client and matchmaker ought to be? Oh, yeah. It's definitely true. We have recently been through some major bonding experiences, and I owe you big-time for getting rid of two people who tried to murder me. Yep. We're involved."

"I agree. I also think we should acknowledge that there is a strong physical attraction between us."

She thought about the kiss in the room at the Rendezvous Inn.

"Yep," she said.

"As far as I'm concerned, that means we are not on a fake date. It's a real date."

She caught her breath. "This is so not a good idea."

"Has it ever crossed your mind that you tend to be a bit overcontrolling?"

She exhaled deeply. "My talent—"

"The fire witch thing. I understand. You do a fine job of controlling your psychic ability, but you don't have to control it when you're with me."

She relaxed a little. "It doesn't make you nervous."

"Nope."

"You don't want to run experiments on me."

"Nope."

"You don't think I'm a real witch."

"Well—"

She narrowed her eyes in warning.

Ethan stretched out a hand, caught her chin, and tipped up her face. "Let's just say that when I'm with you I believe in magic."

"Ethan," she breathed. She turned toward him and wrapped her arms around his neck. *Ethan.*

He wasn't talking Covenant Marriage. He hadn't mentioned any sort of marriage. But he was right. They hadn't had sex, but they shared a relationship that could only be described as intimate. They had been through a lot together in the past few days and the attraction between them was undeniable. The reason the fake date had felt so wrong tonight was precisely because she had wanted it to be real.

"Yes," she said. She took a deep breath and prepared to jump off the cliff. "I am emotionally involved with you, damn it."

Energy shifted in the atmosphere. Ethan's eyes burned.

"I guess that's a step up from an outright rejection," he said.

He started to lower his mouth to hers.

"Wait," she said. "I think I should fire you as a client before this goes any further. Professional ethics."

"So fire me," he said against her mouth.

"You're fired."

He crushed her close and tight. The thrilling energy of desire that she had worked so hard to suppress stormed through her. She was suddenly shivering with the force of it. She and Ethan were not the only source of heat in the vicinity. The elemental energy of the psi-laced greenery infused the atmosphere with an earthy, intoxicating tingle.

What they had between them might be temporary, she thought, but it was real and it was more than enough to fuel an affair. She gave herself up to the magic of the night, the man, and the moment.

CHAPTER THIRTY-SEVEN

A tremor went through Ravenna when she felt Ethan's fingers on the zipper of her gown. A moment later he peeled the dress down to her waist. The built-in bra went with the rest of the bodice.

Ethan broke off the kiss and looked down.

"Beautiful," he rasped.

He touched her breasts with a hand that shook a little. Knowing she had that effect on him filled her with a glorious sense of her own sensuality. She fumbled with his bow tie, because her fingers were quivering, too, and finally managed to undo the intricate knot.

He pulled back long enough to shrug out of the black jacket and toss it over the railing. She unfastened the front of the formal shirt, a sweet tension building deep inside. When she got the garment open, she flattened her palms against his chest, savoring the feel of the strong muscles beneath his warm, firm skin.

He pulled her across his thighs, cradled her with one arm, and kissed her again. His hand slipped up under the skirts of her gown. A long, breathless moment later she felt his palm on the inside of her thigh. The anticipation of a more intimate touch stole her breath. Her nails dug into his shoulder.

When his fingers slipped inside the silky scrap of her panties, she almost climaxed then and there. She had never been so hungry for release. The hot kiss in the motel room had let her know what to expect if she and Ethan ever made it to bed together. There was no bed tonight, but they were together and that was all that mattered.

And then he was stroking her, discovering her secrets. She was clawing at him now, soaking wet, desperate for release. When he eased his fingers inside her and found the taut bud of her clitoris with his thumb, she went over the edge.

The thrilling pulsations of her climax swept through her, stealing her voice and her breath. Her body clenched around his fingers.

"Yes," he whispered. "Just like that."

The night stood still.

When it was over she sank against him, into him. The urge to laugh or shout was overwhelming, but she was too spent to summon the energy, so she closed her eyes and smiled a very smug, very satisfied smile and kissed his bare chest.

"Fire witch," Ethan said.

He sounded enthralled. Enchanted.

For once the words did not bother her. She was a fire witch. She raised her lashes to tell him that . . .

. . . and saw the little shower of fireworks that was already fading inside the gazebo.

"Oh, shit." She struggled to sit upright on his thighs, horrified by the loss of control.

"Let it go," Ethan said. He gripped her waist, lifted her, and turned her so that she sat astride him. "We have more important things to worry about."

"Such as?" she shot back.

And then she realized that the front of his trousers was open. His erection was fierce and full.

"That is . . . very impressive," she whispered.

"I want you, Ravenna. I've been waiting all my life for a fire witch."

She forgot about the unplanned fireworks and wrapped her fingers around him. He did not try to conceal his hunger. She could not take him all at once. Instead she eased herself slowly down on his rock-hard length until he was deep inside her.

When his release struck in pounding waves, he took her with him. She could have sworn that for a moment their auras were locked together. The sense of intimacy was unlike anything she had ever known.

The night burned.

Adelaide and Natalie stood together on the veranda. The muffled music and laughter of the ballroom seemed to come from another dimension. From their vantage point they could not see the gazebo, but there was no mistaking the sparks of paranormal energy that danced in the atmosphere at the edge of the lake.

Adelaide smiled, satisfied. "I think I see fireworks."

"I do believe I see them, too," Natalie said. "If he breaks her heart, I swear I will destroy him."

"You won't have to do it alone. You'll have plenty of backup from the rest of the family. But according to Jake Sweetwater, the real problem is that she might break Ethan's heart. Evidently when the Sweetwaters fall, they fall hard."

"So do the Chastains," Natalie said.

Adelaide smiled. "Yes, they do."

CHAPTER THIRTY-EIGHT

"I can't go back in there," Ravenna announced. "Not after that scene in the ballroom. And not looking like I've been having wild sex in a gazebo."

"Okay," Ethan said. He fastened his shirt and tucked it into his trousers while he watched Ravenna pull up the top of the evening gown. He was feeling much too satisfied, too content, to argue about anything, including the merits of making another appearance in the ballroom. "I doubt that anyone will be expecting us to do an encore."

"Good. That's good."

She turned around so he could zip the back of the sadly crushed gown. Something about the small act of putting her back together struck him as delightfully intimate. Her body was still warm from the lovemaking, and the scent of passion whispered around her. When he got the zipper up, he leaned forward and kissed the curve of her throat.

"I'm not inclined to go back into that ballroom, either," he said. "But for the record, the wild-sex-in-a-gazebo look is good on you."

She turned back to face him and gave him a slow once-over with sultry eyes. "The look works for you, too."

"A win-win. We should do it more often."

The heat in her eyes faded. "This makes it official, doesn't it? You are no longer a client and we are having an affair."

"I'm not sure there is anything official about an affair," he said. "We could fix that with a Marriage of Convenience if you want some legal paperwork."

"Absolutely not. MCs are tacky. Professional matchmakers can't be involved in Marriages of Convenience. It sends a bad message."

"But an affair is okay?"

"As long as we are discreet it will be okay. Unmarried matchmakers are allowed to date. We do have social lives, but we are expected to avoid scandals. There will be a big one when Ms. Ottoway realizes we are not actually engaged. I've decided the best thing I can do is resign as soon as we get back to Illusion Town. That way I won't put the agency's brand at risk."

"You're going to quit your job because we're not really engaged? That sounds a little screwy if you ask me."

"Trust me," Ravenna said, "matchmakers have to walk a very narrow line."

"Even in Illusion Town, where just about anything goes?"

"People take Covenant Marriage seriously in Illusion Town, just as they do everywhere else," she said.

He took his jacket off the railing. "Does this mean you'll have to change careers again?"

"No, I don't think so." Ravenna sat down on a bench and slipped on the high heels. "My friend Sybil says I'm welcome to enter into a partnership with her. She's trying to build a niche market by matching high-end, hard-to-match talents."

"If Willis and Hatch are examples of the dates she's arranged for you so far, I can't say I'm impressed with her agency's work."

"Anomalies, I'm sure," Ravenna said. "Even professional matchmakers can make mistakes."

"I've noticed that," Ethan said.

CHAPTER THIRTY-NINE

"I can't believe we got through breakfast without anyone asking us about last night," Ravenna said. "I was sure Mom and Grandmother would grill me. I thought my dad would try to pin you down, too. Instead everyone acted like nothing happened. I guess no one wanted to embarrass us."

She settled deeper into the passenger seat of the Slider and watched the mountain scenery glide past. Ethan was at the wheel and Harriet was riding in her favorite position on the back of the front seat. She clutched a new pen. It was bright purple and it was engraved with the logo of the Silver Lake Lodge. Ravenna suspected it had come from the small desk in her room.

She had dreaded the big farewell breakfast, but to her relief it had been a warm, cheerful family event. There hadn't been any sly glances—okay, maybe one or two from her younger nieces, and she had heard a few giggles when Ethan went through the buffet line—but no one had demanded an explanation of what she would always think of as the Great Meltdown.

"I hate to break this to you," Ethan said, "but I'm pretty sure no one asked any personal questions this morning because everyone knows exactly what happened last night."

She winced. "I was afraid you were going to say that. It didn't help that your grandfather got into the act with that phone call he made to my grandfather."

"Are we going to argue about who is to blame for last night?"

She gritted her teeth. "No. I'm well aware it was my fault."

"Exactly."

"Excuse me, but I think you should be a little more supportive. It's not every day I have a major meltdown in front of my entire family."

"They did seem a little stunned at the time, but it's clear they have recovered."

She decided that comment did not warrant a response. She decided to sit back and enjoy the scenery. Her silence did not seem to affect Ethan, which was annoying, so she searched for a neutral topic of conversation.

"I asked the hotel kitchen to refill the picnic basket," she said, going for bright and cheerful. "Can't wait to see what's inside."

"Something to look forward to," Ethan said.

It was a perfectly polite response, but for some reason it irritated her. She had to swallow a snarky comeback. Ridiculous. It was just road food, for goodness' sake.

This was not going well, she reflected. It dawned on her she was apparently spoiling for a fight, and she had no idea why. She and Ethan had settled things last night. They were having an affair. Fine. She was going to resign from Ottoway and relaunch her career at the Banks agency. Fine. When they got back to Illusion Town, Ethan was going to help her investigate the strange behavior of two men who had recently tried to kill her. Fine. Okay, so that meant she was still in his debt, but—fine.

There was nothing to argue about, but she wanted to keep rezzing Ethan's buttons. That was just dumb.

It was time to be honest with herself. She knew why she was in such a bad mood. She wanted more from Ethan than a vaguely defined affair. She wanted a commitment. She had no right to ask for that, not after such a short time together. There was nothing to suggest they would be a good match long-term. Then again, how did she know they wouldn't be? A matchmaker who tried to match herself had a gambler for a matchmaker. When it came to Covenant Marriage, mistakes were very, very costly.

The last truck stop at Grimley Pass was several miles behind them, as was the series of warning signs to motorists—*Do Not Attempt to Cross Desert After Dark, No Services Until Connerville, Don't Forget Extra Water, No Cell Service Until Connerville, Do Not Stop in the Hot Zone*—when she got the ping.

She was reaching into the back seat to grab the picnic basket and thinking of asking Ethan if he might be interested in registering at the Banks agency—just as a matter of curiosity, to see if by some chance they might be a good match—when she suddenly chilled. Something was wrong. She hauled the basket over the back of the seat, set it on her lap, and fastened her seat belt.

She realized Ethan was paying too much attention to the rearview mirror. The energy around him was charged. Harriet seemed aware of the change, too. She was still fluffed up, but she had opened her hunting eyes.

"What's wrong?" Ravenna asked.

Ethan glanced at the rearview mirror again. "I may be a little paranoid these days, but I think there is a possibility we're being followed."

"*What?*"

She turned in the seat to peer out the rear window and saw a muscular SUV in the distance.

"Shit," Ethan said quietly. There was no heat or alarm in the word, just an acceptance of reality. "We've got a problem."

Ravenna settled back into her seat and saw that he was checking the instruments on the dashboard.

"You're sure we're being followed?" she asked. "That vehicle is quite a ways behind us. It doesn't seem to be trying to close the distance."

"The SUV is a problem, but not our first priority. I'm getting a warning signal from the car's security system."

"Engine trouble?"

"No. Someone planted a tech device on the car. It was activated a few seconds ago by remote control."

"What kind of device?"

"I don't know, but I'm pretty damn sure it won't be helpful. When I say run, do it."

It was her turn to say *shit*, but she refrained because her mouth had gone dry with tension.

The battered sign appeared at the edge of the road.

WARNING

MIRAGE LAKE AND NIGHTMARE CAVE AHEAD
YOU ARE ENTERING A HOT ZONE
DO NOT STOP FOR NEXT THIRTY MILES

Ethan braked sharply. Harriet almost lost her grip on the back of the seat, but she deftly recovered her balance. Ravenna jolted against the seat belt restraints.

The Slider rocked to a halt.

"Out," Ethan ordered. He unlatched his seat belt with one hand and flipped open the console to grab a flamer with the other. "Now."

She was having an affair with a man who packed a tux and a flamer when he traveled. Her life had become very strange lately.

She got her seat belt unlatched. Without stopping to think, she grabbed the handle of the picnic basket because it was there on her lap and in her way.

She opened the door and leaped out.

"Harriet," she called.

Harriet was already bounding down to the ground. No longer playing games, she was sleeked out, all four eyes showing. Ethan rounded the
hood of the Slider and grabbed Ravenna's hand.

"The cave," he said.

"I was afraid you were going to say that."

They ran.

"I don't think they will try to follow us inside, but if they do, we're
better off in the cave than we are out here in the open." Ethan glanced
down. "What the hell? Drop the picnic basket."

"Sorry," she muttered. She opened her hand and let the basket fall to
the ground. "Wasn't thinking."

Even from a distance the currents of energy that wafted out of the
mouth of Nightmare Cave pinged her senses, and not in a good way.
Dread whispered through her. But this wasn't the time to discuss the
merits of what was obviously the only available cover in the vicinity.

"Ambush?" she gasped as they scrambled up the rocky hillside.

"Yes," Ethan said.

At least she wasn't wearing stilettos this time.

Harriet was racing alongside them. Her six paws made her more
nimble on the pebble-and-boulder-strewn ground. She reached the
shadow-drenched cave entrance first and paused to issue a series of ur-
gent, encouraging chortles.

Ethan propelled Ravenna into a sea of churning energy. Instinctively she
heightened her senses to suppress the force of the heavy psi. Before she could
adjust to the atmosphere, Ethan was tugging her down to the stone floor. He
fell on top of her, covering her body with his own. Harriet crowded close.

Down on the highway, the Slider exploded in a ball of flames.

CHAPTER FORTY

Most of the force of the explosion was blocked by the sheltering walls of the large cavern, but not all of the sound waves were stopped. Ethan's ears rang in the aftermath.

He shook his head in an attempt to clear it, levered himself up on his forearms, and looked down at Ravenna. Her eyes were closed and she was not moving. Panic shot through him.

"Ravenna."

His voice sounded muffled to his own ears, as if he were speaking underwater.

Harriet, still sleeked out, all four eyes glittering, huddled close to Ravenna's face and muttered encouragingly.

Ethan felt a shudder go through Ravenna, and then she opened her eyes. Relief flashed through him.

"Are we still alive?" she asked.

Her voice was slightly muffled, too. He shook his head in an instinctive attempt to clear his ears.

"Looks like it," he said.

Satisfied that she was all right, he lifted himself away from her, got to his feet—and nearly lost his balance. The sea of swirling energy inside the cavern made it difficult to focus, let alone stand upright.

He recalled his first visit to the cave and raised his senses to suppress most of the effects of the paranormal energy. He went to the mouth of the cave and leaned around the edge of the opening to see what was happening down on the narrow highway.

The Slider was engulfed in flames. The SUV closed in slowly and stopped a safe distance away from the roaring fire. Four men in khaki and leather climbed out of the big vehicle. They were carrying mag-rez pistols.

Of course they were carrying the pistols, Ethan thought. Aboveground the weapons were far more effective than flamers. Greater range and more stopping power. No smart hit team would bother with flamers on the surface. But this was a hot zone, and that made all the difference.

"There are four of them," he said.

He sensed a small movement at his feet and looked down. Harriet was crouched next to his boot. The dust bunny was in full battle mode.

"There are three of us," Ravenna said.

He glanced at her. She was on her feet, bracing herself with one hand planted on the wall of the cave. She radiated an aura of grim determination. He almost smiled, remembering how he had described her to Gabriel Jones. *Small but fierce.*

"Yes," he said. "There are three of us." He took a few seconds to survey the cavern. His ears finally stopped ringing. "What's more, we have a fortress."

Ravenna followed his gaze, taking in the forbidding interior of the cave. She got a knowing look. "You're thinking we can leverage the heavy psi in here."

"Yes, assuming they are dumb enough to come looking for us. With luck, they may conclude we died in the Slider."

Ravenna pushed herself away from the rock wall and moved forward to join him at the mouth of the cave.

The flames of the car fire were starting to falter. The members of the hit team moved in cautiously, two on either side of the burned-out Slider. It did not take them long to realize there were no bodies in the front seat.

"So much for luck," Ravenna said.

There was some agitated shouting, and then the four men began searching the rough terrain. They spotted the cave and headed straight for it. One of the four, a muscled man with a shaved head, barked orders. The guy in charge, Ethan decided.

The gang clambered up the hillside.

"That's our cue," Ethan said.

"What's the plan?" Ravenna asked.

"We move to the back of the cavern and keep out of sight. Unless they are all strong talents they won't be able to spend much time in here. Their mag-rezes won't function well, if at all, in this energy, and they aren't carrying flamers."

She glanced at the weapon in his hand. "But you are. What made you bring a flamer?"

"I knew we would be traveling through a hot zone. I like to be prepared. Let's go. Tell me if it gets too hot in here."

He led the way deeper into the cave. Ravenna and Harriet followed.

The energy rose rapidly and became more disorienting. Ethan had to pull more talent to deal with it. He knew Ravenna was forced to do the same. It wasn't long before the hallucinations set in. *Things* materialized and then disintegrated, a parade of nightmares.

"Shit," Ravenna said. But she kept moving.

Of course she did, Ethan thought. This was Ravenna. He reached out and grasped one of her hands. She tightened her fingers around his. The hallucinations receded.

"Better?" he asked quietly.

"Yes."

It was a basic rule of survival in a strong paranormal environment—two auras were more powerful than one when it came to suppressing the effects of heavy psi.

Ravenna reached down and scooped up Harriet. Ethan was surprised to feel the additional whisper of energy from the dust bunny's small but sturdy aura.

They were a team.

The cave narrowed dramatically at one point, forming a tunnel that was wide enough for only one person. That was good, Ethan thought. It meant that if the men hunting them got this far, they would have to advance single file. He could deal with them one at a time.

Daylight did not reach far into the depths of the cave, but the paranormal radiance infused into the surrounding stone grew stronger in the darkness, illuminating the interior.

The tunnel abruptly opened onto a vast, glowing cavern. Glittering stalactites hung from the high ceiling, giant icicles made luminous by strange minerals. A forest of sparkling stalagmites thrust upward from the floor.

It would have been an ideal hiding place if not for the pool of crystal clear, utterly transparent water that covered most of the floor. Ethan almost stepped into it. He was holding Ravenna's hand so tightly he knew that if he had fallen into the pool, he would have dragged her in with him.

It was Harriet's warning growl that saved them. Ethan froze. He felt Ravenna do the same.

"What is it?" Ravenna asked in a hushed voice.

"A cave pool," Ethan said. "Fed from a deep spring or underground river. No telling how deep it is, but the real problem is that there's no way to know how powerful the currents are. If you fall in, there's a good chance you wouldn't be able to climb out."

"It's hard to see."

"Optical illusion," Ethan said. "The paranormal light in here doesn't reflect off the surface of the water the way normal light would. We've got to move slowly and carefully so that we stay on the edge."

He bent down and scooped up a handful of glittering pebbles. One by one he tossed them around the space. Some of them sank without a trace into the pool but a few landed on hard rock and bounced.

"It's dry for a few feet near the wall," he said. "But it looks like that's as far as we can go."

They followed the path that had been cleared by the pebbles and stopped to assess the situation. It was far from ideal, but some nearby stalagmites provided a little cover.

He flattened his back against the wall. Ravenna, with Harriet still perched on her shoulder, did the same. Voices rumbled in the outer cavern. At least some of the team had been strong enough to enter the hot atmosphere.

"Fuck, it's hot in here," one muttered.

"You inside," another man yelled. "We're Guild security. We're here to help."

Shaved Head, Ethan decided.

Ravenna looked at him, her eyes widening in a silent, shocked question. He shook his head.

"We're chasing the guys who planted that bomb under your car," Shaved Head continued. "We didn't know the vehicle had been sabotaged. Glad you two made it out alive. Whoever is after you is not playing games. Come on out. We'll provide protection for you and the woman until we get back to Illusion Town."

When the offer was met with silence, Shaved Head shouted again.

"You don't want to spend the night in here. Trust me. That sign you saw out on the highway is for real. This is a no-go zone after dark. You think this cave is bad now? Just wait until nightfall when the lake effect hits."

Ethan listened intently. As far as he could tell, only two of the four men had followed them into the cave.

"I don't see any sign of them," the second man said. "Maybe they didn't make it in here. Maybe they went in another direction."

"They're in here," Shaved Head said. "There's no other cover for miles. They must have gone through that tunnel. Let's go."

"Fuck it, I'm not going any farther into this damn cave," the other man said. "Not getting paid enough to deal with this kind of heat. You're the guy in charge, Joyner. If you want to go in after those two, that's on you."

"If I bring 'em out, I collect the whole fee, not a quarter of it," Joyner warned.

"You're welcome to it, but you're wasting your time. You won't be able to follow them, not through that energy. My guess is they're both brain fried or dead by now. I'm out of here. The job is all yours."

"Get lost, but don't come whining to me when it's time to get paid."

There was no response from the second man. Ethan heard one set of footsteps beating a hasty retreat out of the cave.

He raised the flamer and waited.

Boots echoed from the other side of the narrow passage.

"Fuck you, Sweetwater. You're worth just as much dead as you are alive. You want to stay alive, come out now."

More footsteps. Joyner was inside the tunnel that separated the two caverns. In another few seconds he would be in the pool cave. Once he stepped out of the tunnel he would see his targets, assuming he looked in the right direction.

Ethan picked up a small rock and hurled it against the rock wall on the opposite side of the tunnel opening.

It clattered against the stone and tumbled to the floor. The noise was amplified and distorted by the thick currents of psi.

Joyner emerged from the tunnel, but he did not see Ethan, Ravenna, and Harriet. He was following the sound of the rock. But he was running hot in order to deal with the energy in the cave, and in his tense state he overreacted. He panicked and rezzed the mag-rez again and again.

There was a series of clicks, but nothing happened.

"Fuck it," he shrieked.

He rezzed the pistol one more time. The weapon glowed with an ominous heat. Joyner yelled and hurled it away from himself. It landed near the entrance of the tunnel and exploded into flames.

Joyner screamed. The sound rang off the stone walls, adding more energy to the paranormal currents in the atmosphere. The flames of the burning pistol got brighter and hotter, feeding off the strong psi that swirled in the chamber. Within seconds the fire crossed the spectrum and became a wall of flames that blocked the tunnel and any possibility of escaping back into the outer cavern.

Joyner's face twisted with shock and horror. He scrambled madly to put some distance between himself and the furnace of a tunnel. One of his boots skidded on the wet rocks.

Ethan realized what was about to happen. "Shit."

He lunged forward. He was fast—all the Sweetwaters had excellent reflexes—but he was not fast enough. Joyner slipped on the rocks. He flailed, but he could not regain his balance. He went into the pool with a resounding splash. The water roiled and seethed as if some great creature was emerging from the depths in search of prey.

Joyner thrashed wildly, trying to get to the edge of the pool. He groped for and found the rocky rim but he could not maintain his grip. His hands slipped off. He looked up at Ethan, stark terror glittering in his eyes.

"Help me," he shrieked. "There's something in here. It's pulling me down. Get me out of here."

So much water had been splashed around the edge of the pool, it was more difficult than ever to see where the rock ended and the water began. Ethan stopped at what looked like a reasonably safe distance and stripped off his shirt. He gripped one sleeve and tossed the other to the struggling man.

Joyner managed to snag the sleeve. He clung to it with both hands. "Hurry. I'm telling you, there's something in here."

Ethan hauled on the shirtsleeve, drawing Joyner through the churning water until he was able to land him like a large fish. Joyner scrambled to safety and collapsed, unconscious, on the wet stone.

Ethan turned toward the wall of paranormal fire that blocked the tunnel.

It was gone. Ravenna stood in its place.

Ethan smiled slowly. "You're good."

"I can start a paranormal fire," Ravenna said. "And as long as it's not too big, I can put one out."

CHAPTER FORTY-ONE

Ravenna went to the mouth of the cave and watched the strange mist coalesce into thunderclouds above the mirage of the lake. The three other men on the hit team had waited outside the cave until it became clear that Joyner was not going to return. Not wanting to risk a night drive in the desert, they had departed a couple of hours before sunset.

Now darkness was settling quickly. A storm shot through with the eerie radiance of paranormal energy was gathering over Mirage Lake. The wind was picking up. It seemed to be laced with the wails and shrieks of lost souls. She shuddered.

"You're right," she said. "As unpleasant as this cave is going to be tonight, it's safer than the storm that's brewing out there."

"It'll get a lot worse in here, too, but at least we'll be out of the wind and the lightning," Ethan said.

She turned around and watched him crouch beside the unconscious man. Joyner lay on his side, his wrists secured with his own belt. He had come out of the pool soaking wet, but his clothes had mostly dried in the warmth of the cave energy. He had moaned a few times as if in the throes of a nightmare, but he showed no signs of regaining consciousness.

"I wonder if he'll ever wake up," Ravenna said. "There's a lot of energy in that water. He may be in a coma."

Ethan's jaw flexed and his eyes tightened dangerously. "I'd like to ask him a few questions."

"He probably doesn't know anything more than the pair who chased us into the Underworld the other night. You heard what the other man said. Grabbing you or killing you is just a job as far as they're concerned."

"True." Ethan went methodically through Joyner's clothing. "And that confirms that Spooner knows how to deal with the brokers who handle contract killings."

"No surprise there." Ravenna hesitated. "Assuming that Spooner is behind the attacks against you."

"That's the only assumption that makes sense. I wasn't having these problems until after I tried to get a fix on his sig frequency."

"I understand why he wanted to get rid of you back at the start," Ravenna said. "He was trying to stake a claim on Glass House and he thought you were in his way. But he failed to grab the antiquity. Gabriel Jones and the Illusion Town Guild got there first. Now Glass House belongs to the government. In business you win some and lose some. Spooner lost. Why would he take the risk of trying to murder you now? What purpose would it serve?"

"Some people don't take losing with what you could call grace. There are those who get really, really pissed."

"And want revenge?"

"Yes." Ethan removed a braided leather bolo tie from around Joyner's neck. He sat back on his heels to take a close look at the stone. "This is interesting."

"What is it?" Ravenna asked. She took a few steps closer. "Looks like quartz."

"It's a burner com. Tuned so that it can be used once and once only to send a signal on a unique frequency. One-way. It can't receive a signal, so it won't function as a tracking device."

"Why would that guy need a burner communicator?"

"To send a signal indicating the job was finished." Ethan rose to his feet. "I need to get back to the lab and run some tests."

Ravenna looked out at the intensifying storm. "We have to get through tonight first."

"We'll use the buddy system," Ethan said. "Two auras and all that."

Ravenna smiled. "Plus we have Harriet."

Harriet popped up from behind a tumble of rocks and chortled at the sound of her name.

"It's going to be cozy," Ethan said.

"Now aren't you glad I rescued the picnic basket?" Ravenna said.

When the SUV and the crew of hit men had given up and driven off, Ethan had left the cave long enough to salvage the basket of road food she had dropped earlier.

"Very glad," he said. "We're going to need the energy and the hydration before the night is over, and we sure as green hell wouldn't want to drink the water in that pool."

Ravenna angled her chin to indicate the unconscious Joyner. "What about him?"

"He's on his own," Ethan said. "As long as he's unconscious he can't help us suppress the bad energy. For all we know, he's going to have it a lot easier than us. He'll probably just sleep through the night."

Joyner moaned again and whimpered softly.

Ravenna shuddered. "I don't think he's having pleasant dreams."

"I don't know about you, but I plan to save the sympathy for us."

"It's going to be a long night, isn't it?"

"A very long night."

CHAPTER FORTY-TWO

The demons, goblins, and monsters came out in full force after nightfall. The hallucinations were auditory as well as visual. The startling, unnerving, frightening visions were accompanied by howls, cries, and shrieks that seemed to emanate from the bottom of hell.

"Or that pool in the other chamber," Ethan said. "It's probably the source of the energy in here."

Ravenna rezzed her senses to suppress an army of the living dead tromping toward her. She assumed the vision sprang from some horror movie she had watched in her youth. She managed to dampen it, but another hallucination immediately took its place.

Exhaustion was going to be the biggest threat, she thought. If she and Ethan let down their guards, there was a risk they would get sucked into a nightmare. The more terrifying danger was that they might not be able to find their way out. Storms of paranormal energy could do strange and unpredictable things to the human mind.

They were sitting back-to-back on the floor of the cave, comrades in arms, drawing strength from each other's energy fields. Harriet was lounging against Ravenna's thigh, munching a dainty pate a choux filled with chocolate pastry cream and contributing the heat of her own aura to the battle.

As far as Ravenna could tell, she wasn't affected by the nightmares swirling around the cave. She seemed to have at least some immunity. Dust bunnies were, after all, native to Harmony. They were at home both aboveground and down in the Underworld. But Harriet evidently sensed that the humans had some serious problems with the sort of energy that swirled in the chamber.

"Do you think there is a monster in that pool?" Ravenna said, mostly to keep the conversation going. Talking helped—at least it helped her. It kept her focused on reality.

"Who knows?" Ethan said. "Our pal Joyner certainly panicked, but I've got a hunch we would have panicked, too, if we had gone into that water."

"For sure. We humans have only been here on Harmony a couple of hundred years. We're still adapting. There's so much we don't know. We haven't even begun to map the surface, let alone the Underworld. We've only been able to make a serious start in the last seventy-five years or so."

After the Curtain had closed, cutting off all hope of return to Earth, the First Generation colonists had been forced to focus on survival. With all of their Earth-based technology failing, there had been little time to explore and chart their new world. Then, just as they had begun to recover, Vincent Lee Vance had fired up his cult and attempted to take control of the fragile governments of the four city-states via a guerilla-style war in the tunnels. It wasn't until after the rebellion had been crushed by the hastily established Ghost Hunters Guilds that the descendants of the First Generation settlers had finally been able to begin the process of discovering the secrets of Harmony. In an ironic twist, Vincent

Lee Vance had died in the Underworld without ever knowing his impact on history. It was the rebellion he had orchestrated that had made the four city-states unite in what had become the Federation.

"What are we dealing with?" Ravenna asked.

"Something called Vortex, evidently," Ethan said. "And according to Gabriel Jones, the Arcane Society seems to think Vortex may be as big a threat as anything the Aliens left behind. They are convinced that it's got to be stopped before it really gets off the ground."

"What is it?" Ravenna asked. "A super-powerful weapon?"

"No one seems to know for sure, but Jones told me the goal of Old World Vortex technology was to artificially enhance natural human psychic talents and expand the range of the senses."

"Talk about playing with fire. There's so much we don't know about the mind-body connection. The brain is still very much a mystery."

"That's why that kind of research is illegal."

Ravenna suppressed another storm of visions. "This Vortex project sounds like a conspiracy theory, doesn't it?"

"Some conspiracies are real."

"Think this one is?"

"If someone like Spooner, with his money and his power, believes in Vortex enough to take the risk of committing murder, I'd say that makes it real enough to cause trouble."

"True." Ravenna pulled the picnic basket closer and examined the remaining contents. "I vote we hold the high-carb goodies for later when we'll need fast energy. Let's stick with the proteins for now."

"Good plan," Ethan said.

She uncovered a tray of exotic cheeses, cured meats, olives, and nuts and set it on the floor where they could both reach it. Harriet finished her pastry and fluttered to the tray to examine the contents. She helped herself to some meats and cheeses and reclined against Ravenna's thigh again to savor the meal.

They all ate in silence for a while. Ravenna was suppressing another wave of visions when Ethan spoke.

"For the record," he said, "I would just like to say that this wasn't what I had in mind for our next date."

"No?"

"I was planning to take you to a nice restaurant and order a bottle of wine."

"Sounds lovely."

"After a fancy dinner I thought we could take a stroll through the Dead City. Enjoy the vibes together."

"Maybe have sex under the stars in your garden?"

"If the mood took us," Ethan said.

"It probably would have."

"It would definitely have taken me," he said.

Ravenna exerted some focus and shut down a hellish scene. "Clearly we're following a somewhat different script here, but you get bonus points for creativity."

"I do?"

"I've never spent a night in a haunted cave with a date," she said. "This is a first for me."

"Same. I appreciate the creativity points, but let's face it, my dating technique still needs a lot of work."

"On the plus side, there's one thing to be said about tonight's date."

"What's that?" Ethan asked.

Another vision spun out of the heavy paranormal currents, a shrieking thing that was all teeth and claws. Ravenna pressed herself more firmly against Ethan's back, taking heat, strength, and comfort from him just as he took the same from her.

"It's another bonding experience," she said.

"True. We seem to be doing a lot of bonding lately."

"I've got a question for you," Ravenna said.

"What is it?"

"Why Illusion Town?"

"I told you, I like the energy."

"But there's more to it than that."

"You must be psychic."

"I'm serious," she said.

He was silent for a moment.

"Illusion Town was as far away as I could get from the people who cared the most about the Kavanagh affair."

"I understand," Ravenna said. "You wanted to move on. Can I ask you a very personal question?"

"What is it?"

"After Covington Kavanagh died, why didn't you and Bethany Kavanagh marry?"

Ethan was silent for a time. "Bethany and I were childhood friends but never lovers."

"What aren't you telling me about your past, Ethan Sweetwater?"

"Bethany was in love with Covington Kavanagh when they married. But he turned out to be a brutal, controlling man. He was a charismatic, high-rez strategy talent. He married Bethany for her money. It costs a lot to go into politics."

"And?"

"And he had another talent, one no one knew about. He was an aura disrupter."

Ravenna let out her breath. "A monster. I think I see where this is going."

"Kavanagh terrorized Bethany with his talent, but he was very, very clever about it. There was never any physical evidence of abuse. Nothing that could be used to prove intolerable cruelty. Nothing that could prove he was one of the monsters. She was afraid he would eventually murder her."

"You offered to pretend to have a very high-profile affair with her. You knew that in his rage, Kavanagh would try to kill you."

"I knew he would try to kill me *first*," Ethan said, his tone very even. "And then he would murder Bethany."

"Kavanagh tried to destroy your aura, didn't he?"

"Yes."

"Obviously he failed. How did that happen?"

"I'm a pretty good engineer."

CHAPTER FORTY-THREE

"What happened to your car?" the trucker asked. He studied the remains of the Slider through the wraparound windshield of his big rig. "Looks like one heck of a fire."

He had introduced himself as Calvin Miller, and Harriet had taken to him immediately. Ethan considered it a good sign, but Ravenna had warned him that the dust bunny's judgment might have been heavily influenced by Calvin's huge truck. Whatever the case, Harriet had offered Calvin the last pate a choux. The trucker had been charmed.

Calvin had been the first trucker through the hot zone that morning, barreling down the highway shortly after sunup. He had braked to a stop when he spotted the small group at the edge of the highway. As far as professional truckers were concerned, the code of the road dictated that you didn't leave anyone at the side of the highway in the middle of a vast stretch of desert, hot zone or not.

At dawn, Joyner had begun to surface, but he was only partially conscious when Ethan loaded him into the back of the truck cab. He did not seem to have any notion of what was going on, and every few minutes he dropped back into a troubled sleep. Ethan had managed to keep him awake long enough to get the code needed to send confirmation of the hit to whoever was on the other end of the one-way communicator. The device was sophisticated tech, however, which meant it wouldn't work until they got to Connerville.

"It was a very bad fire," Ravenna said.

Ethan glanced at her. She was squeezed against him on the wide passenger seat. She looked more petite than ever, wedged between himself and Calvin. You'd never know she could set the entire front of the cab on fire if she took a notion to do so. He smiled at the thought.

Calvin put the truck in gear. The massive vehicle rolled forward, picking up speed. Harriet got excited.

"Any idea what caused the fire?" Calvin asked. "Engine problem?"

"The cause is in the back of your cab," Ethan said.

Calvin glanced at the rearview mirror. "Figured you weren't best friends. Road pirate?"

"Yes," Ethan said. He and Ravenna had concluded that was the easiest explanation under the circumstances.

Calvin made a disgusted sound. "Should have left him back there in Nightmare Cave."

"We definitely gave that some consideration," Ravenna said. "But in the end we concluded it would be best to turn him over to the authorities."

"What did he use on your car?" Calvin asked.

"Some kind of explosive," Ethan said.

"Those pirates are bastards, but never knew 'em to operate in this zone," Calvin said. "Too dangerous. That guy back there must not be real bright. Any idea why he went after you two? Pirates usually work in gangs and stick to trying to stop us long-haul guys. We're not easy targets, but they figure the cargo is worth the risk."

"How do truckers defend themselves and the cargo?" Ravenna asked, neatly sidestepping the question of motive.

"We're all armed," Calvin said. "But our main defense is the truck itself." He patted the dashboard with its array of gadgets. "These rigs are built like fortresses. Drivers aren't afraid to plow straight through a road-block and anyone standing in our way."

"I've looked into the engineering on these long-haul rigs," Ethan said. He surveyed the interior of the cab. "You're right, they're designed from the ground up to protect the driver and the cargo. Mag-steel frames and side panels, bulletproof glass, high-rez locking mechanisms, and interior sprinklers."

"And that's just the basic defense system," Calvin said. Enthusiasm energized his voice. "You should see what I've got in the engine compart-ment. Turbo-charged six-forty. Out here on the open road this bad boy can cruise at a hundred for hours without breaking a sweat."

"No kidding?" Ethan said. "I'd like to take a look at that setup."

"Sure," Calvin said. "When we get to the truck stop at Connerville we'll get some coffee and take a few minutes to stretch our legs. I'll pop up the cowling and show you the works."

Ethan realized there was a subtle smile flickering around Ravenna's mouth. "You probably aren't real interested in looking at an engine," he said.

"No," she said, "but I am very interested in coffee and a restroom. I'm looking forward to the truck stop."

Calvin glanced at her with a sympathetic expression. "How bad was it last night in that cave?"

"It was a bonding experience," Ravenna said.

Ethan couldn't tell if she was joking or not. He decided it was safer not to ask.

No question about it, he had to level up his dating game. It was as-tonishing that Ravenna had agreed to an affair. He was pretty sure every other woman of his acquaintance would have given up on him by now. But Ravenna wasn't like any other woman. He had known that the moment he walked into her office at Ottoway Matchmakers.

Ravenna nudged him with an elbow. "I wasn't joking."

He relaxed a little. "I knew that."

When they reached Connerville, Ethan took out Joyner's pendant and rezzed it, sending the code that meant the hit team had been successful.

"What are you doing?" Ravenna asked.

"Buying some time," Ethan said.

CHAPTER FORTY-FOUR

His real name was Dex Forrester, but on the dark side of the rez-net he was known only as the Concierge. He was in his luxuriously appointed office on the first floor of his mansion in one of the most expensive gated communities in Illusion Town when Ethan Sweetwater came through the door.

Forrester stared at him. "You're dead."

"Not yet," Sweetwater said. "We've got a few questions for you."

He was not alone. Gabriel Jones and two Guild men were with him.

Forrester was stunned. He had been going about business as usual, updating some files. In his profession, you could not risk hiring a secretary. Sooner or later everyone talked, especially if there was something to sell. He had a lot of valuable data on some very rich, very well-placed, very dangerous individuals.

The sudden appearance of Sweetwater and the Guild men came as a shock, but he had an emergency procedure in place for just such an occasion. After all, when you catered to a clientele that valued discretion and silence above all, you had to offer the ultimate in anonymity.

He also had to protect himself. That meant guaranteeing that no embarrassing information pertaining to transactions with clients ever fell into the hands of the authorities. Of course he kept excellent records—you never knew when you might have to blackmail a client—but those records existed only on paper, and all of those potentially damaging files were hidden in a chamber in the Underworld. He was the only one with the key, a locator that contained the coordinates. The locator was locked to his signature frequency.

He did not hesitate. He immediately began to channel some energy into the amber in his ring. It would send the emergency destruct frequency into the miniature locator that he wore around his neck under his clothes. He did not have to worry about destroying the coordinates. He had a backup.

But something was wrong. The amber in his ring was not responding. He began to sweat. He kept trying to send the destruct order while he mustered the natural outrage of an innocent man.

"What is the Guild doing in my home at this hour?" he demanded, rising to his feet. "You have no right to break in like this. I will sue."

"I've got a warrant to search this office for evidence of attempted homicide," Jones said. "You can save everyone a lot of time and effort if you turn over your files."

"You want my computer?" Forrester gestured at the device on his desk. "Help yourself. You can have my phone, too. But you're going to regret this, Jones."

"Forget the computer and the phone," Ethan Sweetwater said. He was studying his watch. "Looks like he's got a locator on him. Under his shirt."

Panic crackled through Forrester. "I want a lawyer."

"You'll get one," Jones said. "Right after we confiscate the locator."

Forrester rezzed his talent one last time in a final, frantic attempt to send the destruct signal. Nothing happened. He stared at Ethan. "What are you doing to me? What kind of talent are you?"

"I'm a pretty good engineer," Ethan said.

Forty minutes later Ethan stood with Gabriel Jones. Together they looked at the old-fashioned metal filing cabinet standing in the middle of the green quartz chamber.

"You were right," Gabriel said, "Forrester didn't trust computers."

"A good hacker can get into any computer eventually," Ethan said. "Forrester figured he would be safe if he kept his client files on paper and stashed them in the Underworld. There's just one problem with hiding stuff down here."

"You have to know how to find what you've hidden," Gabriel said. "And the only way to do that is by keeping a record of the coordinates."

"Let's see what we've got."

They walked across the space and stopped in front of the cabinet. Ethan examined the lock.

"Nothing special," he said. "Just hardware-store tech. We could break it with a hammer, but as it happens I've got a lock pick."

"So do I," Gabriel said. He slipped off his backpack. "Better let me do this. I'm the one who's supposed to be in charge down here."

"It's all yours."

Gabriel used a small pick to get rid of the lock. He opened the top drawer. "Well, damn, will you look at that? Forrester kept very neat files."

It took only minutes to find the right folder.

"Looks like Forrester was right," Gabriel said. "According to this file, you're dead."

"With luck, I'll stay that way long enough to finish this job," Ethan said.

. . .

Gabriel got on his phone as soon as they emerged from the Underworld. "Aiden, I need two reservations on the next rez-lev train to Frequency."

The high-speed rez-lev train was by far the fastest way to get to Frequency. With a top speed of over three hundred miles per hour, it beat the only other viable alternative: a car. Illusion Town did not have an airport. The powerful, unpredictable energy in the vicinity made air travel far too risky.

Ethan took out his own phone and called Ravenna. She was at home, which was where she had been since they had made a very low-profile return to Illusion Town late yesterday afternoon.

"Gabe and I are on our way to the train station," he said.

"Spooner?" she asked.

"Yes."

"Promise me you'll be careful."

"Sure. As far as he knows, we're both dead. Assuming all goes well, I'll be back on the midnight train."

"Good."

"Will you wait up for me?" he asked.

"Are you kidding? Of course I will. I'll want every detail of the takedown."

That wasn't quite what he had hoped to hear, but it would have to do for now. What mattered was that he would see her that night.

He ended the call and looked at Gabriel. "Well?"

"Aiden got the reservations," Gabriel said. "We're going to nail Spooner and find out what the hell is going on with Vortex."

CHAPTER FORTY-FIVE

Taggert Spooner was standing in front of his office window, contemplating the spectacular view of the Dead City of Old Frequency while he savored his revenge, when his phone pinged.

Melody Palantine's message was short and shocking.

Sweetwater is on the way to your office. He's alone. I've notified security.

Taggert went cold. This could not be happening. Sweetwater was dead. The Concierge had sent a message informing him that the hit had taken place in a hot zone in the Mirage Desert and that the bodies might not be found for a few days, if ever.

Don't panic. You can handle this. There's no proof. Nothing. He can't touch you.

The plan came together in a heartbeat. It was perfect. Should have done it this way in the first place, he thought. Simple. Elegant. Neat. He really had no choice. His destiny was on the line.

He sent a message to Palantine.

Hold security until you hear from me. I will deal with this.

He was sitting at his desk, both hands planted on top, when the door opened. Ethan Sweetwater strolled into the room. As Palantine had said, he was alone. That made things so much easier. It was a bit surprising, though. Apparently Ethan was not the most well-tuned chunk of amber on the family tree.

"Did we have an appointment?" Taggert said politely.

"No."

Ethan closed the door and sat down with a cool ease that was unsettling. He looked very sure of himself.

"Out of curiosity, how did you get past security downstairs?" Taggert asked.

"I didn't come through the lobby," Ethan said. "I used the emergency exit and took the stairs."

"The emergency exit is locked and alarmed." Taggert leaned forward and stacked his hands one on top of the other. "There are cameras in the stairwells."

"I noticed. Good tech, too. Straight out of one of your company's labs. But I've developed this really cool jammer. I'm in the process of getting a patent on it as we speak."

Spooner Technologies produced some of the most sophisticated technology on the market, but the locks, alarms, and cameras installed throughout the building were not yet on the market. The fact that Sweetwater had made it all the way up to the CEO suite without being detected was not good. Not good at all. Taggert told himself he would worry about the issue later. He had to deal with Sweetwater first.

"Why are you here?" he asked. He was pleased with the way the words came out. Cold. Calm. Controlled.

"I dropped in to tell you that I had a chat with the Concierge," Ethan said.

Shit. Another jolt of panic shot across Taggert's senses. It was followed by hot rage. It took everything he had to control his fury.

"I've heard of the Concierge," he said. "Something of a legend on the dark rez-net, I believe."

"You hired him to get rid of me," Ethan said. "Twice. The fact that I'm sitting here in your office indicates you should have employed better talent."

No, I should have handled it personally, Taggert thought.

"I don't know what you're talking about," he said. "But I am surprised you were able to find him. They say he's just a ghost online."

"His business model was good," Sweetwater said. "But there is always a weakness in any operation, isn't there?"

"You tell me."

"I was able to find him because he couldn't avoid using tech altogether. He needed to communicate. What can I tell you? Good communications are at the heart of every successful business."

"What the fuck are you talking about?" Taggert said.

"The Concierge made sure the leader of the hit team that was sent after me had a burner com. The leader was supposed to send a confirming code when I was dead. I sent the code for him. The Concierge, naturally, had no way of knowing who was on the other end of the communicator. He just assumed it was the team leader. After all, who else would be able to rez it?"

"You couldn't have rezzed a burner com, not without the code."

"Yet here I am."

Taggert's palms prickled. "That's impossible. Even if you managed to use a burner, you couldn't have used it to find the Concierge. Burners self-destruct after one use."

"You're a tech guy, Spooner. You should know that the process of destruction can be analyzed and reverse-engineered just like any other process. If you know how something fell apart, you can re-create it. It's true the original quartz was shattered in the burner. It couldn't be made to work again. But I was able to analyze the pattern of the destruction.

Once I had that information, I had the original frequency. I figured out the resonating frequency, locked onto it with a tracker, and followed it to the source. The Concierge was surprised to see me, too."

"No," Taggert said. "No, that's impossible."

"I might be able to overlook the attempted hits on me. Business is business. I might have left the problem of the murdered prospector to the police. But you went too far. You put my matchmaker in the line of fire. She nearly got killed *twice* because of those hit teams. That can't be allowed to stand."

Taggert got a little light-headed. He forced himself to think. "You can't prove that I paid the Concierge to send a hit team after you. If you could, you wouldn't be sitting here in my office. Why are you here? What do you want?"

"I want to know about Vortex."

Should have seen this coming, Taggert thought. He took a steadying breath. He had a plan. He was going to kill Sweetwater today. But he needed a few more answers.

"I have no idea what you're talking about," he said.

"Let's start with what I already know." Ethan leaned back and steepled his fingers. "Arcane has a long history with Vortex, and the Sweetwaters have a long history with Arcane. We know that anything connected to Vortex is extremely dangerous, because it involves artificially enhancing the human para-psych profile by means of overstimulating it."

"Nonsense. Everyone knows that can't be done. Something about the sensory overload damage."

"Let me try to clarify this for you. If you are messing around with Old World Vortex technology, you are trying to create monsters."

"That is pure ghost shit," Taggert said.

"I don't think so. Got a hunch you've been running a few experiments on yourself. That explains the loss of control after you missed out on the Glass House Antiquity. The Taggert Spooner who built Spooner Tech would not have tried to handle that situation on his own. He would have assembled an in-house team and come up with a plan."

"Shut the fuck up."

"When the plan failed, he would have known when to cut his losses. He would not have opened a contract with an anonymous rez-net broker to take out a Sweetwater. He would not have let the desire for revenge get the better of his common sense. You're losing it, Spooner. I think Vortex is the reason."

Taggert shot to his feet, hands clenching. "Stop talking."

"You've changed, Spooner. I'm willing to bet it's because you've been fooling around with your new version of Vortex. You're turning yourself into one of the monsters, aren't you? Fascinating."

Taggert began to rez his talent. The exhilarating sensation swept through his senses, the same euphoric rush of power that he'd experienced when he stopped the prospector's heart.

The transcendent experience replaced all other emotions. He was no longer fighting to suppress the hot rage. The panic was gone. He was in complete control. Powerful.

He would have liked to acquire more information from Sweetwater, but it would not be a good idea to let this go any further. He had a plan, and it was time to implement it.

"You made a mistake coming here today," he said.

"Think so?"

"You won't be leaving this office alive. You are going to suffer a heart attack and die."

Sweetwater frowned. He wiped the back of his hand across his forehead.

"Like the prospector you left in a Shadow Zone alley?" he asked.

"Exactly," Taggert said. "I admit Bowen played me. Not many people can say they've done that. But he paid for it. You should have seen his face when I stopped his heart. Can't wait to see your face when I do the same to you."

He generated a little more talent, taking his time. He wanted to savor the kill.

"Your previous two attempts to take me out failed," Ethan said. He shook his head a little as if to clear it. "What makes you think this time will be any different?"

"Because I am going to handle things myself," Taggert said. "You were right about one thing. I made a mistake hiring the Concierge to get rid of you. I won't repeat the error. In case you are wondering why you don't feel very well, it's because I am using my new talent to kill you."

Ethan closed his eyes. His breath came in hoarse gasps. "You're an icer."

"It's my new talent—my third, to be precise. I was born with two, you see: one for strategy and one for technology. Vortex provided the third."

"You made yourself a triple? You must be insane. Oh, wait. Most triples do go mad, don't they?"

Taggert walked around his desk and angled himself on the corner, one foot off the floor. He rezzed a little more talent and smiled when Ethan shivered.

"Triples who are strong enough to handle the increased sensory load do not go mad," he said. "They become extremely powerful. They say Vincent Lee Vance was probably a triple."

"Look what happened to him."

"He almost took control of the four city-states."

"The key word here is *almost.*"

Taggert waved that off. "He made a mistake by trying to use a cult as his power base. The model is flawed. Eventually all cults self-destruct. Yes, I am resurrecting Vortex."

"It's illegal to experiment with artificial para-senses enhancement. But you know that, don't you?"

"As I'm sure you're aware, there's a fine line between cutting-edge scientific research and illegal experimentation. To date I am the only living evidence of the success of the Vortex machine, and you are the only one who knows that. My lab people don't have a clue. As far as they are concerned, they are working on proprietary medical technology that will one day revolutionize the treatment of patients who have suffered serious para-psych trauma."

"Congratulations. You're driving yourself insane."

Taggert kicked up his talent to the max. "This has gone on long enough. I have work to do."

Ethan sucked in a rasping breath. "My family isn't going to like this."

"The Sweetwaters will have questions. They will no doubt put pressure on the police to investigate. There will be an autopsy. But ultimately there will be nothing to find, because you are going to die of natural causes."

"Not today," Ethan said.

His voice no longer shook. He got to his feet.

This was not how it was supposed to work, Taggert thought. He tried to strengthen the fix.

A sudden, disorienting sensation slammed into him with the power of a wave crashing on a beach. He could not breathe. He clutched at his chest. A terrible darkness rolled toward him. The oppressive miasma emanated from the walls, floor, and ceiling. He could no longer see the door.

In the center of the unnatural shroud of night stood Ethan Sweetwater.

"You're right," Ethan said. "That icer vibe is one hell of a talent. And you combined it with two other talents. No wonder you're as mad as a ghost-burned prospector."

Taggert grabbed the edge of the desk to keep from collapsing. He tried to refocus his talent on Ethan, but nothing happened. *What are you doing to me?*

Ethan reached inside his jacket. Taggert figured he was going for a pistol. Even knowing that Sweetwater was about to shoot him dead didn't produce the energy he needed to fight back. He had never known such exhaustion.

But Ethan didn't take out a mag-rez. When his hand reappeared Taggert saw that he was holding a pen that glinted and sparked in the light.

"What?" Taggert managed.

"Mirror amber," Ethan said.

"Nobody uses mirror amber," Taggert rasped. "It's just for decoration."

"It's true that most people can't resonate with it, but it works for me. I can tune it and I can use it to reflect the wavelengths of most forms of paranormal energy, including those of the human paranormal spectrum. It works even more efficiently if the wavelengths are already unstable. Wavelengths like yours, for example. Instability creates weakness in the aura, but I'm sure you know that."

Understanding crept into Taggert's cloudy brain. "No. Impossible."

"As a tech guy yourself, you'll be interested to know that right now everything you are throwing at me is being reflected. The currents are rebounding straight back at the source—your aura. I suggest you cut that icer shit before it kills you."

Taggert struggled one last time to generate more talent but he got no response. All of his senses, normal and paranormal, were fading. His heart was pounding erratically.

He fumbled to open a desk drawer, desperate to grab the mag-rez he kept there, but he could not muster even that much effort. He was dying.

He abandoned the effort to focus his talent. The waves of hellish darkness retreated immediately. He was no longer on the point of complete collapse, but he was exhausted. He stumbled back behind the desk and fell into his chair. He knew he had very nearly died.

Numbed by what had happened, he watched Ethan take out his phone.

"I got what we needed," Ethan said to whoever was on the other end of the connection. "It's recorded. He's all yours now."

The door slammed open. A team of grim-faced people carrying guns swept into the office. They wore FBPI vests. The one in charge stepped forward.

"Taggert Spooner, you are under arrest for the murder of Travers Bowen and the attempted murder of Ethan Sweetwater and Ravenna Chastain. You are also charged with engaging in a murder-for-hire plot."

"You can't prove any of that," Taggert snarled.

"I think I forgot to mention that Gabriel Jones and I found the paper files the Concierge kept in the Underworld," Ethan said. "The details of the contracts you took out on me are all there. You yourself just confessed to Bowen's murder. Plenty of evidence."

Taggert shook his head. "It wasn't supposed to end this way."

"You're wrong," Ethan said, his voice lethally soft. "When you put Ravenna Chastain in danger, you sealed the deal. This is the only way it could end."

Taggert stared at him in disbelief. "She's just a matchmaker."

"She's *my* matchmaker," Ethan said.

Two agents put Taggert in handcuffs and steered him out the door and into the hall. He saw Melody Palantine in the doorway of her office. She stared at him, open-mouthed with shock.

"Mr. Spooner," she said, "what should I do?"

"Call my lawyer," Taggert said.

"Yes, sir," Melody said.

She fled back into her office and grabbed the phone.

CHAPTER FORTY-SIX

"What I keep coming back to is the fact that your profiles of Garrett Willis and Clark Hatch completely missed their stalker sides," Ravenna said.

"I've been losing sleep over that, too," Sybil said. "There are several different kinds of stalkers, though, and some evade detection more easily than others. I had my IT consultant install trip wires in the program that are designed to ping when certain personality disorders are detected, but no system is perfect. All I can tell you is that neither Willis nor Hatch triggered any red flags. I just don't understand how I could have been so wrong, not just once, but *twice*."

"You and me both," Ravenna said.

"You get a pass because you're the client."

"Willis and Hatch were the last two dates you arranged."

"So?"

Ravenna thought about that while she listened to the steady drumbeat of the rain. It was eight o'clock in the evening. The thunderstorm had moved in on Illusion Town late that afternoon and showed no signs of letting up. It was the kind of wild weather only the desert could conjure, the kind that sent sudden flash floods roaring down normally dry creek beds and lit up the sky with lightning.

It would have been nice to share the spectacular energy of the storm with Ethan, but he and Jones were still in Frequency, finishing up the interviews and accompanying paperwork that were always involved with an FBPI operation. She could only hope the storm would not delay the midnight rez-lev train.

She and Harriet had dined alone on pizza delivered from Ollie's House of Pizza. *All four food groups in each delicious bite. Featured in the movie* Guild Boss.

Afterward, Harriet had disappeared through her private door. Ravenna had settled down to watch a murder mystery on the rez screen but had discovered she was too restless to pay attention. She had given up and called Sybil.

"Harriet missed the red flags, too," Ravenna said.

"You said she liked both men," Sybil mused. "But she's a dust bunny. Who knows how she forms opinions about people?"

"She's pretty good when it comes to sensing a threat. Well, an imminent threat, at any rate."

"That's just it. Neither Willis nor Hatch gave off any threatening vibes before they attacked you."

"What are the odds that all three of us would be wrong about two different men?"

"I don't know," Sybil admitted.

"Neither do I, but my intuition tells me they are not good. We can no longer ignore the possibility that my talent is the problem. Thirty-six dates and no hits. Then I suddenly attract two stalkers. Let's face it, there's something very wrong with this picture."

"Stop," Sybil said. "Don't go there. I've told you a gazillion times, your talent is not the problem. Case in point, Ethan Sweetwater does not appear to have any issues with your psychic side."

"Ethan is . . . different."

"How?" Sybil demanded.

"Damned if I know. He just is. I'm going to hang up now, Sybil. It's been a rather stressful few days."

"No kidding."

"I'm going to pour another glass of wine and read until Ethan gets back from Frequency."

"Good idea." Sybil hesitated. "But call me if you get any insights into what went wrong with Willis and Hatch. I'm worried, too. I'm starting to wonder if there's a major error in my program. If so, I need to find it before there's another disaster."

"Right. Talk to you later."

Ravenna ended the call and went into the kitchen to pour a therapeutic glass of wine. She sank into her favorite reading chair and settled back with a novel of romantic suspense. She was midway through chapter three when she was distracted by the memory of an observation she had made earlier to Sybil.

Why the most recent two dates? Why not number five or number sixteen or the wellness spa guy?

Willis and Hatch both seemed like nice men. But wasn't that what everyone said after the cops arrested the serial killer next door?

Actually, most of the time, there were a few red flags, but the neighbors ignored them because they didn't seem important. It was only when they looked back that they realized a monster had moved among them.

But good matchmakers did not ignore even the smallest warning signs.

Ravenna put the book and the unfinished wine aside, got to her feet, and went into the study. She sat down at her desk, opened a drawer, and took out the little black book. She reached for the rez-Valentine pen that Ethan had given to Harriet.

When she touched it, she got the familiar little thrill of awareness. She knew the pen had not been intended for her—Ethan had planned to give it to his Covenant Marriage bride, whoever that turned out to be. But it felt good in her hand. Somehow it made her feel a little closer to Ethan, who would soon be on his way back to her.

Ethan, who didn't give a damn about her psychic talent.

It occurred to her she was no longer worried he might be a member of a clan that resembled a mob family in certain respects. He was an engineer—most of the time.

She tightened her grip on the pen and went to work. She had been an excellent criminal profiler, and now she was a very good matchmaker. She knew how to do this. The first step was to take herself out of the equation and review the evidence with fresh eyes.

In the past few months she'd had thirty-six matches from the Banks agency. Of those, thirty-four dates had passed without any major incident—so far. Why the problems with the last two, and why now?

She worked steadily through her notes, paying particular attention to the para-psych profiles of the thirty-six men. Most had been strong talents of one kind or another. Some, like Willis, were in the gaming industry. There had been a few para-psychologists, a couple of surgeons, a handful of business executives, two tech people, a journalist, a professional daredevil, and the wellness spa guy.

She paused over the entries for Willis and Hatch, absently tapping the pen against the page. Her intuition whispered.

She took out her phone and called Sybil.

"You thought of something, didn't you?" Sybil asked, her voice tight with tension. "Is it my program? Tell me the truth."

"I don't think it's your program," Ravenna said, choosing each word with care, because she was not entirely certain where she was going. "But what if someone hacked into it?"

Sybil fell silent for a moment. "It would have to be a hacker with mad skills. My programmer is very, very good, and he has an excellent reputation in the tech community. He installed all sorts of security protocols."

"No program is perfectly secure."

"True, but even if you're right, it doesn't make sense. Hackers want something—usually money. There haven't been any ransom demands."

"People crack computers for a variety of reasons, sometimes just for entertainment."

"Yes, but how does this connect with the fact that Willis and Hatch both tried to kill you?"

"What if someone sent them after me with the goal of murdering me? That individual started with the most recent files in your database because they came up first when my name was searched."

"That's a ghastly thought, and again, it doesn't add up. Even if someone wanted you dead, what would make that person think Willis and Hatch could be used to carry out a murder? There's nothing in my files that indicates either man could be convinced to do such a thing. They're rich. Successful. *Nice.* They aren't in the murder-for-hire business." Sybil paused a beat. "That I know of. And there's something else."

"What?"

"Quite frankly, they are both too smart to go after you the way they did. Why take the risk? In this town, people like Willis and Hatch know how to contact professionals who do that sort of work on a contract basis."

Professionals like the Concierge, Ravenna thought. But neither Willis nor Hatch had contracted out her murder. Each had come after her on his own.

"Both men evidently underwent a major personality change," she said. "Obviously."

"I do know someone who would like to see me dead," Ravenna said quietly. "And he has a talent for manipulating people."

"That self-appointed witch hunter? Clarence Fitch?"

"Yes."

"But he was declared criminally insane. He's sitting in a locked parapsych ward."

"He escaped once before."

"If he got out, wouldn't someone have let you know?"

"Not necessarily. I left the FBPI several months ago. I'm sure the team has forgotten me. I've got to hang up now, Sybil. I need to call someone."

"All right. While you do that I'm going to contact my programmer and ask him to see if there's a possibility someone got into my files. You've got me scared to death."

"Right."

Ravenna ended the call and scrolled through her contact list, searching for a familiar name. Luckily she had not deleted him, otherwise she would have had to spend time tracking down the number.

Max Collins answered on the first ring. "Ravenna? Hey there, good to hear from you. Been a while. Looking to rejoin the task force? No problem. You were a good member of the team."

"Yes, I was a good member of the team. You owe me, and I've got a question for you."

"What's that?"

"Is Clarence Fitch still locked up in an asylum?"

"Sure, why?"

It had been a shot in the dark, Ravenna thought. And the more she thought about it, Fitch just wasn't the most likely suspect in this case. Yes, he had motive. She had seen the rage in his eyes when the agents had led him out of the chamber, but he lacked the organizational and planning skills it took to carry out such a complicated revenge. For that matter, he hadn't had the skill set required to build a cult. And yet.

There were motives other than rage that could drive a person to a murderous revenge. Fear could do the job. So could envy. A combination of the two would make for a very dangerous para-psych profile.

"I want you to check out another name for me," Ravenna said.

"Okay, but make it fast. I've got a meeting with the team."

She gave him the name. Collins didn't have to check the files. He knew the answer.

"Got out three months ago on a technicality and hasn't been seen since," he said.

"You should have told me," Ravenna said. She clenched her fingers around the amber pen. Her chest got tight.

"Why would I do that?" Collins asked. He sounded honestly bewildered. "You're no longer involved with the Bureau. How is Illusion Town, by the way? Getting bored with the matchmaking business? I knew you wouldn't like it."

Ravenna hung up on him. She had to think. But the scent of an exotic perfume distracted her. She wondered if she had left a window open. The rain had stopped, but the energy of the storm might have released the scents of a nearby garden. Or maybe Harriet had returned earlier than usual and the fragrance had followed her through the dust bunny door.

She got to her feet. "Harriet?"

There was no answering chortle. Not Harriet, then. The flowery scent was stronger now. It no longer smelled sweet. Instead it was infused with a dark, summoning vibe that triggered a memory. It was the scent that had clung to the clothes that Willis and Hatch had worn.

Not bad aftershave. Poison.

The acid energy of panic splashed through her veins. She had to get out of the house. She lurched through the doorway of the study, barely able to maintain her balance. A terrible lethargy pulled at her senses, threatening to drag her down into oblivion. Halfway along the hall she realized she would never make it to the front door.

She stumbled toward the basement instead. If she could get downstairs she would be able to escape to the safety of the Underworld. She was wearing tuned amber in the form of an ankle chain and a bracelet. She would be safe.

She was only a few feet from her goal when she saw Harriet lying motionless on the floor. She realized the dust bunny must have sensed the danger and had returned to the house but had been overwhelmed by the poisoned gas.

"Harriet," Ravenna whispered.

Ravenna struggled to get to the dust bunny but the fumes were too strong. A fog of green-tinged gas filled the hall, overwhelming her senses. She tried frantically to rez her talent. A few small sparks appeared in the fog, but they winked out in an instant. She went down on her hands and knees and covered her nose and mouth with the hem of her pullover. She'd had some vague notion of escaping the gas by going low, but there was no escape.

Two monsters loomed in the fog that swirled through her home. Not monsters, she decided, men wearing gas masks. They had come for her.

"The boss said to grab her phone," one of them said. The mask gave his voice a robotic quality.

She realized she was still clutching Ethan's pen. She summoned what little energy there was left in her swiftly failing senses and managed to shove the pen into the pocket of her sweatpants.

CHAPTER FORTY-SEVEN

The anticipation that had been built during the seemingly end-less train trip evaporated in a flash when Ethan got out of the cab in front of the little cottage on Midnight Court. There were no welcoming lights inside. The sight of the darkened windows sent slivers of ice through his veins.

He was an engineer who made it a practice not to jump to conclu-sions, but he was also a Sweetwater with a hunter's intuition. Something very bad had happened inside the cottage.

He took the small flamer out from under his jacket and went up the steps. The door was unlocked. When he got it open, traces of a familiar, deeply unpleasant scent wafted down the hallway. His heightened senses told him that no one was lying in wait.

He left the door open to air out the space, covered his nose and mouth with the hem of his shirt, and went through the house, room by room, flamer in hand.

He found Harriet in the hall. The dust bunny was dazed but alive. Ethan picked her up and tucked her under one arm.

He continued down the hall and went into the study. There was a page of notes on her desk. The last entry was a name. Next to it were the words *fear* and *envy.* There were other descriptors as well: *Delusional. Organized. High-rez hypno talent?*

Harriet stirred and perked up. She opened all four eyes and growled.

"We'll find her," Ethan said. "But first we need some answers. We want to make sure we're hunting the right witch."

CHAPTER FORTY-EIGHT

Garrett Willis was sitting behind his desk when Ethan Sweet-water and his aunt were ushered into his office. They were not alone. There was a dust bunny cradled under one of Ethan's arms. The critter looked limp and exhausted.

Garrett got to his feet. "What happened to the dust bunny? Was it hurt?"

"Long story," Ethan said. "This is Harriet."

Garrett raised his brows. "Ravenna Chastain's pal? I didn't recognize her. Harriet and I are friends. I gave her a pen."

"Unfortunately, your relationship with her got complicated," Ethan said. "I'll explain."

"You do that, right after I greet Zora the Mysterious." Garrett moved around the desk to kiss Zora's hand. "Welcome to the Lucky Quartz. I'm honored by your visit. I'm a fan. One of these days I hope you will play the Hot Quartz Room here in my casino."

"Thank you," Zora said. She gave him a gracious smile. "I would be delighted."

Garrett turned to Ethan. "What is this all about? Considering that it's well after midnight, I'm assuming this isn't business related."

"Let's start with a question. What do you remember about Ravenna Chastain?"

"I'm registered with the Banks matchmaking agency. Miss Chastain was a date arranged by the agency. I enjoyed her company and I think she enjoyed mine, but we agreed we would continue to date other people. Why?"

"Do you remember waking up in an alley in the Shadow Zone?" Ethan asked.

Garrett winced. "Gossip travels fast in this town. I was hoping to keep that incident quiet. Not my finest hour, that's for sure. How did you hear about it?"

"I'm the one who left you in that alley," Ethan said. "I believe I owe you an apology."

Garrett went very still. "I think you had better explain."

"That's exactly what I intend to do," Ethan said. "Afterward I'm hoping you will allow my aunt to help you recover your lost memories."

Garrett frowned. "Of that night, do you mean?"

"Yes," Ethan said. "And maybe another lost memory as well."

Garrett narrowed his eyes. "What in green hell is this about?"

"Ravenna Chastain has been kidnapped. I'm hoping you have the key I need to find out who is trying to murder her."

CHAPTER FORTY-NINE

"I remember perfume," Garrett said. He spoke in the unin-flected voice of one who is in a deep trance. "It was pleasant at first. Sweet. Flowery. But it got stronger. Cloying."

"Go on," Ethan said.

Zora frowned. "Don't rush him. He needs time to organize his recovered memories."

"Sorry," Ethan muttered.

He was in a great hurry for answers. The sense of urgency that had been riding him hard since he had returned from Frequency was growing stronger by the minute.

Garrett appeared unaware of the low-voiced conversation between Ethan and Zora. He continued to speak in the same unemotional tone.

"A woman entered my office. She was wearing a gas mask. Said she was a consultant and that she had something important to tell me. She said it concerned Ravenna Chastain."

"What did she tell you?" Zora asked quietly.

For the first time since she had put him into a trance, Garrett seemed confused.

"I don't know," he said. "No, I do know, but it's not a real memory. It's the memory of a dream, a nightmare. I would never have done what the woman told me I must do. I wouldn't have hurt Ravenna."

Ethan went very still. He looked at Zora. She understood.

"What did the consultant tell you to do?" she asked quietly.

"She said I must kill Ravenna Chastain. She told me I had been stalking Ravenna. Said I'd left items related to fire on Ravenna's doorstep. She explained exactly how to do it. When. Why."

"Why were you supposed to murder Ravenna?" Zora asked.

"Because she was a witch who intended to destroy my casino."

"Wake up, Garrett," Zora said quietly.

He snapped out of the trance, shaken. "Shit. What happened to me? What did I do?"

"It's all right," Zora said. "You were hypnotized, but you didn't hurt anyone."

"You're sure?"

"Yes," Zora said. "Do you remember going to Ravenna's house?"

"Yes." Garrett frowned. "I took a cab to the edge of the Dark Zone and walked to Midnight Court. I . . . had a mag-rez. It's a nightmare. It didn't happen. It's not possible. I like Ravenna. She listened to me talk about my plans for the Lucky Quartz for hours."

"Can you describe the woman who told you that you should kill Ravenna?" Zora asked.

"The consultant," Garrett said. "Attractive, but very focused. I mean scary focused. There was some bad energy around her, I can tell you that."

Ethan held up his phone to show Garrett the image on the screen. "Is this her?"

Garrett peered at the picture. "That's her, all right. She was wearing a gas mask when she walked into the room, but after a while she removed it. Weird eyes, even in a photograph. Who is she?"

Ethan thought about the notes he had found on Ravenna's desk. "Her name is Louise Lace. She thinks she's a real witch, and she's out to get rid of her rival."

CHAPTER FIFTY

Ravenna opened her eyes to the familiar glow of a green quartz chamber and strong currents of energy. She was in the Underworld.

The feel of unyielding stone under her back told her she was lying on the floor. Groggy and shaky, she turned onto her side and managed to lever herself up to a sitting position. She took a few deep breaths to calm her rattled senses and queasy stomach. She was in a mag-steel cage, the same kind of cage that Fitch the witch hunter had used to imprison her the first time.

There was no sign of Harriet. The memory of her small body lying unconscious in the hallway of the cottage brought a rush of anguish.

Cautiously she tried to rez her paranormal senses. There was no response. Panic threatened to choke her. The poison gas had flatlined her talent. There was no way to know if the effects were temporary or permanent.

She checked for her rez-amber without much hope and was not surprised to discover the bracelet and ankle chain were gone. Not that they would have done her any good as long as she was locked in a cage.

Consciously and subconsciously she had always relied on her talent for manipulating fire. It might be a problematic talent when it came to finding a husband, but it had served her well as a means of self-defense. She had, however, learned a few things during her time with the Bureau, one of which was that there were a lot of items that could be used to defend oneself against an assailant.

She made herself conduct a detailed head-to-toe inventory. Sweatshirt, sweatpants, sneakers.

Ethan's pen. It was still in one of the deep pockets of her sweatpants.

Whoever had stripped her amber had missed the pen. That made sense. It was made of mirror amber, not rez-amber—attractive, but only for decorative purposes. It wouldn't have caused a nav amber sensor to ping.

Just a very pretty pen, but one that had been tuned by a very good engineer to serve as a rez-Valentine gift. If she sent the signal, Ethan might pick it up when he came down into the Underworld to look for her. And he would come down sooner or later, because this was Ethan.

The fog of poison gas had flatlined her two strong talents, but it didn't take a lot of psychic power to activate a resonating Valentine. All it required was an act of will. Anyone with an aura could focus that much energy.

She closed her eyes, gripped the pen very tightly, depressed the small sunset-red mirror jewel on the pen cap, and concentrated. *My heart resonates with yours. I love you.*

Footsteps muffled by the heavy currents of psi sounded in the hallway outside the chamber. She took her hand out of her pocket and gripped one of the bars of the cage. A man appeared in the arched doorway. Overmuscled, dressed in a lot of khaki and leather, his thinning hair caught back with a strip of leather, he looked as if he moonlighted as a bouncer at a downscale nightclub in the Shadow Zone.

"About time you woke up," he said. He snorted in disgust. "The boss says you're a genuine fire witch, but it looks like she got that wrong. My partner and I didn't have any trouble at all grabbing you. You aren't exactly setting any fires in here, are you?"

Ravenna gave him a dazzling smile. "Your boss is delusional and paranoid, but she is smart and she's organized. When she's finished with me, she won't need you or your pal. She'll put the two of you in a trance, strip your amber, and send you on a long walk in the tunnels."

"Huh?"

Bouncer Guy moved a few steps into the room, stopped, and squinted at her. She got the feeling he was trying to come up with a suitably threatening response, but he was too slow.

"That's enough," Louise Lace said from the doorway.

She was no longer posing as the adoring acolyte of the insane leader of a witch hunting cult. The long black robes were gone. Tonight she wore a sharply tailored business suit, pumps, and some discreet amber jewelry. Her hair was cut in a stylish bob. She looked as if she had just walked out of a business meeting.

She looked normal. Except for the eyes.

Louise motioned with her right hand. "Wait out in the hall, Meeks. I want to have a private chat with our guest."

"Whatever."

Meeks shot another wary glance at Ravenna and stomped toward the doorway.

When he was gone, Louise moved closer to the cage.

"I hadn't planned to take care of this personally," she said. "But you left me no choice."

"You were the one running the witch hunting cult, not Fitch," Ravenna said. "You used him as your front man. You organized the whole thing. You arranged for him to escape the asylum. You brainwashed and hypnotized the recruits, and you used the rez-net to identify your targets."

"Congratulations. You're the only one who managed to figure it out."

"I'm embarrassed it took me so long. I never would have tumbled to it if you hadn't tried to kill me by remote control. You're convinced you're a real witch, aren't you? You think your psychic side is actually an ability to work magic. You tried to hunt down those of us who looked like real witches, because you were afraid we might be more powerful than you."

"You just proved you're a witch," Louise said. "Only another witch can see the real me. I can't allow that. If the public finds out about my true powers, I will be in danger."

"Are you a triple talent? That would probably explain the delusions. Everyone knows triples run a high risk of para-psych instability."

"Shut the fuck up." Louise's face contorted with rage. She raised the flamer and took a step closer to the cage. "I'm not unstable. This is exactly what I mean when I say I have to make sure no one recognizes me. As long as people like you can see me, my life is in danger."

"Are you out for revenge against every member of the FBPI task force that took down your witch hunting operation?" Ravenna asked. "Or am I special?"

Louise's smile was now ice-cold, but her eyes glinted with a dangerous energy. "You're special, all right, because you're a real witch, like me. But I am far more powerful."

"Nope, you're just very good at navigating the rez-net. Speaking of which, do you know how easy it was to get your attention? Well, okay, at the time I thought I had gotten Fitch's attention, but it amounted to the same thing."

"You used the craft," Louise shrieked. "Magic."

"No magic involved. I just took a close look at the three women Fitch flatlined. I realized the one thing they had in common was that they had all registered at the same online ancestry research website. All had strong but highly unusual talent ratings. I registered at the same site, set up a similar profile, and the next thing I knew, your enforcers kidnapped me."

Louise took another step closer to the cage. She was only inches away now. Her face twisted. Energy writhed in the atmosphere.

"Why can't I hypnotize you?" she rasped. "Tell me."

The last piece of the puzzle slipped into place. Ravenna smiled.

"I get it," she said. "Now I know why you came looking for me after you walked out of prison. You realized you couldn't control me when you had me kidnapped the first time. You can't stand knowing I'm immune to your hypno talent."

"You're the one in the cage, not me."

"For now."

"I stripped you of your psychic senses."

"You had to use poison to do it, not your talent. You have to keep me locked in a cage because that's the only way you can control me."

Louise made a visible effort to pull herself back from some inner brink. "I need to know why I can't put you in a trance."

"You want a technical reason? I come from a long line of psychics. The Chastains were powerful talents back on Earth. When my ancestors came through the Curtain and adjusted to the paranormal environment here on Harmony, their senses got stronger. *And so did their ability to control those senses.*"

"I don't understand."

"The reason you can't use your hypnotic powers on me even though you've suppressed my psychic senses is because I've still got the strength required to control my talent. It goes hand in hand, you see. If you don't develop the power required to handle big talents, you end up in a para-psych asylum."

"*No.*"

"My family has had generations to develop control. You can kill me, but you can't put me into a trance."

"Then I will just have to kill you."

"But not yet," Ravenna said. "You're insane, but you've got a strong sense of self-preservation. You won't murder me until you're sure you can get away with it. If you get caught again, you'll end up in a high-security para-psych hospital, not prison. They'll suppress your hypnosis talent with drugs, and you'll never escape."

"I can kill you now and leave your body in this chamber. No one will ever find you."

"We both know it's a little more complicated than that. First, you have to get rid of your two witnesses out there in the hall. After all, they're just hired muscle. Why wouldn't they sell you out for the right amount of cash?"

"They won't be a problem," Louise said. "When they have served their purpose, I will dispose of them."

Meeks suddenly loomed in the doorway, flamer in hand. "What the fuck are you talking about?"

Another man armed with a flamer appeared behind him. "I knew we shouldn't have taken this job. Told you the bitch was crazy."

"The good news is that she hasn't hypnotized you yet," Ravenna said. "That's because she needed you to be able to carry out the complicated business of kidnapping me. Hypnosis is unreliable in situations like that. But now that she doesn't need you—"

"Shut up," Louise shrieked.

Ravenna felt energy pulse in the atmosphere. Louise was raising her talent again.

"Better run," Ravenna said to the two in the doorway. "She actually is a pretty strong hypnotist. If she gets control of your mind, she can send you into the tunnels without amber. No problem."

"I say we get rid of both of them," Meeks said. He raised the flamer.

"Fine by me," the second man said. "Guess this means we don't get paid, though."

"Not a good plan," Ravenna said. "She's a really strong hypno talent."

"Shit," Meeks whispered.

Louise screamed in rage. Meeks stared at his hand. The flamer trembled in his grasp. He started to raise the weapon, turning the barrel so that it was aimed at his face.

"She's doing something to me," Meeks yelped.

Ravenna gripped the bars of the cage. "Hey, Louise, I've been thinking. I know how you can improve your pathetic control."

Louise rounded on her. *"Stop talking."*

The short distraction shattered Louise's focus, and therefore, the trance. Meeks sucked in a shaky breath and stumbled back out into the hall. He collided with his companion.

"I've had enough of this weird shit," the second man said.

Both men disappeared. Footsteps thudded in the hallway, and then there was silence.

"Your big plan is falling apart," Ravenna said quietly. "Those two are witnesses, and they'll talk. They'll sell you out in a heartbeat. By now Ethan Sweetwater will be searching for me. You probably don't want to be in the vicinity when he shows up."

Louise hesitated for a few seconds, but in another beat, the heat returned to her eyes.

"I'm leaving, but you're coming with me," she said. "If Sweetwater or the Guild gets in the way, you're my ticket out of here. There's a sled in the hall."

"You'll be better off if you escape on your own," Ravenna said. "A hostage will slow you down."

"Shut up." Louise unlocked the cage, stepped back, and aimed the flamer at Ravenna. "It's set on max rez. At this distance I can't miss. *Move.*"

Ravenna walked slowly out of the cage and started toward the door. Louise followed close behind, the barrel of the flamer pressed against the back of Ravenna's head.

They were halfway across the room when Harriet raced through the doorway, sleeked out, all four eyes open and a lot of teeth on display. A rush of joy and relief slammed through Ravenna.

"Harriet," she said.

"Stop it," Louise yelped. "Make the rat stop or I swear I'll kill you first and then flame it."

"Not now, Harriet," Ravenna quickly. "Please. Stop."

"You can stand down, Harriet." Ethan appeared in the doorway, a flamer in his hand. "I've got this."

Harriet scrambled to a halt but remained in attack mode.

"It ends here," Ethan said from the doorway. "Drop the flamer, Lace."

"Die, Sweetwater," Louise screamed.

Energy shuddered in the space, but it was chaotic, unfocused.

"She used to be a pretty good hypno talent," Ravenna said. "But she's losing control. Can't hold a focus."

"Explains why I can't reverse her wavelengths," Ethan said.

"Stop talking," Louise shrieked, "both of you."

Ethan looked at Ravenna, a question in his eyes.

"She knocked out my talent with some really bad aftershave," Ravenna said.

She opened her right hand just enough to show him the pen. She had managed to slip off the cap, revealing the sharp metal point.

"Got it." Ethan raised his brows. "So, no special effects this time?"

"Not from me," Ravenna said.

"No problem, sometimes the old-fashioned ways are the best," Ethan said. "Whenever you're ready."

"I swear I'll burn her if you don't drop the flamer, Sweetwater," Louise shouted. "Get rid of it. Now."

"Sure," Ethan said.

He started to lower the weapon, moving slowly and deliberately.

"I said drop it," Louise screamed.

She was shaking with rage and panic. Her attention was focused on Ethan.

Ravenna clenched the pen in her fist and drove it back, straight into Louise's upper thigh. She felt the point bite through fabric and into soft flesh. It was too small to do much damage, but it got Louise's attention.

Already unnerved and frantic, she reacted instinctively. She yelped and twisted violently away from the source of the pain.

Ravenna dropped to her knees, getting out of Ethan's line of fire. He rezzed the flamer. A bolt of lightning flashed.

Louise convulsed. The flamer she had been clutching clattered onto the quartz floor. She stared at Ethan.

"I'm dying," she rasped.

"No," Ethan said. "But you aren't going to be a problem for a while."

Louise convulsed again and fell to the floor. She did not move.

Harriet, once again showing a strong resemblance to a wad of blue-eyed dryer lint, chortled and dashed across the room. Ravenna scooped her up and hugged her close.

"I've been so worried about you," she said.

Ethan looked at Ravenna. The lenses of his glasses did little to diminish the impact of his molten amber eyes. "Are you okay?"

"I don't know," Ravenna said. "I was telling you the truth when I said she flatlined me with that gas."

Ethan crossed the space and crouched to secure the flamer Louise had dropped.

"Don't worry," he said. "You'll be fine."

"How can you possibly know that?" she whispered.

"I talked to Garrett Willis tonight. She used the gas on him, too. His talent has returned."

"That's very reassuring." Ravenna looked at Louise. "She's definitely unstable. Probably a dual or triple talent. Couldn't control the power. Thinks she's a genuine witch. But she's deteriorating rapidly."

Harriet chortled.

Ravenna looked down at her. "You do know how to live in the moment, don't you? Nice talent you've got there, pal."

"Wish I had the same ability," Ethan said. He rose to his feet. "I may have to take to my fainting couch when we get home."

"Ethan—"

"Hush." He gathered her into his arms. "It's over. It's going to be okay."

Harriet, squeezed between the two of them, wriggled free. She tumbled to the floor and immediately set about investigating the chamber.

"There were two men working with her," Ravenna mumbled into Ethan's jacket.

"Not anymore," Gabriel Jones said from the doorway. "When they ran out of this room they ran straight into my men. Looks like everything is under control in here."

Ravenna lifted her head and gave Gabriel a misty smile. "You and Ethan make a very good team."

"The Sweetwaters and the Joneses have been working together for quite a while now," Gabriel said.

Harriet bustled across the chamber, an object in her front paws. She offered it to Ravenna.

"My phone," Ravenna said.

CHAPTER FIFTY-ONE

"How did you find me so quickly after I rezzed Harriet's pen?" Ravenna asked.

"By the time you activated the Valentine, Jones and I were almost at your location," Ethan said.

Ravenna smiled. "Harriet led you to me, didn't she?"

"Nope. She didn't really wake up until we were already in the sled and on our way."

"Okay, I demand an explanation," Ravenna said. "How did you manage to find me in the Underworld?"

Last night's storm had passed, leaving a fresh buzz in the atmosphere. Night was falling fast, as it always did in the desert. Illusion Town was lighting up with a mix of paranormal and normal energy.

She and Ethan were reclining in lounge chairs on Ethan's patio. They were drinking wine, munching pretzels, and savoring the radiant garden.

Harriet was scurrying around in the foliage, investigating the landscape.

From time to time she appeared and disappeared in the eerie green shadows. Her latest acquisition, a pen bearing the logo of the Illusion Town Guild, was clutched triumphantly in one paw. Ravenna was not sure if she had thieved it when they were all gathered in Gabriel Jones's office earlier that day or if Gabriel's administrative assistant, Aiden Shore, had given the pen to her.

"You helped me locate you," Ethan said. He crunched down on a pretzel. "I found your notes about the witch hunter case."

"I remember writing down Louise Lace's name. How did that help?"

"You also wrote the words *delusional, envy,* and *fear.* I was pretty sure you were detailing motives. Your phone was gone but I grabbed a photo of Louise Lace off the rez-net, and then Aunt Zora and I had a chat with Garrett Willis. Zora uncovered his memories. When I showed him a picture of Louise Lace, he recognized her as the woman who had used the gas on him."

"Okay, you had the probable identity of the kidnapper. I repeat, so?"

"So, I contacted Gabriel Jones, who contacted the FBPI. We found out Lace had been released on a technicality."

Ravenna grimaced. "I'll bet she hypnotized a few people."

"Apparently. The FBPI was embarrassed about the failure to identify Lace as a strong hypno talent, but they do keep decent files. When Louise Lace was taken into custody, someone noted that she used signature amber and included the frequency along with fingerprints and a description. I figured there was a good chance that after she walked out of prison she had gone back to the habit of using tuned amber. You can't change your signature frequency."

Ravenna smiled. "You set your snazzy locator to her frequency and it led you straight to her."

"Yes."

"You are a very good engineer."

"Thanks."

"What do you think will happen to Lace?"

"She'll probably spend the rest of her days in a high-security para-psych hospital for the criminally insane," Ethan said. "She's been diagnosed as a burnout for now, but the authorities aren't going to take any chances."

"What about Taggert Spooner?"

"The mirror amber did some damage to his aura but I don't know how much. On top of that, there's no way to know how the Vortex experiments affected his para-psych profile. For now he appears to be a total burnout. The FBPI is taking apart the Spooner Technology labs looking for evidence of illegal para-psych research, but if Spooner himself was the only human test subject, they won't have much of a case. Regardless, he'll be doing time. He confessed to killing the prospector and hiring the Concierge."

They drank their wine in silence for a while. Eventually Ravenna stirred.

"About the rez-Valentine pen you gave Harriet," she said.

"What about it?"

"I used it thinking it would act as a distress signal that might just possibly lead you to me."

"I understand. It worked as you intended."

There was no emotion in his voice. He was back in unreadable mode.

"I think you should know that when I rezzed the signal, I wanted to send two messages," Ravenna said. "Yes, I was trying to let you know my location, but I was also sending the message that the Valentine was intended to send."

Ethan went very still for what seemed like an eternity. Then he set his wineglass down with great precision and sat up on the edge of the lounger. He leaned forward and braced his forearms on his thighs, his fingers casually linked together. His eyes burned.

"A rez-Valentine is meant to tell the recipient, *My heart resonates with yours. I love you*," he said.

Ravenna swung her legs off the lounger and sat up. She put her own glass aside.

"I know," she said. "I realize you gave the pen to Harriet because you had given up on finding someone to love at Ottoway Matchmakers, but—"

"No," he said. "I gave the pen to Harriet because I was pretty sure she would sense that it was meant for you. I hoped that eventually you would get the message and rez the Valentine to send the message it was designed to send. Instead you used it as a distress signal. Don't get me wrong. I was thrilled to get the signal tonight, because it meant you were still alive. But at the same time, I knew I couldn't take it as a sign that you loved me."

She caught her breath. "I do love you, Ethan."

He stretched out a hand and brushed his fingers against her cheek. "I fell in love with you the first time I walked into your office. I knew I wanted to marry you."

Dazed, she stared at him. "What?"

"I said, I knew I wanted to marry you. You didn't make it easy for me. I had to walk through the fires of hell before I could get a date with you."

"Excuse me? The fires of hell?"

"Nine lousy dates before I could land a fake date. Definitely hell."

Her professional pride kicked in. "Those nine dates were good matches. I worked hard to find them in our database."

"I don't care how hard you worked. I was never interested in any of them."

"According to the after-action reports, you didn't give any of those very nice women a chance."

"I tried to be polite, but I admit I was impatient, because I knew I was wasting my time."

"If you didn't like the matches I selected, why didn't you ask for another matchmaker?"

"You're missing the point here, Ravenna. I went out on nine boring dates because it took me that long to figure out how to get a date with you."

She spread her hands wide. "You could have simply asked me out on a date."

"That was the one thing I couldn't do. You would have said it was unprofessional for matchmakers to date their clients."

"It is unprofessional. And it isn't smart for matchmakers to try to find their own matches."

"You made those things very clear," Ethan said. "Naturally I was a desperate man. That was when I got the bright idea of asking you to assess my dating techniques. I couldn't believe my luck when you asked me to escort you on a fake date to your grandparents' anniversary celebration. Everything seemed to be falling into place. And then my brilliant plan went to green hell thanks to Louise Lace, Taggert Spooner, and Vortex."

She smiled. "In hindsight, there were a few complications."

"The situation continued to stagger along until that night in the gazebo at Silver Lake. Talk about a real bonding experience."

"One might even say transcendent."

"One might, if one were a wellness spa guru instead of an engineer. But all you seemed to want was an affair. Still, I figured I could work with that. Then we almost got killed and had to spend a night in Nightmare Cave and things got even more complicated. For a while there it was just one snafu after another."

"I'm not so sure about that." Ravenna tried for somber and serious, but inside she was flying. "Our time in Nightmare Cave was definitely another bonding experience."

"We need to stop bonding like that. I don't know about you, but I am ready for a normal relationship."

She leaned forward and put her arms around his neck. "Speaking as a professional matchmaker, I don't think there is any such thing, and who wants normal, anyway? I'd much rather have what we have, whatever that is. I love you. I have from the beginning. It just took me a while to realize it."

"Ravenna."

He didn't just say her name; he breathed it as if it were oxygen.

"I told myself it was physical attraction," she said. "I told myself I was a professional and that I shouldn't get distracted. I reminded myself that matchmakers are notoriously bad at finding their own matches, that I couldn't trust my own judgment. I was not interested in a flirtation or an affair. I was committed to finding a forever husband. But after the trip to Silver Lake I realized I wanted to be with you and that maybe you wanted to be with me, not just for an affair but forever. I hoped maybe you just needed time."

"I told myself you were the one who needed time." He rose and drew her to her feet. "I would have signed up for a Covenant Marriage with you that first day at Ottoway, and I can prove it."

"Is that so? And just how would you do that?"

He reached into his pocket and took out a tiny velvet pouch. He opened the little bag and tipped the contents into his palm.

Ravenna looked at the ring, which gleamed in the moonlight. It was a band of gold set with elegantly cut fire amber—tuned fire amber. The stone glowed with power.

"I bought this that same day," Ethan said. "Tuned it myself. It's a signature frequency. *Your* signature. No one else can use it. Just you."

"It's beautiful," she whispered.

She shivered a little when he slipped it onto her finger.

"I love you, Ethan."

He tightened his arms around her and pulled her close. When his mouth came down on hers, she abandoned herself to the radiance of the garden and the joy of love.

Fireworks danced in the night.

CHAPTER FIFTY-TWO

"I can't begin to tell you how grateful I am for your capable assistance, Ms. Palantine." Walter Willoughby surveyed the office that, until a short time ago, had belonged to Taggert Spooner. "I admit I'm feeling a bit overwhelmed by the responsibility. I still don't understand why the board of directors asked me to step into Spooner's shoes."

Melody Palantine gave him a reassuring smile. "Obviously they selected you to take the helm of Spooner Technologies because they are sure you are the best person to guide the company through the difficult weeks and months ahead."

He grimaced. "Either that or they set me up to take the fall if the company goes under."

That was the truth, Melody thought. She was, however, more than a little surprised that Willoughby sensed what had actually gone on at the last board meeting. Until his sudden promotion into the C-suite, he had been an obscure mid-level manager in charge of Shipping & Receiving.

"Trust me, Mr. Willoughby, you will save Spooner Tech," Melody said. "We have work to do, but together we will navigate the troubled waters the company is facing."

Well, strictly speaking, she would steer Spooner Tech through the FBPI investigation and the public relations disaster that the arrest of the company's president and CEO had created.

Willoughby was right to be bewildered by his sudden rise up the corporate ladder. What he didn't know was that she was the one who had used her computer skills and her talent for manipulation to convince the board that he was the best person for the job.

It had been a complicated project begun several weeks earlier when she had picked up on Taggert Spooner's growing paranoia and instability. Mystified by the change in his personality, she had tracked him to the Vortex lab one night and watched, shocked, as he subjected himself to the radiation of the machine.

When the personality changes set in, she was not entirely surprised. She had dug deep into the history of Vortex. Thanks to a certain Old World journal, she was sure she knew what was happening to him.

And thanks to Spooner's increasing recklessness, she learned of his plans to meet with the prospector in Illusion Town. She knew a golden amber opportunity when she saw one. She made sure the appropriate rumors reached Arcane and the Guild Council.

The operation had been a success, delivering results that were even more spectacular than she had imagined. Not only had Spooner been arrested, he was apparently quite ill and deteriorating rapidly.

The next step had been to make sure the board installed the right individual in the head office, someone who would be overwhelmed by the responsibility and turn to her for guidance and advice. Willoughby was perfect for her purposes.

"Don't worry, sir," she said. "I am here to support you in any way I can. With you at the helm, this company will move forward into a brighter and more profitable future. I would suggest that we start by changing the name of the firm. People have short attention spans. A new brand will help ensure that clients and the investment world soon forget Taggert Spooner and the humiliation he brought down on this company."

Willoughby looked at her with a pathetic mix of relief and gratitude. "That is an absolutely brilliant idea, Ms. Palantine."

"I'll draw up a list of possibilities immediately," she said. "Once we make our selection, I will coordinate with marketing and publicity."

She went briskly out the door, entered her office, and sat down at her desk. A grand sense of certainty swept through her. After a moment she took out her secret phone and pulled up the images of her notorious ancestor.

She was going to succeed where Vincent Lee Vance had failed.

You have a destiny.

For all intents and purposes, she was now in charge of Spooner Tech, a company that boasted some of the most advanced research-and-development labs on Harmony. Even more importantly, she had the top secret documents relating to the Vortex project. The FBPI would discover enough data to make them destroy the lab, but they would not find the machine. She had made certain it was safely concealed in the Underworld.

Under her leadership, research would continue. Vortex was the key to power, the means by which she would fulfill her destiny.

But first, a name change. She opened a drawer and took out the list of possibilities she had made. Decision time. Branding was important.

CHAPTER FIFTY-THREE

The dust bunnies were lined up on the tiered quartz benches when the sled arrived in the underground theater.

Ravenna, seated on the front seat with Ethan and Sybil, surveyed the crowd.

"They got here early this time," she said. "I wonder how Harriet communicates with her buddies."

Harriet, riding on the dashboard, chortled a greeting to her guests. A chorus of excited chortles responded. Several of the dust bunnies were so overcome with anticipation they bounced up and down.

Ethan brought the sled to a halt. "Something tells me this is the place."

"Welcome to Dust Bunny Theater," Ravenna said.

"We found it one day when we did some exploring," Sybil explained. "Ravenna put on a little show, just for kicks. Harriet was thrilled. Somehow she got the word out to her pals."

"This is amazing," Ethan said, stepping down from the sled. "I've never seen a chamber like this in the tunnels."

Sybil looked at him. "If you bring the cauldron, I'll get the popcorn."

Ethan chuckled and gave Ravenna a knowing look. "Cauldron?"

Ravenna glared at Sybil. "It's a very large popcorn kettle, obviously. The *cauldron* thing is Sybil's idea of a joke."

"Sorry," Sybil said. "Couldn't resist."

"Right." Ethan hoisted the huge kettle out of the cargo bay of the sled. "Where does the cauldron go?"

"Set it on the platform in the center," Sybil said.

She picked up the large package of popcorn kernels from the back of the sled and followed Ethan to the stage. He set the kettle down. Sybil removed the glass lid with a flourish and dumped the contents of the package into the pot. At the sound of the kernels rattling on the bottom, another round of chortling went up.

"That's a lot of popcorn," Ethan said.

"The dust bunnies love the process as much as the munching," Ravenna said. "Stand back."

Energy sparked in the atmosphere as she rezzed some talent. Paranormal flames leaped under the kettle. When the first kernels popped, the audience went wild.

Ethan, Ravenna, and Sybil returned to the sled and sat down on the front seat. Ravenna reached into the back of the sled to get the wine. Sybil lined up the glasses on the dashboard.

The popping was louder now. It wasn't long before the fluffy popcorn filled the kettle, pushed the lid aside, and overflowed. Ravenna cut off the flames.

The dust bunnies surged forward to chow down on popcorn.

Ethan sat on one end of the sled bench. He braced a booted foot on the floor of the chamber and drank some wine while he watched the dust bunnies.

"They know how to have a good time," he said.

"Maybe that's why we find them so charming," Ravenna said. "They remind us that we should take time to enjoy life."

Sybil raised her glass in a toast. "They also remind us that it's good to have friends."

"I'll drink to that," Ravenna said.

Ethan put his arm around her. "So will I."

"By the way," Sybil said. "I have a little surprise for you two."

Ravenna looked at her. "What?"

"Ethan dropped by the office of the Banks agency, paid his money, and filled out the questionnaire. I ran it through the computer, applied my professional expertise and superior talent to the problem, and came up with the perfect match."

Ravenna narrowed her eyes. "That match had better be me."

"Of course it's you," Sybil said. "There was never any doubt. Ethan made it clear it had to be you. Think I want trouble with the Sweetwaters? You told me they looked a lot like a mob family."

Ethan gave her an innocent smile. "Actually, we're in the amber business. I'm sure I put that down on the questionnaire."

Ravenna shot him a warning look and turned back to Sybil. "Are you two serious?"

Sybil laughed. "Yes, I'm serious. Don't worry, my programmer fixed the bug that allowed Louise Lace to gain access to my database. This is a straight-up, legit match. Don't you think I'd tell you if it wasn't? If I didn't like it, I would recommend that you enter a Marriage of Convenience, have lots of great sex, and get it out of your systems. But the match is excellent, so relax. When it comes to a Covenant Marriage, you can bank on Banks."